daydreams
undertaken

daydreams undertaken

Stephen L. Antczak

For Robin—
Here's to the pursuit of
many pleasant daydreams.
—Steve Antczak

MARIETTA PUBLISHING
MARIETTA, GEORGIA USA
AN IMPRINT OF MEISHA MERLIN PUBLISHING

PUBLISHED BY
Marietta Publishing,
An Imprint of Meisha Merlin Publishing
Bruce R. Gehweiler, Publisher
PO Box 3485
Marietta, GA 30061-3485
http://www.mariettapublishing.com

Daydreams Undertaken © 2004 by Stephen L. Antczak
ISBN 1-892669-25-0

"Be My Hero" — first published in *Dragonlaugh* (2001)
"Captain Asimov" — first published in *Superheroes* (Ace Books, 1995)
"The Monster Lab" — first published in
    Gahan Wilson's Ultimate Haunted House (Harper Paperbacks, 1996)
"Nail in the Coffin" — first published in *Descant* (2003)
"The Other Side of Light" — first published in *Tomorrow Speculative Fiction* (1995)
"Reality" — first published in *Adventures in the Twilight Zone* (DAW Books, 1995)
"Reed John-Paul Forever" — first published in *In Dreams* (Victor Gollancz, Ltd., 1992)
"Pop Goes Weasel" — first published in *The Third Alternative* (1995)
"Space Aliens Ate My Head" — first published in *In Your Face* (John Benson, Publisher, 1996)
"Virtual Day" — first published in *Dreams of Decadence* (1997)
"Way Down" — first published in *Not One of Us* (1995)

Printed and bound in the United States of America by Lightning Source, Inc.
10 9 8 7 6 5 4 3 2 1

Design: Robert Sommers
Cover Art: Georges Jeanty
Copy Editing: Kimberly Hays

Dedicated to the Memory of Jack C. Haldeman, II.

For his encouragement, his friendship,
his stories, and his spirit. We'll miss you, Jay.

Acknowledgements

The short stories herein owe their existence not entirely to me. The following people, most of them fellow writers with their own tales to tell, helped in many different ways. Sometimes it was with constructive criticism, sometimes with emotional support, sometimes with financial support when the going got tough, and sometimes it was just the right amount of encouragement at just the right time. James C. Bassett, Rob Sommers, Gregory Nicoll, Johna Till Johnson, Wendy Webb, Tina Bushnell, Allen Steele, Michael & Linda Moorcock, Roger Baker, Holly Sommers, Lawrence Watt-Evans, Gary Kim Hayes, Brad Strickland, Brad Linaweaver, Tom Fuller, members of the Dark River Writers, plus my parents and David Weinell in the very early days...if I missed anyone, well, I'm an idiot.

Contents

Foreward

THE TITLE *DAYDREAMS UNDERTAKEN* AS much describes a process as it does the stories herein. When I latch upon an idea for a story, especially a science fiction or fantasy story, one of my main tools for figuring out the various elements of the story is, of course, daydreaming. I suspect this is true for most writers, at least most of the writers I know personally. I've also read accounts by different writers that this is how they work. I am sure that none of them daydream in the same manner. Doubtless the various implements needed for successful daydreaming vary from person to person. For some it may require a hammock hung between two trees on a breezy Spring afternoon. For others an ice cold beer, or two, or three, may be helpful.

Daydreaming for me requires music. The music can't be intrusive, which means I generally prefer classical or music I once heard referred to as 'dream pop.' The latter for me means acts like Dido, Sinead Lohan, Lush, or Shea Seger. Bands like Mono, Sneaker Pimps, and Olive also work. Generally, a soothing female voice or a string section lulls me into that daydream-state. In the past this has not always been the case, and the music that worked for me ranged from Butthole Sufers and Scratch Acid to Nine Inch Nails and Ministry, to bis and Bjork. Lately, jazz has worked pretty well, especially 'Kind of Blue' by Miles Davis.

The other necessary ingredient for me has always been a rocking chair. Generally, any kind of rocking chair will do, whether it's a bentwood or a swivel, spring rocker, or a rattan rocker, a glider, or even a porch swing. Constant movement is absolutely necessary for me to feel comfortable. I think this is because my mother used to rock me to sleep while she was pregnant with me.

The whole point is to get to where I can free-associate in my daydreams. I try to direct it by thinking about whatever writing project I'm working on at the time. The funny thing is, I know that I will always, eventually, be able to figure out that missing element that's keeping my project from reaching fulfillment, whether it be a short story, a screenplay, or a novel.

The most amazing feeling is when you're sitting there and suddenly the elements come together, or they're coming together slowly but somehow you know they will eventually get there and make the story work.

I think daydreaming helps in the "where do you get your ideas?" department. Story ideas come from all over the place, but for me they almost never come fully formed. Usually I hurriedly tack a working title to it and write that title down. The title acts as the metadata for the story, a key word that unlocks the story elements in my mind. Generally, a look at a title brings to the fore of my mind the basic concept, theme, and plot. Sometimes even characters.

I don't write the story in my head like I've heard some writers do. I use daydreaming to come up with a beginning and an ending. Once I've started fleshing out the plot or even writing the story, daydreaming is a great way for me to figure out how to overcome plot problems in the middle of a story.

Once I actually start writing, anything can happen, of course. The story can completely change, the title can change, everything can change. Daydreaming doesn't make writing any easier. But it sure is a nice way to spend time. And don't let anyone try to tell you that daydreaming is a waste of time. It is an indispensable tool for any creative soul. At least, it is for me.

daydreams
undertaken

This story originally appeared in the paperback anthology Adventures in the Twilight Zone *edited by Carol Serling, the widow of Rod Serling, and published by DAW. It has also been available on the Web at Alexandria Digital Literature, and has consistently made bestseller status there. A lot of people consider this to be my strongest story. Anyway, I wrote this story at about the same time as I wrote "Captain Asimov." This was during one of lowest moments, at the end of a relationship. I truly was in the pit of despair when I wrote these two stories.*

"Reality" came about because I'd gotten interested in the mobile sculptures of Alexander Calder, and had also read a little about knot theory. The idea that the universe can be described mathematically, and that the resulting equation could then be turned into a representative shape is certainly nothing new, but it grabbed my imagination. What if an artist came along who could, like a savant, simply make the leap between the real object and the representative shape derived from its equation without having to figure out the equation itself first? What if he created an art object that represented the universe, that was true to the equation of the universe? Would it have some sort of connection to the universe?

The concept that came to me while daydreaming, the concept that for me made the story worth writing, was this: What if the power of the sculpture was, possibly, imagined? What if the entire town where the sculpture resided had fallen into a form of mass hysteria about it, and our main character had snapped out of it?

Of course, then the question remains, is he wrong, and does the sculpture really have the power the townspeople believe it has?

Reality

RUSTED METAL RODS INTERCONNECTED TO form a chaotic framework around a space big enough to walk through, following a twisting pathway that curved in on itself, spiraled, zigzagged, wobbled through the industrial behemoth called *Reality*. Throughout, along the path, were placed knobs, levers, switches, cranks, chains, and wheels. Turn a knob or a wheel, throw a switch, pull a lever or a chain…the sculptor had intended the piece to be interactive. A twist on a crank, and part of *Reality* shifted, changed, made the sculpture different.

daydreams undertaken

Stephen L. Antczak

The plaque that stood at the "entrance" said: *Reality is Art. This piece represents reality. Like reality, you can walk through it, and like reality, you can affect it. But be careful, once you alter something, you may never be able to put it back the way it was before.* It was the centerpiece of Random, Oregon's town square. Random had a population of around 10,000, not much bigger than in the early part of the century when *Reality* was built. Located in the midst of an old growth forest, surrounded by the wilds of the northwest, Random was as isolated as it could be. Highway 26 passed to within 15 miles of Random at its closest point. Stories about Big Foot, man-eating grizzlies, ghosts, Aryan Nations encampments, and the like abounded, but in a quiet, accepted sort of way. The folks of Random weren't trailer park hicks, but neither were they a community of Mensa

However, it was no longer legal to walk in and turn any of the knobs or pull any of the levers. That didn't stop someone like Osgood Kramer from casting sidelong glances of desire towards it whenever he passed by, to and from lunch over at Pete's Grill, which was across the street. Sometimes Osgood would sit there and let his coffee get cold while he stared at it. Even at Home Depot, where Osgood did customer service in the complaints department, he'd daydream about walking into *Reality*, and pulling a particular lever he'd already spotted and *knew* without a shadow of doubt would change what he'd decided needed changing. Once the deed was done, he didn't worry about whether or not he'd get arrested or anything, because things would be *different*, and that was the whole point.

One morning, when Osgood's coffee at Pete's had become lukewarm, the town sheriff, Jake Sky, sat in the same booth, across the table from him.

"Mind if I join you?" the sheriff asked, but the question was more or less rhetorical since he'd already effectively joined him.

But Osgood nodded anyway and said, "Sure, have a seat." Jake grinned at him like a wolf facing down a moose. The sheriff was a big Cree Indian, known for his joviality and ready chatter. He waved at Bea, the waitress. She didn't bother to walk over, but yelled out asking if he wanted his usual, and he gave her the thumbs up and looked at Osgood, rolling his eyes.

Osgood knew it was an act, though. He knew why the sheriff was lavishing this attention on him. But that didn't matter. Nothing mattered, or none of it *would* matter once things changed.

"What's up?" Jake asked, amiably enough.

"Not much," Osgood said, which was usually true. Nothing much in his life was ever what he would term "up". Nothing bad, just nothing great. Maintaining status quo was what Osgood had been best at ever since he could remember. Status quo was like a drug for him, a syringe filled with mind-numbing heroin he injected into the pulse of his existence. It kept him warm, safe, and sound of mind and body, or so he fooled himself.

Reality

"Anything on your mind?" Jake asked. "Anything you want to talk about?"

"Not really," Osgood answered. Playing the game, but this wasn't a game, it wasn't a joke, it wasn't a scene in the school play. It was *Reality*.

"Sure?" the sheriff persisted. "You've been looking rather…contemplative, lately."

Osgood concentrated on the patterns in the linoleum table top, imagining it as the speckled surface of some gigantic eggshell. "Yeah," was all he managed to say, which wasn't what he'd wanted to say. You have to say *something*, though, when the town sheriff expects you to.

"You know," Jake was saying, "I oftentimes wonder…what life would be like if the white man had never made it to America. What if he'd never taken blacks as slaves, or forced Chinese immigrants to build his railroad across the red man's land? Sometimes I think these things when I look out the window of my squad car and see that big ol' sculpture towering over the town square."

Osgood regarded the big Indian with some caution. Jake Sky was talking along a thin blue line, saying things most locals wouldn't say to their best friends. He felt that maybe Jake expected him to say something *now*, while Jake paused to let Bea set his food on the table. Ham and cheese on rye, with hot mustard, Polish dill on the side.

"But you know what?" Sky continued. "I wouldn't do anything to change the past, not one thing. Because how do I know it would actually make things better? How do I know native Americans wouldn't have wiped each other out, or wouldn't have been conquered by someone else? I don't, I *can't*. And besides, some of my best friends are white, and black." He paused to eat part of his sandwich, then said, "Haven't met any Chinese yet."

Now Osgood realized he *had* to say something if he intended to keep the sheriff at bay. "I wouldn't change anything that major, even if I could."

"What about something small?" the sheriff asked. "Something that wouldn't affect anything else."

Osgood shrugged. "I can't think of anything offhand. Besides, I have enough trouble changing the *now*. You know me."

"That's the problem," Jake said, "I *don't* know you. Not really."

Enough of this, Osgood thought. It was all but right there on the table between them, next to Jake's sandwich. He decided to put it there.

"Okay, Sheriff," he said. "You're afraid I'll mess with *Reality*, right? You're afraid I'll walk in there and pull some lever and suddenly the Sun'll be green or something." That got the attention of a few eavesdroppers, each of whom reacted with a cough or a start. One even dropped a fork. Jake Sky ignored everyone but Osgood.

"This isn't something I normally discuss in a public place," Jake said, his voice lower than before. "But since you've already, ah, broached the subject, let me say this: Remember Sarah Cole. Remember Jack Kennesaw. Then, last of all, remember Haver Compton. Think about them, then do what you're best at doing. Keep on keepin' on. Make no waves. Don't rock the boat. Understand?"

Osgood nodded, quelling the urge to make a remark about extensive cliché usage. He got up to leave, throwing down money for the coffee he didn't even drink.

It was cold now, anyway.

Sarah Cole. Osgood was convinced there had never been a Sarah Cole, not in this reality, not in *any* reality. Supposedly Jake Sky and several others had seen her walk into *Reality*, and before anyone could stop her she had flipped a switch. A metal rod turned, a section of the sculpture swung to hang lower than before, and Sarah Cole disappeared. Whatever effect she'd had on the past had wiped out her existence.

Jake and two of his buddies had been hiding deep in the bowels of *Reality* to smoke hash and drink cheap beer. This was back during their senior year at Random High. One of them had climbed up to sit atop a massive gear, his legs hanging down from between the teeth. When the sculpture changed, that gear moved. Jake's old high school pal was now one of Random's few panhandlers. They called him Legless. He never rolled his rickety, twenty-year-old wheelchair far from the square, where he spent his days staring at the industrial monster that had bitten his legs off with iron fangs. Every now and then Jake bought him a cup of coffee or a hamburger, for old times.

Jake and his friends swore on the graves of every one of their ancestors that this Sarah Cole person had done it, had altered *Reality* and then disappeared. Their reputations were better than good. Jake was a star linebacker on the football team, Legless was a wide receiver, the other was the President of the senior class. Local heroes each of them, which made it real easy to believe their story. When no one remembered Sarah Cole, and speculation arose about the connection *Reality* had to reality.

There was already a bit of superstition surrounding the sculpture anyway. Even before its completion, a group of churchgoing citizens protested its construction, claiming the artist had to be inspired by Satan to even imagine such an evil-looking contrivance, never mind actually build one big enough to loom over downtown like a mechanical sentinel. In a freak accident, the crane being used to build *Reality* malfunctioned and dropped several hundred pounds of scrap metal on the protestors. It had been unmanned at the time

Folks started remembering Sarah Cole. They'd seen her at the prom, seen her shopping with her Mom, who, by the way, also no longer existed. Perhaps Sarah had wiped out her entire bloodline! Like a virus, the memory of Sarah Cole spread from person to person, household to household. It was reasoned that those who lived in the immediate area around the sculpture were less like-

Reality

ly to totally forget what had gone before things Changed with a capital *C*. Why? Who worried about why? This was some bizarre link between the universe and art, two things people accepted as without reason, without design.

Through dreams, through creative interpretations of some fuzzy memories, people rebuilt Sarah Cole. They rebuilt her life, her family, reconstructed memories to include her ghostly presence in the background, a peripheral attendance to their different pasts.

Rebuilt, or built from scratch. Osgood had gotten caught up in it, too, even though he knew in the back of his mind that something was wrong.

There was always a handy blank spot in someone's Polaroid from a Fourth of July parade or birthday party, empty space that invariably wound up being filled by Sarah. Osgood had a picture of him sitting in the driver's seat of his then brand new sky blue '68 Ford Mustang. He looked too happy for someone with *just* a new car. As if the most beautiful girl in town were sitting there beside him in it, and they were about to go on their first date.

Sarah Cole. It was almost too embarrassing to even think about now, but he had to. No sooner had he jumped that bandwagon than he distinctly remembered that first drive in the old 'stang. Cruising the winding roads around town, enjoying the sensation of the 350 vibrating all around him, humming the sacred hymn of a boy and his car with miles of pavement unfurled before them. Absolute freedom, a true release of the spirit to go wherever and whenever he wanted. Just get in his car and *go*.

That was the grin on his face in the picture, as he sat for the first time behind the wheel of a bigger world. *That* was the reality he remembered, the reality that had been, was, and always would be. When he realized this, it was as if he'd been awakened from a dream, snapped out of deep hypnosis, or freed from a hex.

The town of Random was under the same spell, enchanted by a ton of scrap metal bolted and welded together into a crude representation of existence. Osgood knew he had to be the one to break that spell.

Once he had himself freed of the delusion, Osgood found it easy to see contradictions about Sarah, the most obvious of which he was surprised no one else had noticed. There were at least nine different men who claimed to have been the one to "deflower" Sarah Cole. The locales ranged from the backseat of a car (five of those) to a park bench. One claimed it had happened inside *Reality* itself.

A blanket of self-deception had settled over everyone, a nightfall of delusion, a shared sham. It was a town-wide dementia which Osgood understood only he had escaped.

People believed in *Reality*.

Jack Kennesaw. Had it not been for Jack Kennesaw, there would still be *two* moons, two lunar orbs keeping us company, keeping each other company in their otherwise lonely trajectories around the Earth. But no, because Mr. Kennesaw, stepped into the sculpture and interacted with it, touched something, turned something, that second moon ceased to exist forever…backwards and forwards in time. Had never been, would never be. Wasn't, and that was that.

Except, again, for some who dreamed.

Folks seemed perfectly happy to gaze up at ol' Luna and point at the Man in the Moon, and proudly remember that July 20th, 1969 when a man, an American, set foot on it for the first time. There weren't many lights to crowd out the night sky in Random, and a wide-eyed kid with a telescope could pick out the luminaries of the Northern sky with ease. Kindergarten classes drew crayon pictures of the constellations, everyone knew the names of all the visible stars.

Jack Kennesaw had been around for years, and was as basic as a Crayola crayon could have made him. All broad strokes, no subtleties. According to him, he'd been bilked out of triple-dipping into the government retirement fund as an ex-Marine, an ex-Letter Carrier, and a former Park Services ranger. Dismissed from the Park Service without benefits for accepting a bribe by undercover Drug Enforcement agents to look the other way while they grew marijuana on the National Forest land in his charge. Now he took every chance he could to hit back at the government.

Kennesaw had been a Commie-hating patriot of the McCarthy era, a black-list keeper of weirdos and freaks he knew had to be Stalin's foreguard in America. He took credit for wiping out Uncle Sam's most embarrassing failure in the face of the Red Horde by using *Reality* to perform his Patriotic duty to eliminate that other moon from existence. He claimed the U.S. had allowed the Soviets to put a man on that moon in the early '60s, before Armstrong's *Eagle* had landed on Luna, in another reality. He may have actually believed it himself. After Sarah Cole, Randomites were ready to swallow anything, and they ate Kennesaw's story for dinner. Jack Kennesaw had used *Reality* to put the U.S. ahead in the space race! Sure, why not?

Then there was the case of Haver Compton.

His wife had left him, and he was known as a quiet, chronically depressed drunk who spent his time on the porch, sipping malt liquor while staring at their wedding portrait.

His suicide, disemboweling himself with a steak knife, was the culmination of a week-long frenzy of madness brought on by some of the wildest speculation about what the manipulation of *Reality* had done yet. One day someone noticed it had been tampered with, had been changed. No one saw who had actually gone in there to yank on whatever chain, or pull whatever lever, but there was something *different* about it. And while everybody could agree on that point, none of them could agree as to *what* was different about the sculpture.

Reality

Osgood remembered hearing them, standing around it all that Monday morning, trying to figure it out.

"That part there's higher than before."

"No, it's lower."

"It's that section there on the side, it's moved in a bit."

"No, it's moved *out* more."

"That bit up top's shifted to the left."

"To the right!"

"Higher."

"Lower."

"In."

"Out!"

"Left!"

"RIGHT!!"

And on and on and on. They were still at it when Osgood walked across the square to take his usual lunch at Pete's, only the argument had intensified into a screaming mob. He remembered looking at *Reality* that morning going to work, and it looked exactly the same as the day before, but he didn't say anything. They probably would have lynched him, because by God they were all absolutely, positively, one hundred percent certain it had changed. "Higher!" "Lower!" "In!" "Out!" "Left!" "Right!" At least they had it narrowed down.

Eventually someone realized that if *Reality* had been altered at all, then so too reality. The mob paused, ceased being a mob for a moment of being just a lot of folks standing around, and then it became a riot. The fighting only broke out because people were in each other's way as they tried to run home to check those old photographs again, or to catch a nap so as to dream about what might have been. It was at that moment that Osgood first conceived of the notion that there had to be a way to put *Reality* back the way it had been originally.

Among the speculated lost realities that arose then, there was one that, at first, seemed way too outrageous for anyone to take seriously. In fact, Osgood was sure that it had been put forth more as a joke by the skeptical few, maybe a half dozen people, of Random who regarded the whole business with disdain. Their opinion of *Reality* was that the materials it was built out of would have been put to better use at the recycling plant. Their status as art critics notwithstanding, between them there was probably enough imagination to come up with the concept of the Thirdmate.

It went like this:

Humans had originally consisted of *three* sexes. Male, Female, and the so-called Thirdmate. Men and women could not procreate without the Thirdmate. The man provided the semen to the Third, then the Third impregnated the woman with it. Men and women were never meant to interact sexually! That could explain a lot, some folks reasoned.

Osgood watched as the idea caught on, managing to keep his own head above water while everyone else drowned in this newest flood of madness. Why had the Thirdmates been wiped from existence? Who had done it?

Then the anonymous confession appeared, words made up of letters cut from the newspaper, which was found Scotch-taped to the window of the mayor's car, saying, "Our Thirdmate cheated on us so we got rid of *all* of them!" That was it.

People started dreaming of their Thirdmates. Husbands and wives who suddenly realized they didn't "belong" together suddenly found an excuse to file for divorce. The sheriff and his deputies had their hands full with hundreds of nightly domestic situations. Some spouses had affairs with someone they were sure had been their Thirdmate in the other reality, which led to even more problems. Luckily there were no fatalities, although there were a fair number of close calls as jealous husbands and wives turned everyday household appliances into weapons. There were plenty of serious injuries pouring into the emergency rooms at Random General.

Until Haver Compton.

When he performed his unceremonious *hara-kiri*, there was no *kaishaku* there to cut his head off for him. He died from loss of blood and guts.

Poor Haver Compton. Poor, lonely, fever-dreaming, Haver. It so happened that around this time Haver was sick and running a temperature of 104. There was no one around to care for him like his wife had done when they were together. He stared at their wedding picture and wished she were there with him, to ease his suffering with kind words and a cool hand on his forehead. Decked out in his tux, Haver looked smart and full of promise in that picture. His new wife, Melanie, looked rapturous in white. But there was this space between them, a space big enough for a third person.

Thirdmate.

Maybe it was more than Haver could take, to realize then that in another reality, even after his Melanie had left him, he might not be alone. But in *this* reality, because someone had messed with *Reality*, he was alone and miserable. He decided he didn't want to live in this reality.

The town was stunned. Jake Sky, newly elected sheriff a few weeks before, put the town under martial law until things calmed down. He made it illegal to even enter *Reality*, and posted TRESPASSERS WILL BE SHOT signs around the industrial monster. Osgood, who had been going back and forth about whether or not to try and *do* something about all this, finally decided. It had to stop, no matter what.

ARTIST TO MAKE SCULPTURE OUT OF SCRAP METAL was the headline of the morning edition of the Random Times on July 19th, 1911. There was a picture of the artist, Jay Elroy, who disappeared as soon as *Reality* was finished and never resurfaced *anywhere* as far as anyone knew. He'd been heading onward

Reality

to Portland, where he'd hoped to start an art movement there, emulating what Alexander Calder had been doing for a year. Massive industrial sculptures were a purely American form which Elroy was positive would forever alter the face of the art world, and probably have a profound effect on society as a whole. Like every other art movement before and since.

In the two-column interview with him, Elroy predicted that at the very least industrial sculptors, utilizing scrap metal and mechanical means, would spell doom for stone and clay. While he lamented the inevitable demise of marble, he felt sure that eventually scrap metal sculptors would someday be able to achieve a similar, and probably superior effect as they perfected their craft. He stayed in Random for six months while he built *Reality*, the flagship of what he envisioned as a series of sculptures that would ultimately be the centerpiece of every town in America. That was his contribution to the Movement, which he hoped to ignite in Portland with the spark of his own pure devotion.

Osgood figured Elroy probably didn't manage too well in Portland, which wasn't exactly an artistic Mecca at that time, and wound up spending his life slaving in a factory, the ultimate industrial work of art. Maybe he was happy. Not that it mattered.

Osgood had acquired several grainy photographs of *Reality* right after it was finished, before anyone had a chance to "interact" with it. He was almost certain he knew what it had looked like originally, despite the poor quality of the pictures. He studied *Reality* from his usual booth in Pete's everyday at lunch, until he started to see a pattern, and he could trace the different changes the sculpture had gone through over the years to arrive in its current form. That was how he discovered the lever, right near the entrance, that he knew if pulled would revert *Reality* back to its original form, and would show once and for all to everyone, including that stubborn Indian sheriff, that it had no effect on *real* reality.

All he had to do was get to it.

Sky would be watching *Reality* like a mother watching a child. He was thoroughly convinced of the sculpture's power, utterly brainwashed by the hysteria it inspired. When the call to dismantle the thing had risen, Sky sided with those who feared it might be like dismantling the universe. No one knew what would happen, so it was better to just leave it be.

Some folks were even convinced that Jay Elroy had actually been an emissary of God, testing the Faith of the good people of Random by placing *Reality* in their hands, to preserve for Him. It was becoming an underground religion.

The big question, as far as Osgood could see, was this: Would Jake Sky shoot him if he simply walked into *Reality* and pulled that lever? Was the sheriff *that* far gone?

He drank his first cup of coffee while it was still hot, and wound up burning his tongue. When he requested a refill, he also asked for a glass of ice water. He

Stephen L. Antczak

was sucking on a piece of ice now, running it over his sore tongue, and waiting. Breakfast and lunch smells filled Pete's Grill. Bacon, hamburgers on the grill, cinnamon rolls, chicken soup…Osgood took it all in, savoring it. His heart beat rapidly, his palms were sweating. He wasn't sure he'd live through the day.

He almost tried it on his way over, but lost his nerve when he imagined Jake's, or his deputies' guns trained on him as he walked, ready to shoot him down in the street if he even so much as glanced in the direction of *Reality*. So he didn't. He didn't even look. He decided to go ahead and eat his usual lunch at Pete's, and work up the nerve while he ate to do what needed to be done. Besides, if he *was* going to get shot, he didn't want to die on an empty stomach.

The door to Pete's opened, and Jake Sky entered. He nodded greetings to several other patrons, nodded to the cook and to Bea, and walked right up to Osgood's table. This time he didn't bother to ask if Osgood minded, and just sat.

"How do you know?" Osgood asked suddenly, surprising himself as much as confusing the sheriff for a moment.

"Excuse me?" Jake frowned. "How do I know what?"

"How do you know anything'll happen if I…if *someone* changes *Reality*."

Sky leaned back in his seat, the padded bench creaking under his 260 pounds. He absentmindedly reached up to twirl one of his black braids. Maybe not so absentmindedly. Maybe he was reminding Osgood that he was an American Indian, and therefore more in tune with Nature and Reality, or something like that.

"I don't," he said. "Nor do I know *nothing* will happen. I mean, what if it *does* change reality, Osgood? What if it were possible for someone to, say, erase my people's existence from reality, make it so Native Americans never were? I wouldn't like that very much."

"How do you know you wouldn't just suddenly become white, or black? Or Chinese?" It was purely a hypothetical question, but a tic started in Jake's neck. Stepping across the line of racism, Osgood realized, was a tricky business.

"My people would no longer exist," Jake said in a controlled tone. "I still wouldn't like that."

"Come on, Sheriff," Osgood said, leaning forward in his seat a little, trying to appeal to the Indian's common sense, to the intelligence behind the fear of the unknown. "Think about it. Based on evidence that is far too easy to disprove, that is sometimes so obviously self-contradictory I could cry…you're willing to even consider the possibility that altering that piece of scrap metal out there could alter the fabric of reality. Change history, change *now*. I mean, *come on*!"

"Can you prove that it doesn't?"

Osgood and Jake Sky stared at each other for a while. Jake's eyes were impassive, the Indian could probably stare down a grizzly. If Osgood didn't look away, he'd lose his nerve for sure, so he turned to regard *Reality*.

Reality

"Yes," he said, the word almost sticking in his throat like bile. He pointed toward the sculpture. "See that big lever right at the entrance there? If that lever is pulled, *Reality* will return to its original form." Sky was looking, and Osgood knew he'd see it. That was one of the weird aspects of *Reality*, which Osgood couldn't figure out, that one could see a pattern within it, see a change that corresponded somehow with an idea about the real world outside, an imaginary connection to be sure, but still…Pull that lever, that part of the sculpture would dip and that part would spin around and that other piece would slide over, and the next thing you know it's back to the way it was when Jay Elroy first built it. Perhaps he disappeared into obscurity because *Reality* had been his one wad, shot prematurely in a town no one ever visited, his single vision wasted on people who would never understand *Reality*'s connection with reality.

"Maybe," Sheriff Sky finally said, after staring at that one spot long and hard. Maybe.

But Osgood wasn't there.

Sky looked frantically around, only to see the portly, middle-aged Home Depot clerk deftly dodge one of the deputies outside, pushing him backwards over a curb. The others Sky had placed around the sculpture were too far away to catch Osgood before he made it to that lever. He tramped through a flower bed bordering the square, and headed straight for *Reality*. Jake rushed out of Pete's, almost subconsciously pulling his service .38 from its holster.

"Stop!" Jake yelled. Osgood did, maybe ten feet from that lever, and turned to face him. Jake kept a bead on him with the gun, and slowly advanced on him. His deputies had explicit orders not to draw their weapons. If anyone was going to shoot Osgood Kramer, it would be the sheriff.

With his arms outspread, Osgood said, "What are you going to do, Jake, kill me?"

"If I have to," Jake said.

Osgood started backing towards *Reality*. The fear that had built inside him all morning was gone. The air outside was cool, energizing, and he breathed it in as though he'd never noticed it before. Maybe he hadn't. Everything around him appeared with a sharp clarity he remembered seeing only as a child. It was all more real to him at that moment than it had been for the last twenty-five years. He smiled, and saw Jake frown in response.

"You don't have to shoot me," Osgood said, and lowered his arms. "You know I'm right, Jake Sky." With that he turned and began walking toward the lever, taking his time because he knew there was no way either Jake or any of his deputies would be able to reach him before he got to it. Unless Jake shot him.

"Stop!" Jake yelled again, but this time he was ignored.

Osgood kept walking, until he was at the entrance to the sculpture. It towered over him, an industrial Sphinx spouting riddles. They all had the same answer, he realized as he grabbed hold of the lever, then looked at Jake.

The sheriff still had the gun pointed at him, still stood with his feet spread apart, his knees slightly bent, like he'd seen in the movies. *Draw.*

Osgood grunted with the effort it took to pull the lever down, straining against rust and inertia; then it moved, imperceptibly at first, but it moved. His muscles burned, his face was on fire, his breath came out in explosive bursts, but inch by creaking inch, the lever gave.

Then *Reality* changed. A chorus of groaning metal was wrenched from within as it moved, as joints and axles that hadn't been used for years suddenly came into play. *Reality*'s shape altered subtly at first, then dramatically as entire sections slid forth or disappeared within the mass. Osgood ran from beneath it, stumbled in the grass to where Jake stood, his gun lowered now, and watched the transformation. They both watched. It was difficult to pinpoint any single aspect of the sculpture that changed, there was just a perception of differences here and there, but nothing obvious.

It seemed to last forever, seemed to get louder and louder until Jake fell to his knees beside Osgood, both hands over his ears, .38 dropped and forgotten in the grass. All around the square, the deputies, the lunch clientele in Pete's, the businessmen and women, the bums, they all fell to the ground clutching their heads as the cacophony battered their senses.

Then it stopped.

A faint echo of it could still be heard in the high country around Random, but *Reality* was quiet. Sky was the first one to his feet. He retrieved his gun, then roughly helped Osgood stand. They both looked around, at the town surrounding them, and beyond that the world, the universe. Osgood turned to regard Jake with a grin, triumphant yet sober in the face of this new cosmic truth.

"Well?" he asked.

The sheriff shrugged. "We'll see." Then he turned and walked away, back towards Pete's Grill.

A woman, attractive despite the encroaching of middle age around her eyes, walked onto the square and stood beside Osgood. He nodded hello to her, then kept looking at her because she seemed somehow familiar, although he was sure he'd never seen her before.

"It's ugly," she said, nodding towards *Reality*.

"Oh, I don't think so," Osgood said.

Then the woman looked at Osgood. "You should learn to just leave things alone, you know." Without waiting for a reply she started walking towards *Reality*.

"Sarah!" a voice yelled, and Osgood turned to see Jake Sky running towards them. "Sarah, don't!" He didn't catch her. She stepped into the sculpture, walked right up to a certain switch and flipped it without hesitation.

Metal shifted with a baleful moan, and *Reality* changed....

To be quite honest, I generally don't like vampire fiction. Especially so-called "cutting-edge" vampire fiction. To me, vampire stories are only a few steps above writing media tie-in fiction, like Trek novels, which are basically glorified copy designed to help market a product line. That said, I acknowledge from a purely entertainment standpoint that Trek novels and vampire fiction certainly attract an audience. I guess this is where the distinction between art and entertainment comes in, but I don't want to get into that quagmire of aesthetics right now.

The idea that vampires are destroyed by sunlight seemed like an interesting rule to play with, despite the fact that this is actually an invention of Hollywood. In Bram Stoker's novel, sunlight merely weakens Dracula; it doesn't destroy him.

Given that, I decided to analyze this latter-day development in the vampire myth. Why would sunlight destroy vampires? For that matter, why do vampires live forever? Why are they stronger than normal humans? It occurred to me that one reason this could be so is that everyone believed it, thus making it a psychological phenomenon. The vampires believed so strongly that sunlight would destroy them that it actually did.

I've always liked the idea of virtual reality, and it tickled me to imagine an ancient vampire in a cyberpunk setting. What if virtual reality was so good that one could not tell a real sun rise from a virtual one? If you were a vampire and you believed the virtual sunrise was real, what would happen?

This story was originally published in the vampire fiction magazine, Dreams of Decadence.

Virtual Day

KATYA DONNED HER VR UNIT, only the helmet this time, and called Daley. He'd know it was her calling. He had caller I.D. like everyone else, so if he didn't answer she'd know to take it as a personal offense. Then she'd have one more reason to rip his throat open if she ever really did come face to face with him.

"Kat," his voice buzzed in her ears. "Hold on…" A moment later the default image of her own VR unit dissolved, a Victorian library melting away to be

daydreams undertaken

replaced by Daley's. He'd programmed a smoky, loud, crowded bar as his. The initial phase of it occurred automatically as Katya saw his virtual self at the bar. He'd made his icon a slicked up Bogart looking at her through a haze of cigarette smoke, then motioning with his head for her come on over. Without the sensation of walking this time, since she avoided total immersion, Katya drifted over to the empty stool by Daley's icon.

"What can I do for ya, Kat?" he asked. He took a puff on his cigarette and blew smoke in her face. She took the cigarette from his mouth and dropped in on the floor. Nice touch, letting her do that. One of the reasons she'd hired him in the first place was things like that in his programs.

"I ran your program today," she told him. "It needs work."

"It doesn't need work," he replied. "It's perfect."

"That's the problem. You need to put in some random factors, some complexity, make it so every time you run it it's different. Just like in nature."

Daley's Bogart sighed.

"Look," Katya said. "In the contract you signed it stipulated one free tune-up. I'll *pay* you for it, your usual rate, just don't give me any grief about it."

He considered it for a moment, then pulled out another cigarette, his lighter, and fired up. After a couple puffs he nodded.

"Sure thing, Kat."

"And please don't call me that," she said. Before he could reply she disconnected. Only one person had ever been allowed to call her that, and that had been in her life, before Pyotr Bezukhov's bite made her into what she remained today: a vampyr, a creature of eternal nights, feeding on the blood of the fresh kill for the last four hundred years…

During those four centuries she'd commissioned paintings of sunrises and sunsets, then photographs, then she'd produced movies, from the early days of silent black and whites to IMAX extravaganzas…sunlight shining across the waves of a choppy Mediterranean sea, or glinting off the side of a glass-encased skyscraper in Manhattan, or blazing across the airless void as filmed from the space shuttle Endeavor. Then, when virtual reality had gone past the crawling stage and started taking those first hesitant steps on its own two feet, Katya sank as much money into research and development as her fortune could comfortably allow.

The first few years yielded naught for her investments but digital landscapes in crayon-like primary colors awash in static-filled electronic "sunlight." Katya despaired that perhaps she'd overestimated the potential of this new technology. For the first few years virtual reality proved too interpretive, so that while a painting by someone like Van Gogh caused a stirring in her heart, the poorly realized virtual sun failed to. Certainly a movie such as the infamous Warhol realtime tracking of the sun as it moved across the sky warmed Katya's soul in a way VR had yet to even approach.

Virtual Day

However, virtual reality technology advanced rapidly. In twenty years Katya realized she'd been right about it in the beginning. Finally, at long last, she'd be able to not just *see* a re-created sunrise, she'd be able to *feel* it. It would be as good as real, and *it wouldn't destroy her*!

Daley, Alvin Daley. He was as annoying a human being as Katya had ever met. Or virtually met, in any case. She had a feeling that if she ever met the man in person he wouldn't survive the experience. Unfortunately, or maybe fortunately, she didn't even know where he lived. It could be anywhere, maybe right there in Miami where she had a house in ever-trendy South Beach, or maybe in Kiev, her birthplace, or Groznyy, the site of her death and re-birth.

The blood of the fresh kill...which reminded her, it was time for a snack. One reason she liked Miami was the abundance of youthful flesh to sink her fangs into, gallons of young, vibrant blood to suck. The energy the young embodied fed her spirit as much as their precious life fluid fed her body.

Outside a light drizzle gave the night air a slight chill. Street lights cast a yellow glow that glinted off the wet pavement. Clouds shrouded the sky, reminding her of London, where she'd lived for almost two hundred years before coming to America. In Miami, as in every large city in the world, homeless men, women, and children wandered the streets at all hours, begging, stealing, weeping in self-pity at their misery. Katya felt nothing for them. Human lives came and went, as hers had come and gone, and she lived in her own version of Hell just as they did. At least they found peace in the end.

She took the metrorail across the intercoastal to Miami proper, where the clubs attracted students from the University of Miami and Florida International University, not to mention the high school kids with fake barcode tattoos identifying them as old enough to drink. Katya enjoyed walking among them, the Angel of Death all but invisible in the midst of life. She was hungry for Cuban tonight, something tender yet spicy. Young girls out looking to dance and play dangerous games with older men. She knew just where to go: Fernando's in Coconut Grove.

The Grove turned into a fiesta of lights, noise, and humanity every night, the streets clogged with hansom cabs, rickshaws, and bicycles as partyers bar-hopped or cruised. Katya hired a hansom to take her to within a few blocks of Fernando's, then walked the rest of the way. Surrounding herself with so many people did wonders for her appetite.

Drunken revellers knocked into her, men brushed by her suggestively. There was always the scent of danger in Miami, even for Katya, who never knew when she might find herself set upon by the Caribbean voodoo equivalent of a vampire hunter. Cruising these streets was just another way to feel something like...alive.

"Yo, lady," a Haitian Joe Adonis, dressed in gangster pinstripes, his skin black as coal, slurred at her. "You wanna come play? I know a good game for you, you know?"

Katya paused, smiling sweetly at the man.

"I like the eyes you got, lady," he said. "They green like the ocean, you know? I bet they light up when you got a man inside you, you know?"

Katya leaned closer to him, sniffing to get his scent. She'd be able to find him anywhere now, months, even years later. Then she gave him her best predatory grin, letting him see her fangs. His eyes widened and he took a step back.

"We'll meet again," she said with a wink, then continued on her way, hearing him mutter something in Haitian Creole that sounded very much like a prayer.

On to Fernando's and some young meat.

Just outside the door a line of kids waiting patiently to get in snaked along the sidewalk. Katya approached, intending to walk past them and charm Ernesto the doorman into letting her slip by. But then she heard a young voice pleading, in Cuban-accented English.

"Please, Thomas, I'm sorry, okay? Let's just *go*, okay?"

Katya realized no one else around her could hear the girl, not over the racket of traffic, the hoots and howls of partiers. The voice came from down the alley along the side of Fernando's.

"Fuck you, Rita," another voice said, this one definitely anglo and a little older.

"But I said I was sorry—" Someone, Thomas presumably, slapped Rita, cutting her off. Katya abandoned the line into Fernando's to walk down the alley. A yellow light barely illuminated a couple just around the back corner of the building. They were dressed up, he in a beige, loose-fitting suit of raw silk — she could smell it — and she in spiked heels and a red and black party dress, her hair done up with red ribbons. Thomas and Rita, out for a night of Latin dancing and fighting.

"You kissed that guy, and then you started talking in Spanish. I *told* you I didn't want you doing that," Thomas said.

"He was my *cousin*," Rita said, "and he doesn't speak very good English!"

"No one kisses their cousin like *that*," Thomas said. He raised his hand to slap Rita again.

At this point, Katya came around the corner so they could see her.

"Hi," she said. "I couldn't help but overhear your argument."

"Go away," Thomas told her. Oh, yes, he was drunk, so drunk he could barely stand up straight. He had a solid build, but these days anyone with *any* money could afford to get sculpted.

Katya smiled, and said, "Make me."

"I'm not in the mood for games, bitch," he sneered at her.

"I am." She walked up to him, grinning. "You're lucky I'm in a good mood. I could make the rest of your life very, very unpleasant."

"Okay," said Thomas. "If that's the way you want it." He reached for her. She grabbed his arm, jerked him forward, then grabbed his head with two

Virtual Day

hands and twisted. His neck broke with a gratifying snap, and he fell to the ground, limp.

Rita barely had time to register what had happened. She started to scream, but Katya was on her, clamping a strong, cold hand over the girl's mouth, holding her against the wall. Rita's eyes were wide and her body shook with fear. Katya kissed her on the lips, forcing her tongue inside for a moment. Oh yes, tender yet spicy....

"I might have let you live, once," Katya said. "But then I'd only find someone just like you." Rita let out a frightened whimper. "Ssshhhh. It won't be so bad." Then Katya sank her fangs into Rita's neck, and drank. Rita didn't fight, and Katya didn't spill a drop of precious blood.

Feeding reinvigorated her, as always.

She took a cab to a dance club in downtown Miami, the Hot Spot, and burned on the dance floor to techno-rave music and industrial trip-hop until four. The sky had cleared substantially by then.

She hired a hansom to take her across the intercoastal to South Beach, then sat back and looked up at the stars. A beautiful night, reminiscent of nights vacationing in Greece and Italy in the early 1800s, riding in open carriages with Pyotr. She was glad such modes of transportation had come back into vogue, although she could appreciate the brief century of speed humanity had flirted with. Speeding along in an open convertible gave a thrill a lot like the thrill she got during the kill.

Many of the old ways had come back, although modern life became more and more intertwined with high technology. Poor Pyotr, so unlike Katya, had not the stomach for it. He only recently conceded to using virtual reality to speak to Katya, and only because she'd re-created their library from London as her set.

That house had long ago burned to the ground, fallen victim to a mob intent on burning a careless new charge of Katya's. Pyotr now stayed in a suite of rooms in the Turner Tower in Atlanta, posing as a reclusive wealthy investor who'd inherited his fortune, as his father had before him, and his before him.... He'd made use of that ruse continuously since before their days in London. Katya started out with money Pyotr gave her, but lost it all in the London fire. After that, she seduced a string of businessman, married them, gave them the bite but did *not* let them feed, so they lived on for years before succumbing to the release of death.

Now she posed as a wealthy widow, dabbling as a venture capitalist in VR. Which reminded her she had to call Daley when she got back to the house. He was the best at creating the subtle nuances most virtual artists tended to overlook: the difference between the sound of gravel and the sound of dried flora crunching underfoot, for instance. Now she wanted him to work his magic and create a sunrise, an early and late morning, a high noon, a mid-afternoon, an early evening, and a sunset...each with its own particular feel, its own enchantments.

How Katya had dreamed of the sun shining down on her with its brilliance! Until color motion pictures made it possible for her to see it safely, Katya had practically forgotten what the sun looked like. She'd managed to fantasize it into a great glowing, burning yellow ball one could actually see rolling across the sky.

"Now where to, Miss?" the driver of the hansom asked. He was an older black man, an air of true dignity about him. Probably drove the hansom just to keep busy in his later years. Katya looked around, saw they were already in the South Beach area. "What time is it?" she asked him.

"Three fifteen in the morning," he answered.

Katya considered going to the beach, maybe even stripping and going for a swim in the ocean. She liked swimming nude. It made her feel as close to alive as she'd ever felt *after*. Regular feedings kept her figure full, her color rich. She knew men stopped to watch her when she swam naked, hoping to see her body in the glow of moonlight.

Alas, not tonight. Perhaps, had it been an hour or so earlier, but she wouldn't be able to enjoy her swim knowing dawn loomed a few hours away. She'd cut it too close too many times, getting home sometimes a mere thirty minutes before the sun's emergence.

"Take me home, please," she told the driver, then gave him the address.

The first thing she did when she got there was don her VR gear and call Daley. He'd be there, he seemed to *always* be there, which sometimes led Katya to wonder if Daley had programmed an AI to behave like him when he *wasn't* there....

"Hello, Kat," Bogart/Daley said as she glided through Rick's Virtual Cafe. "What's cookin'?"

"Did you work on the program?" she asked him.

He paused to down the remainder of a whiskey on the rocks, then looked her up and down.

"Yeah," he said. "Sure, I finished it. Just like you wanted. No sweat. Speaking of sweat, how'd you like to create some with me later?"

"Sure," Katya replied. "Why don't I just hop on a plane and come visit you...where do you live, again?"

"Sorry, Kat," Daley said. "I'd love to have you over, but I never bring clients to the home office. I'm in the virtual business, baby. I know a nice little Roman bathhouse program we can meet in, though, if you're interested."

Katya shook her head.

"I only do *that* in the flesh," she said. "I'll give the program a try, then get back to you."

"It won't need anymore tweaking," he told her. "It's *finished*, babe."

"We'll see."

Virtual Day

She faded out of Daley's set, back to her Victorian library for a moment. Katya had it set up so she had to pull a book from the shelves, the book representing a program she wanted to run. She found the book with *Virtual Day* inscribed on the spine, pulled it down. Suddenly she found herself standing in a field, the sky gray and the sun blotted out of the sky by dark clouds. All at once the clouds drifted to either side as a wind kicked up, and the sun blazed majestically through the hole. Nice touch, Katya decided. Things still seemed to move a tad quickly, but not *too* much that it ruined the feeling of realness. Daley had come through after all. Maybe he *would* survive a face-to-face with her. Maybe she'd just make him sweat....

Katya stood there, enjoying the sensations, especially the feeling of warmth that played across her upturned face. Sun-kissed at last, after all those years. Pyotr *had* to experience this...The only times Katya immersed herself totally in VR were to feel what she now felt.

Reluctantly, Katya disengaged herself from her virtual day, then back to the library, where she called Pyotr. She could imagine the elegant chimes of his system ringing throughout his apartment. They played a little tune, each one different depending on who called, so like Daley, Pyotr would know it was Katya. Her song was *Fur Elise*. Right now he'd be cursing her name as he closed a book, a *real* book printed on paper and bound in leather, then got up out of his favorite recliner and walked over to the computer.

On the wall of virtual books across from where Katya's icon sat, a screen suddenly shimmered into existence. Two-dimensional, Pyotr looked at her from the other side of an electronic window.

"Pyotr, what are you doing?" Katya asked, consternation present in her tone.

"I didn't feel like putting on that awful helmet and those gloves," he said. "What are you calling about? I was in the middle of *War and Peace*."

"Again? Haven't you read that four or five times?"

He sighed.

"Pyotr," Katya said, "please put the virching gear on. There's something I want to show you."

"Let me guess," he replied. "A sunrise?"

"No."

He laughed at her.

"Katya, I've known you far too long for you to try lying to me."

"It *isn't* a sunrise. It isn't a sunset, either. It's the sun breaking through storm clouds. It really is spectacular. You can *feel* the rays on your skin—"

"Okay, okay. I'll make you a deal. I'll come with you this *one time*, and then you have to promise to leave me alone for thirty or forty years. I've been feeling anti-social lately."

"Deal," Katya said. It amused, and sometimes annoyed, her the way Pyotr seemed to conceive of virtual reality as a *going to* somewhere. She'd tried to explain it to him several times, but it never seemed to sink in that when he put on his virching gear and accessed the Net he wasn't *going* anywhere.

"One of these days this obsession you have with the sun is going to be your undoing," he told her. "You'll get so worked up by all your paintings and movies that you'll want to take a peek at the real thing, and then *pfft*."

"Pyotr," she said, "shut up and put your gear on."

He sighed, then said, "Okay, be right back."

The window faded from the shelves of her library, and Katya waited for him to materialize. She decided to amuse herself by running a subroutine in her library program. The girl, a child of seven or eight years, appeared in the middle of the room, blood dripping from gashes in her arms. She held her arms out and began slowly spinning around, speeding up gradually until the blood flew off her arms, spattering the walls of the library, the books and paintings…It brought Katya back to a time in Paris, a visit to get away from dreary London for a few months, when she had kept the girl, whose name she never learned, alive for a week, feeding off her and watching her dance, humming a little tune to herself, too afraid to stop.

If she didn't pay too close attention, the illusion was enough to cast light in a dark corner of her mind, awakening certain memories, and she could actually *taste* the girl again. Not since then had she tasted such sweet blood.

Suddenly the dancing, bleeding girl flickered and vanished, along with the blood splotches in the Persian rug and on the books and the walls. Pyotr's icon replaced her: Bela Lugosi as Dracula, one of the few vampire portrayals in the movies Pyotr ever admitted to liking. Katya commissioned it for him when she got sick of his default icon, a standard blond-haired, blue-eyed Ken.

"Well, where is it?" Bela/Pyotr asked. "Where's the sun?"

"Hold your horses," Katya said. "Aren't you even glad to see me?"

"I am always glad to see you, Katya," he told her. He walked over, held out his hand to her, and she let him take her hand in his. Then he bent and gently kissed her, pressing her hand softly to his lips. She was glad she'd spent the extra money to have her system upgraded to allow for almost complete sensory input, even if she only rarely indulged in total immersion. Pyotr's touch was one thing she tended to miss when they were apart.

"Here we go," Katya said.

The library slowly faded while being gradually replaced by a field and a wide open sky…Except the sky was gray with clouds, so gray there was barely a hint of the sun. Even in real life, a vampyr could survive for a short time outside in such weather. Pyotr looked around, as if seeking Katya's sun, frowning all the while.

"Just be patient," Katya told him.

Pyotr sighed, but said nothing.

A wind blew across the field, the tall grass rippling like the surface of a lake. Pyotr's cape billowed around him, and Katya caught him grinning at the effect.

Virtual Day

In the sky she detected movement. The clouds were racing, those below blowing across the paths of those above.

She tapped Pyotr on the shoulder and pointed to where she could see, by the way the clouds were moving, a hole seemed about to open. She wanted to make sure he saw it right as it happened, right as sunlight burst through.

And it did. Radiant, glowing, burning through the clouds like a shaft of holy light. The light played across the field, seeming to almost set the grass afire, and washed over Katya and Pyotr. Katya closed her eyes and turned her face up to the warmth. The insides of her eyelids glowed red. Then she heard Pyotr's gasp, and a choked scream.

She opened her eyes. Pyotr/Bela Lugosi had thrown his cape over his head and cowered in the grass. A continuous moan issued forth from beneath the cape, and his body trembled as if he'd gone into a seizure.

"Pyotr?" she asked. Her first thoughts were that the virtual sunlight had seemed too real to him, scaring him. Then she saw his icon losing its clarity, as if the connection had gone bad. Or he tried to rip his virching gear off without disconnecting first.

"Pyotr!" she yelled. "Pyotr, it's *not* real! It's *not real!*"

But he was beyond hearing her words. Whatever held his Bela icon together in her virtual realm of sunlight snapped, and suddenly it collapsed in on itself and disappeared. She stood there, alone, as clouds moved to once again hide the sun.

A little while later, after Katya took her virching gear off, she tried calling Pyotr. No answer. She tried again and again until dawn, wanting to find out what had happened, wanting to make sure he wasn't angry with her. She left several messages, and sleep overcame her as outside daylight scattered the darkness, splintering it into shadows.

The next night she still couldn't reach him, and his messages had not been accessed. This concerned her. When Katya went out to feed, she didn't feel like turning it into an event, so satisfied her hunger with the blood of a homeless man she found drinking malt liquor on the beach.

She returned home, checked voice-mail, nothing, and then e-mail: A message, signatured as from the Turner Tower Authority, awaited her urgent attention. *Would like to speak to you re one Pyotr Bezukhov, deceased. Last known contact via Net with Katya Rostov, Miami, Florida. Please call ASAP.*

Pyotr Bezukhov, deceased.

She replied via e-mail, then waited. Moments later her phone chimed. She answered it, voice-only.

"Yes," she said.

"Katya Rostov?" asked a woman on the other end.

"Yes."

"Sorry to bother at this hour, but we noticed that your contact with Mr. Bezukhov seemed to always occur after dark, and generally after midnight."

Stephen L. Antczak

"That's right," Katya responded.

"Mr. Bezukhov apparently has no relatives," the woman said. "And you're the only person who kept in touch with him on a regular basis, aside from his accountant. You were his friend?"

"Yes, for a long, long time."

"Do you know if he has any relatives, then?"

"No," Katya said. "None that are living."

"I see...He left a sizeable estate, Ms. Rostov. We're not exactly sure what to—"

"Give it to charity," Katya cut her off. "He told me several times that if he ever died...that *when* he died, to make sure all his money went to charity."

"I see. We'll have to consult his accountant, then, but if it turns out that's what he wanted, then that's what we'll do," the woman said. "Thank you."

"How did he die?" Katya asked suddenly. "I'm sorry, but I need to know..."

"I understand. It's kind of bizarre, but they said he died from spontaneous combustion. He just burst into flames. I was told he probably didn't feel any pain at all, it happened so quickly, if that helps. I read about it once, supposedly it happens a couple times a year—"

"Yes, well, thank you," Katya said, cutting her off again. She hung up. Burst into flames, spontaneous combustion. It's what would have happened had Pyotr stepped out into direct sunlight, as it would happen to Katya, and any other vampyr. But it had to be *real* sunlight.

She remembered the first time she took Pyotr to a movie. For the first fifty or so years of movies Pyotr had refused to go, and by then color had replaced black and whites. Later, he got caught up on the older flicks watching late-night TV, then cable and video cassettes. But that first time, when the movie started and *daylight* came up on the screen, Pyotr had screamed and ducked behind the seat in front of him.

He never really grasped that movies were an art form, that what happened in them wasn't quite real. For a time after that first movie, he thought the silver screen was some sort of magic window that allowed people to see things without being observed, and to safely view the sun. He eventually realized that what he saw on the screen, in a theater or on the television, was recorded, and arranged in much the same way as a play. Even into the 1990s, though, it surprised him to see an actor appear in another movie after having apparently been killed in a previous film.

"He thought it was real," Katya whispered to herself. Her virtual sun, so brilliantly programmed to seem as real as possible by Daley, had destroyed Pyotr. But not her. What did that mean?

It was no more than a painting, a photo, or a film to Katya. Another representation of something she'd lost, something Pyotr had taken away from her, so long ago. It was art, and Daley was one of the best artists of his day. Katya

Virtual Day

had always commissioned pieces by the best, by Brady, Da Vinci, Bergman, Lebovitz, Picasso, Scorsese...Artwork no one else knew of, save Pyotr. None of the other sunsets, sunrises, high noons, or any other sun-work had ever actually, physically hurt Pyotr, not even the IMAX film.

Why?

He thought it was real. And that meant that what destroyed him had not been *out*side, but *in*side. Himself. So did that mean the sun, the real sun, might not hurt Katya if she believed it wouldn't?

Dawn approached. She could test her new theory within a few hours. She had a feeling that if she didn't do it that morning, then the longer she waited, the less chance she had of ever trying it. Or the less chance she had of *believing*.

She sat there, waiting for the sun, ready to face freedom or, finally, annihilation. All she had to do was step outside. She played it over and over in her mind, Katya opening the door and walking out into the morning light, feeling the warmth on her skin. Then she would alternately burst into flames, *not* burst into flames, burst into flames, *not* burst into flames....

She pulled the curtain back from the sliding glass door that faced east. Then she sat in a chair, back and to one side, and waited.

Katya had read as much about light as she could. There existed no scientific theory about why the sun's rays destroyed vampyrs, although that was partly because there was no scientific acknowledgment of the existence of vampyrs themselves. *It's all in our heads*, she thought. *Who we are, what we do. All in our heads.*

Did this also mean she would no longer have to drink the blood of mortals? Did this mean that she herself might become mortal once again?

If the sunlight didn't burn her to a crisp.

A shaft of sunlight played across the floor as the sun rose. Katya watched it, seeing the hard edge between shadow and light as a No Man's Land that, up until now, she would never have even considered crossing. She sat still, like a statue, throughout the morning as the clock ticked and the sun burned higher in the sky. The area on the floor being lit widened as the sun invaded Katya's home. It took surprisingly little effort not to let her inner terror take over and send her running to her inner sanctum, a room in the center of the house, no windows, where her coffin and soil from Ukraine waited to embrace her. To keep her safe from the sun.

The shadow's edge moved closer, the sun's probing ray pushing it back.

"Why are you so obsessed with the sun?" Pyotr had asked her once, in the mid-1950s, after she'd talked him into seeing the Western *Duel in the Sun.* "It can only destroy you!"

"It's just...so beautiful," Katya replied.

"Can you not find the beauty in a starlit night?" he asked. "A full moon on a calm lake?"

Katya smiled. "I do find beauty in such things," she told Pyotr. "But I can have them whenever I want them. It's the glory of a sunrise I dream of because I know I can have it only one more time, one final glimpse of it before it consumes me."

"Indeed," he said, "I think it already *has* consumed you."

How ironic, she now thought, that the thing he feared most happened *because* he feared it. A false sun, his fear, had consumed him. He believed so strongly that what he saw would destroy him that it *did*. Could it be the other way around? Could Katya believe *nothing* would destroy her, and then walk out into the sunlight as easily as she swam naked under the stars and moon? It *had* to be!

How else to explain such a ridiculous existence, a vampyr's existence? All in the mind.

Katya grinned. It could be however she wanted it to be, she realized. Poor Pyotr, letting his fear get the best of him, would miss out. After centuries of being what humans feared in the night, he wound being no different from them. Too bad. Well, it was his fault that Katya had missed out on the joys of womanhood, having a lover, carrying a child, having a family.

Now, partly through Katya's doing, Pyotr would never experience the power of being a *vampyr* without fear of the dawn.

Perhaps she could keep certain aspects of her ridiculous existence…She liked the thrill of the kill. And, yes, she liked the night. The world became *hers* when the sun went down.

She looked at the shaft of light that fell across her living room. In it she saw specks of dust floating in the air, and suddenly realized she didn't want to be one of those specks, dancing in the light and disappearing at night. She wanted the night, from dusk 'til dawn, to herself and a very few others.

Those others, she could create herself. Pyotr had taught her much in four centuries. She would not make the mistake she made in London.

"Art frees the soul," a mortal once told her in the 1700s. It didn't matter who.

This can be classified as one of my 'punk rock' stories. When I went to college I had been interested in punk rock music for a few years already, but had kept my distance. During college I went to my first punk rock show. The show was in the back room of a video game arcade on University Avenue in Gainesville Florida, in 1985. The bands were Mutley Chix and Scared of Stares from Gainesville, Jehovah's Sicknesses from Orlando, and Stillborn from New York. At that moment I knew I wanted more.

In the years that followed I immersed myself in the local 'scene' in Gainesville, eventually fronting a band myself, Officer Friendly, and co-writing & co-starring in a video movie called Twisted Issues. *I had never tried to use punk rock in my fiction, though, until "Pop Goes Weasel." The idea for the story came from one of those daydreaming sessions where I was just fishing around in my subconscious mind for an idea, something, anything to use as a story. The idea of someone being accidentally transported through time, but only being able to stay in the past for very limited periods came to me. Obviously this has been done, probably most famously in the play* Brigadoon, *but there was also a rather cheesy sci-fi movie like that with Carrie Fisher in it. Anyway, my idea wasn't about a whole town, nor was it about one specific time period. It was about the effects on those left behind, and on how they dealt with their friend suddenly reappearing among them for ever shorter and shorter periods.*

Making the characters punk rockers in a band just seemed natural. I wanted this to be more about a moment in time for them, too, and less about plot. They represented a tip of my hat to the Gainesville punk scene, although I have since used that whole environment for the setting of a novel. "Pop Goes Weasel" was published first by the small press magazine The Third Alternative *in the UK, and then by the US small press 'zine* Space & Time.

Pop Goes Weasel

TRIBAL BANGING OVERLAID BY THE echo of someone puking into a toilet oozed out the open windows. Like a pneumatic nightmare the latest remixed dance single, "Retch" by the Psychotics, flowed into the night of the backyard lit only by burning wood. They clustered around, the ones gathered again for a secret party, a practiced ritual born in a flash of green lightning at a similar party months before, in that very same backyard....

daydreams undertaken

Stephen L. Antczak

Bone nudged Annabel with his elbow. When she didn't respond, he nudged her again. Her eyes flickered with the flames of the bonfire a few yards away.

"What?" she replied without looking away from the spot she'd been staring at. Staring at for the last two hours. A patch of ground cleared away for a second coming, a third, a fourth, a frequent messiah bringing miracles in his voice, and his touch as far as Annabel was concerned. Her entire being was focused on that patch, where not even the tiniest insect moved that she didn't see it, to measure its progress over terrain that at any moment could explode with green energy and deposit a ghost of a man.

"Beer," Bone said. He held the offering out far enough for her to see without having to look directly at it, and so move her eyes away from that one holy spot. She reached out and grabbed the plastic cup full of foamy Old Milwaukee or Busch or whatever American pisswater happened to be in the discount keg.

"Thanks for the beer," she remembered to say after a long sip, just as Bone was about to leave her wrapped in her silence and rejoin Scary Gary, Natas, Sin, and Candy clustered around the bonfire. The band was all there, all the Psychotics awaiting the arrival of their prodigal front man. Weasel.

"You looked thirsty," Bone told her. He held a half empty plastic cup of his own between his teeth as he drew the leather biker jacket closer around him and zipped up. Black leather, black jeans, black painted fingernails, and shocking blond hair shaved into a mohawk pegged him for a denizen of the VFW hall five-bands-for-five-dollars concert moshing set.

Annabel sipped more beer and brushed a lock of hair out of her face. Her hair was dyed red with henna and was long enough to cover her shoulders like a shawl, which was the only thing keeping her warm in her t-shirt and jeans. It was 40 degrees cold, and she held her own leather bomber jacket in her lap. Also, piled atop a 55-gallon metal drum beside the one she sat on were a pair of old worn bluejeans, socks, and Polish paratrooper combat boots. Weasel's.

"It's a lot warmer by the fire, you know," Bone told her. It was one of his more annoying traits, to care about Annabel when she didn't even care about herself, couldn't, until Weasel was there.

"I know," Annabel answered abruptly, wishing Bone would leave now. She didn't want to deal with his shit tonight of all nights, and she knew she would have to when Weasel would be there needing her. It was fucked up enough without Bone adding his weird trip to it. He knew there'd be rules before they'd started spending their nights together, hot and wet and soulless, but at least together. He knew Weasel was going to pop back into Annabel's life again and again, and he'd accepted that. Or said he did.

"You're just gonna stare at the ground, then, until Weasel's here?"

Annabel nodded. "I want to see him appear. I've never seen that instant when he appears, and I want to."

"Whatever."

Pop Goes Weasel

She heard him walk away with heavy steps crunching grass and life beneath them. "Thanks for the beer, though." An afterthought of kindness. An attempt, anyway.

"You said that," his voice floated back to her, almost gone in the cracking laughter of the fire. It made her want to catch a glimpse of him, made her look *away*, made her avert her gaze because really he *was* her steady thing when Weasel wasn't around, and Annabel had to admit that *was* most of the time. Not that it was Weasel's fault. Still, she didn't need to be pissing Bone off every time this happened—

POP

—and realized she was somewhere else when she had wanted to be right *there*, and now she missed it.

Again.

"Weasel!" Annabel screamed and jumped off the drum when she saw the blood. Coming from his head, just above the left ear. He started and spun to face her, his eyes wide with terror. He staggered forward and she caught him. He was light, barely a child in her arms, her child at that and lighter because of it. She eased him to the drum with the clothes on it as the others came running. Scary Gary, the drummer always tap-tap-tapping with his fingers wherever a solid surface presented itself, was the first one there. "He's hurt," Annabel told him, as if the blood running down the side of Weasel's face wasn't enough.

"Shit," Gary said. "I'll get something." He ran inside the house. The others kept their distance. This was Annabel's thing, even though they were all part of it. The Psychotics. Up until the night of green lightning Annabel and Weasel had been *it*. Weird thing was, Bone had been Weasel's right hand then, and the three of them had been the three of them. No more, no less, and no one knew there was anything hidden behind the surface of Bone's pleasantly nodding facade. Maybe a hint should have been when Bone kicked the needle habit right after Weasel was gone. Or so they thought.

Here he was, back again for a repeat performance. But each show was getting shorter and soon he wouldn't be around long enough to sing the first note to the first song.

Annabel managed to get him into the clothes, including the leather bomber, and seated against one of the 55 galloners. Gary rushed back out with some paper towels and a bottle of hydrogen peroxide. Weasel started trying to fight Annabel off after the third dab of a peroxide soaked towel, but he didn't have the strength.

"Hey, Gary," Bone said, staying back by the fire. "How long we got him for this time?"

"Dunno for sure," Gary replied, not watching as Annabel doctored Weasel. "Maybe a half hour. Or less."

"Everything set up inside?"

Stephen L. Antczak

Gary nodded.

"No fucking way," Annabel suddenly said. She was helping Weasel to his feet, but he was still unsteady. "He needs food and he needs to rest. Fuck the demo. Next time—"

"*Next time?* Next time he'll probably disappear after five Goddamn minutes!" Bone screamed. He crumpled his cup and threw it in the fire which jumped and spit at him like the red cobra tattoo entwined around his arm. "We gotta do this tape, Annabel. It's the only shot we got!"

"It's the only shot *you* have, you mean," Annabel returned viciously. Bone's face was distorted by the light thrown across it by the bonfire, but Annabel could see her remark had hit marrow. Bone stomped off, away into the darkness ready to close in on them once the flames died. His plastic cup had become molten slag amidst the sticks in the fire, and the stench of burning plastic wafted into the air on black smoke.

"Way to go," Weasel croaked. His face sported a weak grin, recognizably Weasel's trademark smart-assholiness despite his depleted state. "Gimme somethin'..." he said, his voice trailing off.

"Food?" Annabel asked.

Weasel shook his head. "Beer," he said with that grin. "Need a beer."

Natas, the bass player, got it. "Hey man," he said as he handed the beer to Annabel, who tipped the cup at Weasel's mouth so he could drink. "Hey man, what d'ya say? We playin' or what?"

"Shit, not you too," Annabel said.

Natas shrugged, then nodded at Weasel. "Let the man make his own decision, and don't be such a bitch about it."

"Fuck you."

Weasel didn't reply as Annabel lead him to a chair near the fire. He was able to drink the rest of his beer without her help. The air was alive with sparks, but dead from the weight of tension emanating from Annabel towards the rest of the Psychotics around her.

"I'm gonna find Bone," Sin said, to escape it. No one said anything, so she escaped. Annabel watched her leave. They'd been roommates before the band thing happened, close too, sharing the same bed more nights during the year than not, although nothing ever happened. It was just nice to have someone there. Which explained Bone, and hell most nights nothing ever happened with him either because he was too fucked up to get it up. Annabel wondered if there was something going on with him and Sin, and realized she didn't care. Sin was more Bone's type anyway, more punk rock, and she partied harder than Annabel. But then she'd never been Weasel's girlfriend, and maybe that had more to do with it than anything else.

When Weasel finished his beer he belched and laughed at that, then held his cup out to Natas for a refill. Natas obliged and Annabel sighed.

Pop Goes Weasel

"What do you want to do?" she asked Weasel. "You want to play with them?" She nodded towards the band members. "Or maybe we could spend some time alone together…"

"So *that's* why you're being such a bitch," Natas said. "You're horny? Why don't you just go fetch Bone's bone and let Weasel do his thing with the band?"

"I've said it before and I'll say it again. Fuck you, Nate."

Weasel drained off the second cup, then tossed it into the fire where it melted over Bone's, covering it totally. The torched plastic smell didn't seem as intense this time. He held out his hands to Annabel, and she had to lean back to practically lift him up and out of the chair using her weight, almost sticking her ass into the fire.

"Inside," he whispered as his face drew near to hers, their breath mingling for a moment as two mist-demons dancing in a fog, and began stumbling that way, pulling Annabel behind him.

She looked back at the others. Candy, who'd been staring into the fire the whole time, was still transfixed by the burning dance and mellowed by beer and probably some hash, knowing Candy. Scary Gary and Natas with one hand each in a leather pocket, the other holding beer ready, always. Annabel didn't say anything. They wouldn't, either, or at least she thought they wouldn't, but Gary did.

"There isn't much time," he said, as she and Weasel went inside. No reply necessary.

"Don't you want something to eat?" she asked as Weasel rushed through the kitchen. He didn't answer, or his answer was to yank her through the other door, down the hall, and to the back room that had been, and still was, his room. Weasel's room. It wasn't quite the shrine some of the Psychotics had joked it was. Annabel would go there sometimes to get away from the others, to think, and sometimes maybe to talk to Weasel when he wasn't there. Sin or someone had overheard her in there once, and the rumor started that she'd go in Weasel's room to pray to him. Well, maybe she did. She was allowed to, she loved him, and if anyone could hear her prayers it was him. But she didn't pray, not really, she just talked, or she read, or slept. Compared to the habits of some of her friends, nothing she did seemed all that bad.

Weasel's room was pretty much the way it had been the night of the green lightning. A single shelf of true crime books, Charlie Manson and Jeffrey Dahlmer and Black Delilah and Adam Walsh, the only books she'd ever seen him read, screwed into the wall above three blown amplifiers, big black boxes he wouldn't get rid of because of the impossible to replace bumper stickers all over them. Ramones from six different tours, 7 Seconds, Scratch Acid, Tragic Mulatto, Big Black, Maximum Rock-n-Roll, Thrasher, SubPop… bands, magazines, and other entities inhabiting the punk rock, underground subculture. Annabel knew she and her friends clung to it even as the whole thing died a messy death from corporate poisoning and MTV infestation. But it was still better than selling out, or buying in even, and working at the mall or being chained to a computer eight hours.

So many nights she and Weasel had reassured each other, told themselves they were doing right even if they sometimes felt empty inside, or lost, or if they missed the safe, stable, suburban, middle-class home life they had growing up.

Now Weasel sat in the overstuffed recliner in the corner, made a face, then reached down and pulled out a thick paperback from under his butt. He looked at the cover of Stephen King's *The Tommyknockers*, then tossed it on the futon near where Annabel was sitting. She picked it up and smiled guiltily.

"Still comin' in here," Weasel said. He was smiling too. Not his trademark, but the one he shared with Annabel alone.

"Yeah," Annabel replied. "Is it a problem?"

"No, not at all. So…how're things with Bone?"

Not what she was interested in discussing with Weasel. In fact, discussion wasn't what she was interested in at all, at least not until she and Weasel were lying together in afterglow with a couple cigarettes halfway smoked. And they only had twenty minutes now.

Or less.

And then *POP* goes Weasel.

"Do we have to talk?" Annabel asked, moving from the futon to kneel before Weasel, her arms across his lap with her chin resting on them. "Can't we just do it? Can't we make love?"

Weasel reached out and gently touched her cheek. Annabel closed her eyes and squeezed his legs with her hands.

"I can't," he told her. "Not after what's been happening. Not knowing that at any time during…any second I could disappear and leave you there alone, probably with your legs sticking up into the air…" They both started to laugh, but didn't quite. The image wasn't all that funny, really. "Besides," he continued, "I'm not up to it. They had me on the run just before this." Annabel knew by "this" Weasel meant the here and now. "Almost got me."

"Who?" Annabel asked.

"Just before I appear back here, I've told you what it's like, right?"

Annabel nodded. "Yeah, I went to the university and talked to some history professor lady and she said it sounds like Colonial America. Probably run by a bunch of fucking Pilgrims. Told her I was doing research for a novel. Don't think she believed me."

"Yeah, well, they caught me…they were waiting for me where I appear, in the middle of the Goddamn town square. They had a net over me and dragged me to a tree. They were gonna hang my ass, Annabel. They thought I was a witch or the devil or something. But I got away and I just ran. I figured I'd disappear before they could catch me again, if I just kept on going, so I fuckin' ran and ran and ran."

"Shit, Weasel, they're gonna be waiting for you again."

"Yeah, but how long will they have me for? Not long enough to do a damn thing."

"Oh fuck, that's right. You're not gonna be around long enough to shake hands with, never mind make love to! You sure you don't wanna…?"

Weasel shook his head no. "Listen," he said. "Scary Gary says that whenever I appear its for less and less time, right? Pretty soon it'll be, like, half a second, then even *less* time, right?"

Annabel swallowed dry fear, unthinkable things, and nodded. "Yeah."

"And *then* what?"

"Well…" She knew what, but couldn't bring herself to say it. Scary Gary had come up with the theory, which she preferred not to think about.

"I'll cease to exist," Weasel said plainly, as if he were stating a simple fact like the sun'll come up tomorrow, bet your bottom Goddamn dollar. "Pretty soon I won't fill any space long enough to…well, to *be*, so then I just won't be, right? I won't have time to exist, that's how Gary put it." Weasel was sitting up in the chair now, leaning slightly forward. Annabel sat back on the floor, more aware that they were no longer touching than of what Weasel was saying. It was just too much for her. Finally having something pretty good, maybe not the best, but pretty damn good, something you think maybe you could spend the rest of your life with. Then ZAP! he gets struck by green lightning and disappears, and you think that's it, end of the song, end of the set, duck those beer bottles and burning cigarette butts and get off the stage because it is absolutely over and out. Then it pops back into your life, again and again, every few weeks for a few hours first, then an hour and a half, then forty-five minutes, then half an hour…and pretty soon he'll pop in and pop out literally in the blink of an eye, and then barely long enough to *be* Weasel, and after that? After that, he won't.

Annabel wasn't too sure she could handle the end of the set again, when before there'd been an encore and this time it didn't look like there'd be anything.

"Maybe that guy from the future, what's-his-name, the scientist who caused all this shit, maybe he'll be able to do something," Annabel said, hoping against hope, telling herself no, stop it, it won't happen so just shut your stupid mouth and live *now* because that's all there is. That's all there ever was.

"Kormin," Weasel said, a telling pull at the edges of his mouth, a memory that didn't seem entirely unpleasant. "No, I don't think so. When I was there, he said he'd made some progress identifying the path I was taking through the space-time thing—"

"Continuum."

"Right. But that was all. That reminds me, though, he sent you a present." Weasel grinned the old grin, and unzipped the bomber jacket.

"How could he send something? Clothes don't even stay with you. Shit, we found your fillings on the ground after that first time."

"Check this out," he said, and pulled up one arm of the t-shirt, baring it to his shoulder. There was a tattoo of a death's head moth, intricately detailed and colored, practically indistinguishable from a real one, covering part of the bicep and tricep of his upper arm.

"Wow," Annabel said, leaning in closer to see better. "That's really cool."

"Want it?"

She regarded Weasel with a frown. "Yeah, right. Of course I want it, but what am I supposed to do, *skin* you for it? No thanks."

"Watch," Weasel said, then proceeded to peel the tattoo off his arm, very slowly, but not removing any skin and apparently not causing him any pain at all. The diaphanous membrane of the tattoo hung limp in his hand, while he held Annabel's arm out with the other. Then he spread the tattoo across her upper arm, smoothed it over, and it looked as real as any of her other tattoos. She rubbed her fingers over it, and felt skin. She tried to find the edges of it with her fingernails, but couldn't.

"Can I pull it off if I want to?" she asked.

Weasel looked disappointed. "Why, you don't like it?"

"No, I love it, but…what if someone accidentally scratches it off, or what if I scrub it off in the shower or something?"

"Oh, don't worry. It won't come off unless you want it to." He leaned back in his chair, obviously pleased.

Annabel brushed her fingers lightly over the tattoo, then regarded Weasel with tears glittering in her eyes.

"Hey, what's wrong?" he asked in a soft voice, Annabel not being one to cry easily.

"It's stupid," she said, wiping her eyes. "I didn't get to see you appear again."

"That's not stupid."

"I only get to see you disappear. I can't do that anymore, especially when the next time might be the last time. I just can't."

Weasel scratched his chin and peered out the window into the black night, as if there was something worth seeing out there. But there was. Green lightning, flickering bonfire, the Psychotics. There was something to hear, too. Bone and Sin grinding themselves into a sweat hidden from moonlight and uncaring eyes. Annabel and Weasel listened with tilted heads, and Annabel laughed.

"It may not work the way Scary Gary thinks it will," Weasel announced suddenly. "In fact, it might be totally the opposite."

Annabel shook her head. "I don't understand."

"Instead of just *not* being, I could end up being everywhere at once. Colonial America, Goddamn ancient Greece, running with T. Rex a million years ago…"

Pop Goes Weasel

"What about here and now?" Annabel asked, trying to keep the hope out of her voice, barely succeeding.

"Everywhere I've been popping in and out of," Weasel told her. "Kormin thinks I'll *never* run out of time to keep jumping from one place to the next, but it'll happen quicker and quicker to the point that I'll practically exist in all those place and all those times at almost the exact same moment."

Annabel closed her eyes against the images flashing through her mind. Like a slide projector whizzing around at mach speed. She saw flickering on a screen in her head some of the things Weasel had told her about, or had tried to, the first few times he reappeared until Annabel couldn't bare to hear anymore. It came to mean so much more just to be with him and not talk, rather to make love, touch, and perform with the band. Even that last, the band, Annabel wished would go away and leave them alone with the small moments they had left. But she knew it wouldn't, because deep down in her own marrow, in Weasel's, in Bone's and the other Psychotics, it was their essence. It was the life they lived together, their group marriage, their nuclear family.

If only she could run away, but she wouldn't be able to run away from herself no matter how far, no matter how fast.

The images from Weasel's odyssey through history and future history were blurred and chopped, mangled like corpses in a car accident, hidden by the twisted metal and shattered glass of her broken dreams. What could she imagine of loping duck-billed dinosaurs pursued by a family of bloody-jawed predators across a plain burning at the edges with volcanic activity? It came to her as a painting from one of the books she read as a child, or stop-motion life and death on Saturday afternoon TV. What good was it to tell her of twisted Puritans in black hats chasing through the black as coal forest, torches riding overhead like Will o' the Wisps to lure Weasel to die at the end of a rope? All she saw were scenes from *The Crucible*. It was the same with the statue of Athena and toga clad Greeks on marble steps, and all the others, and the future.

Oh, especially the unseen, impossible to believe future. A name, that's all. Kormin the mad scientist with wild white hair, Einstein or Edison maybe, or Doctor Frankenstein unleashing a nightmare awakened by a bolt from heaven. Or up from Hell. Who knew from whence green lightning was born? She could not picture the future at all, even what had been so vividly described by Weasel, even what of it she now wore on her arm, which she had to see in the light to believe it was there still. Death's head moth, as close as her skin.

"Everywhere at once," Weasel said. "Can you fuckin' believe it?"

No, she didn't say, I can't. I won't.

"How...?" she started to ask him how did he think he'd be able to handle it, split across time like that, spread out across space?

As if reading her mind, and maybe he could after all, maybe that's what the trademark grin was saying — I know what you're thinking — as if reading her mind, he said, "Kormin thinks I'll be able to focus my existence to wherever, *when*ever I want. So, like, if I ain't into the way things are going here, I can decide to hang loose with Aristotle and the boys, right? Sounds cool, right?"

"I guess."

"Hey, Annabel," and now Weasel's voice was low and heavy like it had been in the past after a few hits off a bottle of gin. When reality wound around them too close, when the light at the end was the beginning of another tunnel. "Annabel, don't try to take this away. I *need* this, to believe I'm set for a fuckin' ride and not about to disappear, wink, gone just like that. Believe with me, okay? Okay?"

"Yeah." She tried on her best smile but realized the fakery before showing it. Instead she tried looking at Weasel the way she'd always wanted to. And she said it, too. "I love you, asshole."

Weasel's head went back, mouth open and a geyser of laughter streaming up to the cobwebbed ceiling. "Yeah! Owww!" He looked at her and his face was contorted almost beyond recognition by sheer joy. Happy, Annabel understood, the first Goddamn time she'd ever seen Weasel happy. "I love you, too, bitch," he said, then heaved himself out of the chair, taking her hand and hauling her ass up while he was at it. "Let's kick it out!"

Psychotics waiting in the living room as if sensing the court was in session, the Honorable Judge Weasel was taking the stand in his own defense. Guilty, of course, but that was okay by them.

Bone and Sin came in the front just as Weasel and Annabel entered from the hallway.

"We gonna do somethin' or what?" Natas asked, annoyed at everyone in sight.

Weasel met Bone's calcium stare with a ready trademark, Sin observed the whorls and swirls in the hardwood floor, Annabel held back tears of melancholy transport, Candy stared through the wall to where the fire still burned, Scary Gary fiddled around with the controls of the mixer.

"Ready," Gary said, after the turn of one more dial, breaking the party up.

"Yeah, let's do somethin'," Weasel growled, all *walk on the wild side* high.

Gary sat behind the drums, surrounding him in a wall of unheard rhythms, reverberating through the whole band as they waited with fluttering hearts.

"Jesus Christ, let's go already!" Natas yelled, already timing the silence to his own pulse.

And Gary came down on the toms with the heavy end of the sticks, once, twice, three times, then four and five and six. Bone punished his bass erotically, thumping with his thumb in and around the toms, weaving and circling like the cobra on his arm. Then Candy, Sin, and Annabel began to hum like the

Pop Goes Weasel

Fates, Natas let his guitar wail like a widow, and Weasel waited like the ocean, waiting to let his tide in and sweep them all out into the deep with him, where his current would carry them away and force them to sink, swim, or just flow with it.

When he finally sang, it was the horn of Gabriel telling everyone the fun's over, come all ye faithful and let's blow this dance and head for the high hills. And then, with all the deadbeats gone, let the *real* fun begin.

His voice was sinister silk, raw meat, a rose with thorns. Except only Annabel could hear, at the heart, the pulsing center of it all, just how fucking *tired* he was, how end-of-the-line exhausted popping in and out was making him. Let it be over soon, she thought, one way or another. The rest of the Psychotics were totally into it, eyes closed and bodies swaying, lost at home at last, engulfed by the tapestry they wove together. Annabel held herself back, though, and couldn't look away from Weasel, his back to her as he sang. There he is, there he is, there he is, there he is, there he is. Over and over she said it to her self, it was the subtext of the primal humanity pouring from between her pursed lips.

There he is.

"*It ain't time I'm wasting,*" was the line he was singing, "*just space!*"
                                    POP
She saw the flash of green, a thin line sizzle down Weasel's back, expand and grow around him before she knew what it was, then that sound of air rushing in to fill his void. The music ground to a shrieking halt, rumbling to a stop like an industrial emergency, settling in on itself like a collapsing skyscraper. When the dust cleared, they knew it was over.

"That was good," Bone said, breaking the silence before it stagnated, as only he could break it because he didn't care.

But yeah, Annabel thought, and she could see the others thought so too. It was.

David Bowie's song "Five Years" inspired this story about the quest for immortality mixed in with the quest for fame and fortune. I did a lot of daydreaming in college while to listening to David Bowie records. I wrote this story when I heard about a new market for short fiction in the UK, an anthology of short stories "celebrating the 7-inch single," edited by British powerhouse authors Kim Newman and Paul J. McAuley. The book was called In Dreams. *It tickled me to find a story of mine sharing a book with a story written by fantasy great Jonathon Carroll, and another by* The Keep *author F. Paul Wilson.*

The element that came to me while daydreaming, the element that for me makes the story, is what the kid, Henri, says at the end. I don't want to give it away, alas.

Reed John-Paul Forever

THE LATEST REED JOHN-PAUL HUMPER, 'My Black Hole,' pounded the air like it pounded Henri's blood. Sent him spinning and whirling, jumping and looping all over the dance floor. He was *gone*, the music hardwired to his body, remote-controlled randomness, death-defying fury. To look at him you might say, *There's Reed John-Paul himself, watch him demon dance, see a living legend.* Henri *was* Reed John-Paul, as far as the eye could tell. The reality would tell a different story.

daydreams undertaken

Reed John-Paul Forever

Henri was a Reed John-Paul *effigy*. A kid with no identity of his own, a culture clone, a wannabe, a nowhere else to run dead end of the road loser with one last shred of glory. One of thousands of screaming Reed John-Paul fans, he was one of those few who took it as far as it could be taken. He could be Reed John-Paul like no one else...except Reed John-Paul.

The humper ground itself out in an ashtray of shrieks and shattering glass, but Henri kept on, convulsing in time to the tune still raging in his head, until the Furious George track put his fire out. Not his smoke, FG. Henri stood there, momentarily dazed by the flood of Furious George effigies taking up swaying ranks around him, liquid human parts flowing to words sung by a drowning man.

He beat the dance floor, swaggering that Reed John swagger — left hip thrown way out there, right hand held out for alms — and cut a path through the mish-mash of painted faces and unnatural hair to the table in the corner where his posse posed.

"You were *gone* out there," Tom Tom, Henri's muscle, told him.

"Ragin' fuckin' *gone*," Haze, his cowgirl at night when the music was quieter, whispered wetly in his ear. Her pierced tongue flicked in for a moment, then traced a snail trail around the cartilage, and she kissed him fast on the cheek.

Henri took a whiff. The air was heavy with toxins from a hundred different kinds of burning weed, and as many distillations of alcohol. It was good to be here, at the club, at *any* club, where the energy flowed into you instead of out, where the things that mattered happened on the dance floor, and in glasses or rolled in paper, and sometimes secretly in bathrooms. Outside nothing mattered except getting *in*. In was belonging, in was creating small legends. Out *there* was boredom, getting old and dying nobody.

He noticed a Betty leaning towards him against a railing around the Pit. Below, Henri knew the retro skins and punks moshed and banged their heads together in a war of fevered, manic fuzz that sent their bodies flying at one another until they dropped. Once in the Pit, the only way out was head first.

The Betty smiled at Henri. She looked mundane, a norm, the hottest I-wanna-be-your-dog he'd ever seen. Her lips seemed to direct pleasure through the air at him. Henri felt a howl building inside.

Haze punched his arm. "Hey, heel," she said. "You told me I was along for the ride. What, is the ride over?"

He looked at her, saw her painted white face frowning with red eyebrows that formed a *V* beneath deep, blue dreadlocks.

"Henri..." It was Tom Tom, pointing with his chin.

Henri looked, and saw...The Betty was approaching the table. Her legs were netted in black, waist circled by a loose, black skirt, chest bare down to the nipples, which were coated in spray-on latex neon blue. Her eyes were focused on Henri, ignoring his posse.

Henri suppressed a grin. Probably just a glamgirl out slumming for a little effigy meat. A glam did that every once in a while, got one of the effs, adopted him, took him around for show and tell, until she grew bored with him sucking it all up like a leech or a vampire. Not Henri's smoke. Haze didn't have to worry.

"I'm Anna," the Betty said to Henri.

"Who fuckin' cares, bitch," Haze spat. She was tensed, ready for a knockdown. Henri put his hand gently, yet firmly, on her leg, and squeezed. *Chill.* Haze didn't move, but she stayed tense.

"Call me...Reed," Henri said, to the snickers of his posse. Anna's eyes caught the light and glittered. His spiked, pink hair, raccoon's mask painted blue around his eyes, black lips that formed Henri's perfected off-kilter grin... all Reed John-Paul.

"Okay...Reed. Come with me for a walk."

"Why?"

"For air."

"There's air in here," Haze said. Anna didn't bother to look at her.

"Then come with me for glory," she told Henri.

"Hey, there's glory in here, too," Tom Tom cut in.

Anna ignored him. "Come on, *Reed,* this could be your big chance. Come with me."

Something in her voice was stronger than Henri's will. Henri's will was like a Berlin Wall waiting for a revolution, and Anna was the Molotov cocktail with her fuse lit and smoking, starting it. Maybe she *was* his smoke after all.

Henri stood.

"Henri," Haze said. "What the f—"

"I'll be right back," he told her without looking at her. Anna took him by the arm and led him away.

Outside it was acid raining again. The burning drops forced them to take the tubes, which took them uptown. Uptown, where people didn't die. The dying were forced to leave before they reached that point. The Immortals lived there...the *real* Reed John-Paul and Furious George.

"Are you one?" Henri asked. Immortal, he meant.

Anna nodded, and that was that.

The apartment had ten rooms, each bigger than any house Henri had ever been in. It was high among the skyscrapers uptown, way above eight-hour workdays and sixteen-hour empty dreams. And it was a shrine to Reed John-Paul.

Lining the main hallway from the front door were glass cases, and in each case stood a life-sized mock-up of the singer, wax effigies, posing the way *he* had posed in the different eras of his career so far. There was the early Reed,

Reed John-Paul Forever

defiant and snarling, and the bare, unplugged Reed of the ripped jeans and old leather jacket tour, and then the dark Reed, all in black and holding a gun to his head...The many faces of Reed, the many lives of an Immortal superstar.

"A fanatic," Henri said.

"You."

He turned to face her. "Effigy," he said. "I want to *be* him, not worship him."

She laughed. "Of course." She slipped her shoes off and walked barefoot across a deep, blue carpet to the kitchen. "Hungry?"

His stomach answered for him, "Always."

So, he wondered, what would she want? Sex? A performance? He could do Reed John like no one else. Except....

"Reed John-Paul," Anna said from the kitchen. "Why?"

"It just happened," Henri said. "That's why. Better than being me, Henri Dupris, loser like the rest. Rather be the best, and that's Reed John-Paul. Right?"

"No arguments there." She brought him a plate of microwaved noodles smothered in white sauce. "Sit at the table, and I'll tell you what's happening."

Henri sat at the table. The noodles weren't too soft, cooked just right, and the sauce had to be clam sauce. Anna poured him a glass of white wine, then sat across the table from him.

"Reed John-Paul is dead," she said.

Henri stopped eating. He shook his head. "Sorry. Heard that rumor before, lots of times. Never believe it, and he never lets me down."

Anna sighed. "I know. That's how it was meant to be. There have been five others before you, and they all said the same thing. And I hate myself for doing this, but it's in the contract."

Henri resumed eating to foster an illusion of non-concern, but in reality he was worried. "What contract?" As far as he knew, he hadn't signed anything. Had he?

"With Prolong. They own the Reed John-Paul contract."

"The life-extension company?"

Anna nodded. "Prolong, the drug, doesn't work on everyone, you know. It worked on me...I was his wife when we made the deal."

Henri stopped eating again, and set the fork down. "His wife? Reed John-Paul...?"

She nodded again. "It didn't work on Reed. Prolong just *didn't work*. In fact, it killed him. He lived the rest of his life in *five years*...All that energy, all that time, compressed into five short years. It pushed him over the top, his shows became legendary, his music was unmatched. But it killed him."

Henri was shaking his head, not believing any of it. "I've *seen* him. *Live*. I saw the Dancing with Death tour last summer." The memory was a flashover in his mind, of Henri and countless others shaking to Reed John's raw sound, hanging on the singer's every lyric, each song like a revelation. "He was *there*. I was in the first row, pressed right up against the barricades. He sang 'Don't Even Try to Stop Me' to the girl next to me! He reached out to her. She tried to get to him. When the security gorillas nabbed her halfway across the stage, she popped so bad she had a seizure. Reed John-Paul wasn't dead *then*."

"You saw...an effigy."

"No way."

"The recording company sold the contract to Prolong because Prolong couldn't allow a failure with their drug to get any publicity. They announced Reed was *resting*, then they had the contests, the Reed John-Paul contests. They needed someone who could move like him, sing like him, *be* like him. They needed me to test him, and to guide him, to be there for him...in more ways than one." She paused, then smiled. "The last one was Benny Jargon. You knew him, didn't you?"

Henri knew him, or had known him once. Benny'd been the best of the best, better than Henri, but Henri never minded because Benny was *that* good. Then one day Benny was gone, just disappeared, no one knew how or why, and Henri became the effigy to watch.

"That *was* Benny," Henri finally said, remembering that last show, coming away from it feeling he now *knew* Reed John-Paul. He figured it'd been the sheer intensity of the performance. *Everyone* left that show bonded to one another through Reed John-Paul, as if they'd formed a new religion and were the first true believers, the disciples. But no...an effigy. Benny.

"And now we need *you*," Anna whispered.

Henri looked at her, met her gaze directly. "I have a choice in the matter?"

She laughed. "That's the first time I've ever been asked, but yeah, you have a choice. There *are* other effigies out there, not as good, but a little surgery, a little neural interfacing with the computer, can change that. The rest comes with the drug."

"And then will I be dead in five years?"

Anna nodded. "Probably. There is the chance Prolong will work, too. It hasn't yet. The company figures it has something to do with the kind of mind it takes to *be* Reed John-Paul. It just rejects the drug."

"If I say yes..."

"You will *become* Reed John-Paul. Oh, maybe a part of you will be there, as a spectator along for the ride, but you will be my husband." Her voice nearly cracked, and her eyes should have been crying, but she's done this too many times. To get her husband back for a few years at a time, just to lose him again and again to the very drug that kept her alive...forever.

Henri thought about it. He could go back to Haze and Tom Tom, people he really didn't know outside the club, people he called friends merely because they were those with whom he associated Inside. Outside, he normally didn't even think about them.

He'd never really given much thought to his *life* Outside, either, but now he had to. Outside, he slept in a two-room flat designed for TV worship and little else. His job, when he bothered to show up, had him unloading uniform cardboard boxes onto trucks. He didn't know what those boxes contained and didn't *want* to know. He was locked out of anything resembling higher education because he just couldn't afford it and he didn't fall into the any of the state-approved minority groups that qualified people for grants and scholarships. And the government couldn't afford student loans anymore. Dancing the effigy dance might get real old some day.

And then...Here was a chance he could live forever, a Reed John-Paul kind of forever. If he died in five years, that would still be five years of glory, five years of *being* Reed John-Paul.

Anna left him alone to think about it. Henri wondered what Tom Tom and Haze would say about this. What were they doing right now? Probably grinding in the bathroom at the club, creating small myths....

Henri also thought of his father. What kind of man was he, really? He wanted to hear his father's infamous Pave Your Own Highway speech again, just one more time. Henri remembered the man as apparently believing his own propaganda, despite being a career backroom filing clerk for some impersonal corporate Goliath.

And his mother, her smile and gentle, brown eyes, her support for Henri's lifestyle. Have fun, do what you want to do, because someday you'll be eighty and it'll all be over.

Stretched out on a cold metal table, naked. Anna standing beside him, smiling, touching his chest tenderly with her hand.

"Henri, this is it."

The first needle slipping into the crook of his arm, entering the vein, and then another one entering his other arm. Suddenly fear washes over him like the cold tide of the ocean late at night, tears rolling down the sides of his face, never feeling so alone.

A spectator.

Hot lights, humping music, oceans of arms and heads waving in the darkness beyond with an undercurrent roar of voices raised to a fever pitch.

A kaleidoscope of moments:

Earphones suctioned to his head as he lay down vocal tracks to the newest Reed John hits, 'Hours to Live,' 'Love is the Last Thing I Need,' and 'I Don't Know Me Anymore.'

Stephen L. Antczak

Making love with Anna, enclosed by her hot flesh and strong arms and legs holding him desperately to her, soft music in the background, and Anna whispering over and over, "Reed, Reed, Reed...."

The news media surrounding him at airports, following through the streets of uptown, waiting for him in restrooms. Shooting a synthtape experience of what it's like to *be* Reed John-Paul, *live, in the flesh*. Chased by the rabid diamond dogs called fans, attacked by jealous boyfriends, dance on stage with a crowd of fifty thousand cheering *you* on!

The spectacle of Reed John-Paul's first Martian tour, nearly cracking the stadium dome with ultrasonics, and then—

Collapse. All systems down. Humping still in the air with smoke and lights fading...fading...gone.

Five years.

Gone. Anna stood beside his bed, smiling, but no tears.

"It's over," she said. "You had fun."

Henri could barely feel his body. What he *could* feel was old. Ancient.

"I remember...some," he whispered. He tried to lift his head, to see his body, to see what Reed John-Paul had looked like in the end, what he *really* looked like. What had all those people reached out to touch?

"Do you remember me?" Anna asked.

"Yes. We made love."

"Every single night."

Then another face came into view, leaning in from the edge of darkness. The face, painted and young, was Reed John-Paul.

"Hey, mate," he said to Henri. "I'm you successor. I'm *you*. Pretty weird, eh?"

"He caught you when you fell off the stage last night," Anna explained. "We knew it was over then. It was a stroke of luck that he just happens to be one of the top effigies around. He's taking the injections tonight."

"Great show," the effigy said. "Wouldn't'a missed it for the world." Then his eyes narrowed and he asked, almost inaudibly, "Was it worth it?"

In those eyes, Henri could see it wouldn't matter if he said no.

Henri closed his eyes, and the lights came back, the chanting by ten thousand voices of his name, the music that drove his heart, pumped his blood, and housed his soul. The song was over, but the melody lingered.

It had been worth it.

"Reed John-Paul *forever*," he said with his last breath.

I originally wrote this story for a specific market, a comic book anthology actually, which rejected it. I sold it to the small press magazine Not One of Us, *which published it in 1995. Interestingly, although not obviously, I feel like this story poses the same question as in "Reed John-Paul Forever." The idea of continuing on in a miserable physical existence or ending your physical existence for a better non-physical existence is as old as religion. Perhaps, some day, virtual reality will actually create Heaven for those who believe.*

Now there's a story idea….

Way Down

JANNY HAD SEEN BODIES BEFORE. Dead bodies, a lot worse than the one she saw now. Broken, violated bodies.

A man, leaning against the wall of a dirty alley, legs sticking straight out like a doll, arms folded across the slight bulge of his stomach. Janny didn't know him, didn't care. Couldn't see his face, but she didn't know *any* men. Men didn't come Way Down. The alley Janny squatted in now was a nowhere off-shoot deep downtown. An alley that might've opened onto a bustling street of shoppers and

daydreams undertaken

businessmen once. Now it was part of the maze that surrounded Way Down. Not Doll Squad territory, but close enough. Smell a man here, Vanissa and her gang would come howling, slashing, cutting, killing. Any girl known to have traffic with a man was gone, way gone, and the Doll Squad would make sure of it. They ruled Way Down, and No Men Allowed was the rule.

Janny couldn't see his face because it was covered by a plastic helmet molded into goggles over his head. They looked like bug-eyes. She wondered what would happen if she took it off. Would multi-faceted fly eyes dangle from the man's head? *Too many vids*, she told herself.

She inched closer and touched the man's left foot, moved it side to side. Nothing, no life. Whatever had been his, was hers now. First she went through his pockets, grey suit jacket and slacks, looking for plastic. No plastic, which she'd hoped to have re-coded in her name, but there was some hard currency, spare change. Not much, but better than nothing.

And the weird helmet. Janny knew what it was. Another word that left a bad taste in her mouth. *Technology.* Men and technology had ruined the world. They sat fat and happy in the outburbs with dull-eyed, domesticated clones of the most beautiful women in history, harems of slaves for even the least of these "XY's," as the Doll Squad called them.

Despite her fear and hatred of these two things, she was, by nature, more curious than anything else. She decided to pull it off. She spanned his torso with her legs, his face right there staring her in the crotch. Janny, imagining for a second what might be happening if he weren't dead and she *did* know men, leaned back and pulled. The helmet held fast, so she leaned further back, felt the wiry muscles in her arms burn. Slowly, as if coming unstuck, unglued, it gave. With renewed effort, Janny pulled harder, as hard as she could, and felt it coming, slipping reluctantly.

Then, all of a sudden, it was off. Janny found herself sitting back against the other wall, holding it in her lap, barely aware she'd just slammed her head into red bricks. Now she saw the dead man's face. His eyes.

One tear, from each eye, slid down either cheek.

Looking right at her.

Janny made herself *gone.*

Later, she slowed down, and felt a little ashamed letting herself get spooked by a dead man. Death stares usually had no effect on her. Usually. But this one, with those eyes, as if he could actually *see* Janny from the other side, see her steal the helmet, and steal whatever came with it.

"Hey, Janny, whatcha got?" Scrounge asked as Janny pushed past the even younger girl. Scrounge, Janny's roommate in what was once a service elevator of a four star hotel that now moved never up, never down. It was in an abandoned Marriott hotel of thirty floors and a thousand rooms, but she and Scrounge were the only tennants. Scrounge. The name fit. She was dirty, always wiping her nose on her forearm, always scratching, scrounging, always picking at already picked bones after the vultures finished. But they were friends, and friends in the city, especially Way Down, were hard to come by.

Janny had never seen a real vulture, didn't know what one was, but the concept survived, *thrived* in Way Down. Janny knew Scrounge was one.

Then there were predators, like the Doll Squad.

She took the helmet to her corner, piles of clothes and blankets worn and threadbare, stained and smelling forever of sweat. But it was her sweat, Janny's, familiar. Home. Safe as a place could be. Any one of the Doll Squad could come in and do anything, to her stuff, to Scrounge, to Janny. Sometimes did, but Janny knew the alternative. The Doll Squad were protection for Way Down, against rovers, against government clean-up squads sent in every now and then to reclaim the inner city.

Scrounge came over to Janny's corner, where she wasn't usually allowed to go, but sometimes they shared the space, arm in arm, holding one another. It was a kind of warmth that was rare, even if it was with Scrounge and not someone…better.

"Whatcha got?"

"Somethin' I found." Janny turned the helmet over and over in her hands, feeling the cool, smooth, plastic surface with her fingertips. Seemed basic enough, just a mold. She held it upside down to look inside. Difficult to make out, the entire inside criss-crossed with printed circuits and thousands of tiny holes. Had it killed the man? Had he cried because he was finally free of it, only too late? Janny didn't think that was it. Even in death, he had not wanted to lose whatever the helmet gave him. Even in death.

"Gonna put it on?"

"Maybe."

"You shouldn't."

"I *know*," Janny said. "I'm not gonna do it because I want to. I *got* to."

"Why?"

Janny exhaled sharply, exasperrated. "To see what it *is*, dumby."

"It's technology," Scrounge said.

"I *know*. I need to find out what it *does*, though."

"Oh."

Janny wouldn't be able to see beyond it once it was on, she realized, meaning Scrounge could do anything at all to her, and she wouldn't be able to react in time. "You gotta leave," she told Scrounge.

"Why?"

"Just *leave*," Janny said with a threatening gesture. Scrounge knew not to push it. With a parting look that wished Janny dead, like a roach caught in the light she skittered out of the elevator. Janny pushed the gate shut, figuring it would make enough of a racket if someone tried to open it to alert her even with the helmet on. The elevator's outer doors didn't close, but it was a *big* elevator. She was far enough back, obscured by shadow and the piles of clothes; anyone looking in wouldn't be able to see her without *really* looking.

She slid the helmet down over her head. It went on easily enough, slipped right on without sticking at all, and then total darkness. She felt something buzz, thought she could hear a faint hum, and the helmet started to get warm.

Then her entire head exploded with pain, pinpricking pain all over it, made her want to scream and rip the helmet off, rip her own head off to stop it. But before she could react, the pain stopped, and a light shined in her eyes.

The light, blindingly bright at first, faded into details, and the first detail Janny noticed was the man standing, naked, before her. It was him, the dead one she'd taken the helmet from. Only here he was not only alive, but he looked...*perfect*. In every way, a perfect body and face with kind eyes and a nice smile. How awkward that thought was in her head. *Nice smile.* It'd been a long, long time since she'd seen a smile that wasn't dripping poison. She looked over his entire body unabashedly, curious. So this was a man. Not like she had never seen one before. Sometimes the Doll Squad caught one alive and brought him Way Down, naked, crying, and made a sport of killing him. "Who are you?" Janny asked. Her voice sounded small here, vulnerable. She didn't like it. It was the voice sex toys used, a voice men liked to hear because it reminded them of little girls, and every girl in Way Down knew what men did to little girls.

"My name's Von," he said. "And you're...?"

"Janny."

Now she noticed the other details, finally able to move her gaze from Von's anatomy. Blue above, dazzled with yellow warmth, green below with scatterings of color. Sky, sun, grass, and flowers. And trees, leaves applauding in the wind. She realized, this was *before*. Before everything went wrong. Before civilization cracked at the seams.

"Like what you see?" Von asked. He was suddenly a lot closer, Janny could reach out and touch him if she wanted.

"Where is this?"

Von tapped the side of his head with his finger.

"We're in a portable virtual reality unit," he told her. "I'm wearing it right now. I programmed it myself, you know. Even programmed a ghost of myself to live here when I'm not wearing it, to keep things going smoothly."

"How did you do that?"

Von shrugged. "Oh, it's nothing. Just wearing the helmet begins the process. The more I interracted in this reality, the more information the AI acquired, until it was able to recreate me the way I appear here. When I put the helmet on, I take control of the ghost."

Way Down

"But *I'm* the one wearing the helmet," Janny told him.

Von frowned. "You are?"

Janny nodded. "I took it off a…off *your* body a little while ago."

"You did?"

"And now I'm sitting in my flat wearing it."

"I see." He turned away from her. Her gaze wandered down his back to his buttocks. She'd never seen a naked man like him before. The Doll Squad made certain of that. The ones they'd brought back had always disgusted Janny. Maybe that had been the idea. But this one didn't seem too bad, if this was what men were really like. Kind of nice, actually.

"I didn't mean to upset you."

Von turned around again to look at her. His eyes were wet, crying again. *Not again*, Janny thought. *This one isn't real, he's a program.* The realization surprised her, even as she realized how obvious it should have been right away.

"I'm not upset," Von said. "Not really. I mean, look around. Long as nothing happens to the helmet, I'll have all this."

"But you're *dead.*"

Von nodded, then grinned. "Maybe, maybe not. I could have transferred my *self*, my soul, spirit, essence or whatever you want to call it, here, in the helmet."

In the helmet. It was difficult to imagine that the breeze she felt, the fresh air she breathed deeply in, that it wasn't even real. She felt a tiny spark of desire ignite within, and she was suddenly jealous that she would have to take the helmet off sooner or later and be back in Way Down, in the present reality of endlessly grey skies, choking smoke…Why did it always rain? Why was everything always dirty? Why did she always hear gunfire off in the distance? She'd heard the terms "total collapse" and "global warming" so many times they didn't mean anything anymore. Sounded like *no one* knew what was going on.

She didn't want to go back to that.

"Why do you think you died?" Janny asked.

"Maybe I stayed here too long, and starved. It would be easy to forget the body while you're in here, I imagine."

Janny realized he was right. She couldn't feel her body. For all she knew, someone could be kicking her in the stomach right now. If she didn't take the helmet off, she'd die eventually, like him. If she got rid of the helmet, she'd probably die soon, maybe a few years, during which she'd live in a grey, violent, wet, cold world.

If she kept the helmet safe, especially from Scrounge, kept it hidden away, she could come back every once in a while….

She closed her eyes, felt the heat of the sun on her body, the wind's gentle caress. She opened her eyes. It wasn't the wind, it was him, his hands, his mouth on hers for her first kiss ever. Warmth exploded inside her now, the brightness that had blinded her at first burned in her heart, and for the first time in her life she felt *real*, living, not just existing. Hungrily her mouth explored his, greedily her hands explored his body.

And then something happened.

Darkness, total, then everything reappeared, flickered around her, the sun, the sky...static erased the setting. Von stepped away from her, opened his mouth to say something, then disappeared. Then pain. Someone had taken a spike to Janny's head, or at least that was how it felt. She was screaming before she knew it, then a jolt to her gut knocked the wind out of her and she stopped screaming.

The helmet came away from her head.

The wolfish grins of the Doll Squad came into focus as her blurred vision cleared. Not the whole Doll Squad, of course, but the ones there were bad enough. Vinessa, Maggot, Loona, and Bett. Scrounge had gone to fetch them, Janny knew, like a good little dog. She saw her grimy roommate, nose leaking ooze around her mouth and down her chin, watching at the edge of the doorway.

Her friend. She looked scared.

"You weren't thinkin' of keepin' this for yourself, now, were you Janny?" Vinessa asked, hefting the helmet in one hand, the other holding a fistful of Janny's hair. Vinessa and the other Dolls were decked out in their urban jungle fatigues, spiked gloves, razor-edged boots, zip guns tucked into their jeans.

Janny didn't answer. Saying anything could get her smacked, she knew from experience with Vinessa before. Some of the Doll Squad were nice enough, if they were alone, but get more than two of 'em together, and there was something to prove.

"I don't think she can hear ya," Loona said, pushing her pockmarked face in close to Janny's. "Maybe she *can't* hear no more. I can take her ears off then, and she ain't gonna miss 'em."

"No," Vinessa said. "We don't cut our own. You know that."

"Let's give her a choice," Bett suggested.

"Yeah, *the* choice," Maggot seconded.

"Okay." Vinessa's grin softened. She'd shown Janny kindness before. Even kept her warm one particularly cold night, a long, long time ago when Janny had first wandered Way Down as a little girl. She'd been with her family, her *real* mother and father, on a bus, leaving the city. They had all their belongings with them, and Janny recalled clutching a worn rag doll to her chest the entire time. But they never made it out. Glass shattered as bricks were thrown through the windows of the bus, people shouted and screamed, the bus stopped, began rocking from side to side, and finally tipped over. The rest was confusion from which Janny ran and ran and ran. The rag doll was gone, her mother and father were gone, and Janny couldn't remember anything before then. Not even their names.

Way Down

"The choice," Vinessa continued, "is this: Give this to us and stay, or keep it and leave Way Down…forever."

Scrounge gasped.

Janny was stunned. She'd never *ever* considered leaving Way Down. Sometimes she hated it, but she hated *all* of the city. Way Down was the safest place for a not particularly strong girl to be. The Doll Squad saw to that.

Didn't they *deserve* the helmet, more than her?

"I…"

"Spit it out, Janny," Loona growled. "Ain't got all day."

"I…"

Scrounge's eyes were already wide. The mere fact that Janny hadn't immediately decided to stay was a shock to her…friend. If only Scrounge would for once in her miserable life say *Please, Janny, I need you here. Please, I care about you.*

But no.

"I'll leave."

Silence. Vinessa shoved the head set into Janny's hands, hard, knocking her back a step.

No goodbyes.

Scrounge was already gone, disappeared.

The four members of the Doll Squad, to whom Janny owed her young life, turned and left without another word.

And Janny ran. Out of Way Down through secret alleys, parking garages, subway tunnels. She slipped through stinking sewage, hopped an autotrain moving toward the 'burbs, bringing giant crates of processed food to the more "civilized" sections. How long later, she had no idea, she finally collapsed in the corner of an abandoned depot, where a dead robot forklift sat in a corner, rusted and rotted out, where the lack of any footprints in the dust told Janny no one would come looking for her *here* any time soon. Eventually, though, someone would come, and find her. Without the Doll Squad protecting her, she had new worries.

Her side and back were raw, tight, pulsing with dull discomfort. She regarded her clothes, her shirt and jeans. They were dirty, as always, but something else stained them darker still. Blood. *Her* blood. Somewhere along the way she'd cut herself, *bad*. She was weak, couldn't go on even if she knew where there was to go. And she was tired. All she wanted to do was sleep, to forget the physical discomfort of her body.

She heard a noise. Something scraping along just beyond the edge of the depot. Janny didn't breathe.

Then she heard a soft, almost whispering, voice say, "Janny, it's me."

Scrounge? Janny frowned. The little brat had followed her!

"Janny, come on, I'm not gonna do nothin'."

Stephen L. Antczak

And Scrounge padded softly into the depot, in a half crouch, ready to bolt out of there in a second. She saw Janny, and smiled, showing yellow and brown teeth. Then she noticed the blood, saw Janny was hurt, and froze.

"Who—?"

"I did it to myself," Janny said. "Fell, or something. Why did you follow me?"

Scrounge shrugged.

"For this?" Janny indicated the helmet, which she now held in her lap.

Scrounge looked at it.

"I'll tell you what," Janny said. "You can have it, but after I'm done with it. I need to use it one more time, then it's yours."

"Okay," Scrounge said. "How will—?"

"Just go away and leave me alone," Janny said. "Come back tomorrow and take it. I'm not going anywhere." She coughed, spit up blood.

Scrounge took a few steps back. "I don't want you to die."

Janny smiled. "I'll be okay. We'll see each other again, Scrounge, in paradise, and I'll show you how things used to be in the world. Maybe we can help make it good again, if we can show enough people what life could be like, if only they…tried."

"I'll be back," Scrounge said. "I'll get help, or something."

"Okay."

Scrounge left.

Janny put the helmet back on.

The pain wasn't as bad this time, the connections had already been made once, the microscopic holes in her head were already there. The light wasn't as bright either, but when *he* materialized, and the sun came back, and the wind blew, and she could feel the grass beneath her bare feet, she knew it could be home if she let it.

"Welcome back," he said, arms open wide for her.

She didn't hesitate, but flung herself into them, felt them embrace her, press her into the warm, firm flesh of a man. Even if he didn't exist.

That was all right, because soon Janny wasn't going to exist, either. She imagined she could feel herself dying outside, but didn't fight it, just let it go. She concentrated her energy inward, creating her new *self* in the helmet, making it as much a part of the setting as the trees, the grass, the sky, the sun. Von.

I wrote this story during another dark stage in my life, after another relationship had ended and I found myself jobless, crashing at the house of my good friend Johna Till Johnson while all my belongings resided in the garage of another good friend, Rob Sommers. Both are solid science fiction writers, but they also both truly exceptional friends.

I got a phone call at Johna's house from Nancy Collins, who was helping to edit a collection of stories for an anthology called Gahan Wilson's Ultimate Haunted House. *She needed more fiction, and had contacted another good friend of mine who was doing great work in horror at the time, Gregory Nicoll. For my money, Nicoll is one of the best short horror fiction writers out there, bar none. The late Karl Edward Wagner, who bought three stories from Greg for his* Year's Best Horror Stories *series seemed to have agreed.*

Greg gave Nancy my new contact information because Nancy still had some slots to fill in the book. Each story in the book was to draw its inspiration from a Gahan Wilson drawing of one particular section of the house. Of the drawings Nancy sent me, the ones that had not yet been chosen by another writer, the one that most interested me was titled "The Monster Lab." Frankly, I was surprised that no one else had chosen that particular drawing, and if I'd had to use one of the other drawings that were still available I seriously doubt I would have been able to deliver.

The drawing immediately reminded me of Mary Shelley's Frankenstein, *a book I love. I have always wanted to write a sort of tribute to it. I decided to do just that. Although the anthology was supposed to be composed of mainly horror stories, if you are familiar with Gahan Wilson's cartoons you know they are basically dark humor. I wanted to capture that, too.*

In thinking about the story I wanted to tell, the element that came to me in a daydream was the rationalization for the ending. I think you'll know what I mean when you read the story. The ending is so often the hardest thing to come up with because it is so often the part of the tale upon which the entire story either stands, or falls.

Nancy Collins did a wonderful job, by the way, as an editor in helping me get this story into publishable shape. The voice, because I was shooting for a certain archaic style, was woefully passive, and she did not use that as an excuse to reject the story out of hand but instead sent me a wonderful letter explaining to me in colorful terms what needed to be fixed. I fixed the story, and she bought it.

The Monster Lab

MELISSA HEARD THE CLATTER OF the horses' hooves and the wheels of the carriage on the cobblestones announcing her uncle's arrival. She went to a window, watching through lace curtains as the ornately carved carriage rounded the cherub fountain in the center of the drive. The driver eased back on the reins, slowing the four black geldings, then stopped the carriage at the bottom of the marble front steps of the Lydecker house.

daydreams undertaken

Roderick Lydecker, Melissa's father, had inherited most of *his* father's fortune, passed down from an ancestor who'd amassed riches trading in slaves from the Dark Continent. The house and property, in upstate New York, made up the bulk of the inheritance: five hundred wooded acres centered around the main Tudor mansion, a stable, servants' quarters, and a guest house. Most of the buildings on the property had fallen into disrepair due to neglect. A smaller portion of the fortune, in the form of a flat cash payment, went to Roderick's only sibling, his younger brother, Jacob. Melissa knew her uncle had invested his money in the shipping and warehouse insurance business in Boston, and amassed a fortune of his own.

The driver pulled down a large trunk, setting it gently on the ground, then opened the door to the carriage. A moment later he was helping a lady climb down from the carriage to the ground. So, Uncle Jacob had a lady in his life. Melissa felt excited at this notion because in all the years she'd known him, her uncle had never had *anyone* in his life but himself. However, no one else emerged from the carriage. The lady was alone, and Jacob had apparently not yet arrived.

Disappointed, Melissa went into the foyer to summon her father's only remaining servant.

"Nob!" she called. "Nob!"

A moment later she heard heavy footsteps upstairs and a large, hunchbacked, nearly hairless man appeared at the top of the wide, spiral staircase.

"A lady has arrived," Melissa told him, "and she has a big trunk with her. Please bring it in, and show her in as well."

Nob nodded obediently and came down the stairs, which creaked and moaned under his immense weight. Nob had been Roderick Lydecker's trusted servant since before Melissa's birth, and had even outlived her mother's attempts to have him discharged. Melissa's mother later died from falling out an upstairs window she was apparently trying to clean. Nob had been helping her, and for a while afterward Roderick suspected the misshapen mute of *murdering* her. Melissa managed to convince her father that without her mother around, they'd need Nob more than ever, so he eventually dropped the matter.

Next to Nob's bulk Melissa felt like a small child, although alone, or around men of normal stature, she felt womanly. Petite, yet shapely, she had pronounced breasts and wide hips, and thick curls of auburn hair fell across her shoulders. She also liked to think her blue eyes were lit with a lust for life, like her father's, where Nob's brown eyes tended to reflect his dull and docile nature.

Melissa waited until Nob went out the front door before running to the back stairs that lead to the basement and her father's "workshop." She opened the door and, not daring to actually venture down without Roderick's express permission, called out to him.

"Father, come quick! There's a *lady* here to see you!"

The Monster Lab

A few moments later she heard a door open and close, the jangle of iron keys and the snap of a lock falling home, and her father's muttering voice.

"A lady?" he said. "To see *me*? What on God's Earth...? What lady? Who could she be?" All the way up the stairs he muttered, until he paused to kiss Melissa on the forehead and sigh in exasperation. He too towered over her, although his frame was straight and true, not warped as Nob's. He kept his black-as-oil mustache and hair tightly trimmed. His piercing blue eyes always seemed to be looking beyond the here and now.

"Perhaps she's with Uncle Jacob," Melissa ventured, "and he's sent her on ahead while he tidies up some business back in Boston."

"Perhaps," her father said, although he didn't sound too convinced. He walked a few paces past his daughter, stopped to straighten out his shirt and coat. He ran his fingers through his hair, and buffed his fingernails on his sleeve; then he continued towards the front door. Nob held it open to let the lady in.

"Hello, Roderick," Melissa heard the unmistakably soft voice of her uncle say.

"My God...*Jacob*?" sputtered the eldest Lydecker brother.

Melissa rushed to her father's side to see for herself.

At first she thought that the lady before her stood taller than most women, and had larger bones. She wore a long, dark green dress, a black petticoat embroidered in gold, long black velvet gloves, a dark green scarf, and a black hat underneath which Melissa saw the face of....

"Uncle Jacob!" she gasped when she saw *Jacob's* face smiling at her. His light blue eyes, lacking the sharpness of Roderick's, seemed somewhat glazed. His blond hair played out under the scarf; he'd let it grow to shoulder length. He powdered his face, too, like a true lady.

"Melissa, dear," Jacob greeted her. "My, you've grown! Look at you, you're very nearly a woman!" Had she not spent a large portion of her childhood hearing her uncle's voice, Melissa thought she could easily have mistaken it for a female's.

"And you, Uncle," Melissa said, "you've, umm, *changed*."

Uncle Jacob laughed. He sounded *quite* feminine, light and airy.

"I'm still your *Uncle* Jacob," he said. "Don't you worry."

"But...but you..." Roderick stammered. He took a deep breath. "You look like Mother!"

"Do I?" Jacob asked. "Well then...thank you, brother. I'll take that as a compliment."

"What's happened?" Roderick asked. "An accident of some sort...?"

"No, no," Jacob answered. "I will tell all, but first..." He nodded in the direction of Nob, who stood silently by holding the trunk.

"Oh." Roderick seemed to snap out of a trance. "Right. Nob, take that up to the guest room I had you prepare for my...brother."

Nob, without so much as a *by your leave*, carried the big trunk upstairs. The other three watched, as if glad of the distraction. But then Nob was out of sight and down the second floor hallway, and Melissa and Roderick turned their attentions back to Jacob.

"Do you have any brandy?" Jacob asked. "It was quite a chilly ride here..."

"Oh, of course." Roderick, still acting as though a real lady were in the house, rushed away to prepare the study for them, leaving Melissa alone with her uncle.

"You look very pretty," Melissa could only say.

"I know," Jacob replied. All the same, Melissa couldn't help but notice, now that the initial furor of his arrival had died down, that her uncle also looked very tired indeed. Bone-weary.

"Father's been looking forward to seeing you again," Melissa continued, to avoid the awkwardness of silence. "He's been telling me stories of your childhood together in Salem."

Jacob smiled.

"Oh, yes, our childhood together. We were the best of friends as well as brothers."

"That's what Father says. He says you did everything together."

"Oh, yes, we did." He smiled wistfully and his eyes seemed to focus beyond Melissa, beyond the present of 1908 and into the distant past.

A moment later her father called them into the study.

The pungent aroma of leather-bound books permeated the study, where Roderick had poured three glasses of brandy. Melissa realized she had been invited to sit with them for the first time in her life, probably because her father needed her for moral support just then. Indeed, she noticed the pallor of his face, and his skin seemed waxen. Brandy had been a good idea.

They sat, and sipped their drinks in silence for a moment.

Finally, Roderick spoke.

"I assume there's a good reason for your masquerading as a woman, Jacob?"

"Of course there is, although it may seem silly to you at first. You must trust me in that, until I arranged my 'transformation,' my life was becoming a living Hell."

"I'm listening."

"You haven't seen me in over two years," Jacob began. He paused to sip more of his brandy. Then he continued, "And in that time my condition has deteriorated drastically."

Melissa knew all about his condition. Jacob, she knew, had suffered for a number of years from an unidentifiable malady that doctors told him would gradually siphon off his strength, shorten his breath, and render him feeble and old well before his natural time. In short, he did not expect to live beyond the age of forty, and she knew he was in his late thirties now, since her father had recently turned forty-one.

The Monster Lab

"I found, as a man, that other men I had dealings with, both socially and professionally, regarded my weakened condition with contempt. I discovered that several of my close associates schemed behind my back to wrest control of my insurance holdings away from me! And these men I counted among my most trusted friends! So I devised a plan. It occurred to me that the very traits they found distasteful in me, they very much admired in *women*. Well, I realized that my physique, if you will, wasn't exactly *manly* anymore, and in fact I had acquired a distinctly *feminine* appearance, even dressed in trousers and a shirt with the sleeves rolled up! I concocted a female identity, Roderick, a *sister* who'd been married off at a young age and whom we'd not been in contact with for years, who suddenly found herself a widow and in need of male sponsorship. So I began spreading it around that I had found a potential cure for my ailments in the Far East — Katmandu or some such place — and that I would be leaving our *sister* in charge of my affairs while I ventured off to begin treatment!"

Jacob paused for a moment to sip his brandy, while Roderick absorbed these revelations.

"Sister?" Melissa's father could only mutter by way of comment.

"Yes," Jacob said. "Andrea. Dre, for short. She's the baby, three years younger than me."

"I see."

"I've always wanted an aunt," Melissa said. Jacob smiled at her.

"Life got so much easier after that, I must say," Jacob continued. "Because I was a woman with male sponsorship, suddenly my associates adopted a code of ethics they enforced with each other when dealing with me. I even had a few marriage proposals—" Roderick suddenly gagged on a sip of brandy. "—which I declined, of course. One of my suitors commited suicide, you know. Poor thing!"

"God," Roderick said, setting his drink down and rubbing his face with his hands. "Sounds like you created a monster!"

Melissa broke into a fit of giggles. They watched her, Roderick with exasperation, Jacob with bemusement, until she calmed down.

"Sorry," she said quietly.

Jacob looked at his older brother. "When I got your note, Roderick, I barely took the time to get my affairs in order. I hired a firm to take charge of things—"

"Which firm?" Roderick asked, frowning, suddenly all business.

"Boyle and Leech."

Roderick nodded his approval.

"I came right away," Jacob said. "When I read that you could cure me...You said, *I am positive I have discovered the means of relieving you of your bizarre illness and can guarantee you a new life unfettered by the shackles of infirmity...*"

Stephen L. Antczak

Jacob took a deep breath. "I don't think I'll last through the winter, you know, especially if it proves to be too severe. Not in the pathetic condition I'm in now."

"Then we must begin your...treatment as soon as possible. Tomorrow."

Jacob's eyebrows rose. "Tomorrow?"

"Yes. Until then, however, let us sit a while, and sip our brandy, and talk of happier days. I don't think Melissa has ever heard the story of the time I wrapped you up in bandages and convinced you you had died and become a mummy..."

Jacob groaned. "Does she need to hear it now?"

Roderick looked at his daughter with a twinkle in his eyes. "I also managed to convince him that he had to obey me, because whoever raised someone from the dead became their master."

"Father!" Melissa exclaimed, laughing. "You were so cruel. I'm glad *I* never had an older brother!"

"Indeed," said Jacob, "but I must say this: I am quite glad to have an older brother this day, especially one who is a genius, if a bit mad, and who cares enough about his sickly little brother to devote the vast quantities of time and money it must have taken to discover a way to cure him." With that, Jacob raised his glass in salute to Roderick. Melissa followed suit, and the three of them sipped their brandy in a silent toast.

"What else are big brothers for?" Roderick asked then, after they had emptied their glasses. He got up to fetch the bottle and fill them again.

Next day, breakfast was served in the dining room at eight. The kitchen and dining room smelled of bacon and sausage and fresh brewed coffee. Jacob came late, wearing a flowing dressing gown of linen and lace. Roderick, busy reading a book of Byron's verse, didn't notice him at first. But when he did, he stared in disbelief.

"I have no men's clothing with me," Jacob explained. "How would it look, in the event of an accident or other emergency, for a woman to be travelling alone, yet with a man's clothes in her trunk?"

"I see."

"Anything of yours would hang too loosely on me. Besides, this is quite comfortable. It's about the only thing I wear these days. I don't know why women don't rebel against the outrageously uncomfortable clothes we make them wear!"

"I'm sure I don't know, either," Roderick said. Both men looked at Melissa, as if expecting some revelation, but she just shrugged and sipped her coffee.

"So, Roderick," Jacob said, "will the procedure take very long?"

"It may take a while, yes."

The Monster Lab

"Days?" Jacob asked. "Weeks? Months?"

"The actual procedure won't take long, but the recovery period could last a while. A few months, perhaps."

"Will it be particularly painful?"

"Painful?" Roderick frowned. "Uncomfortable is probably more like it. There will be a certain amount of disorientation. Just remember at all times that you're in good hands, and not to panic. Always keep in mind what the alternative is."

Jacob nodded gravely.

"Death," he said. "Slow, undignified, dishonorable…I do not wish to waste away like that. Rather, let me die undergoing some experimental treatment so that I may at least contribute in some small way to the cause of science."

"You sound like Father," Melissa noted. "He's always talking about the great cause of science, but I think he's just having fun. I think he *likes* tinkering around downstairs in the Monster Lab by himself."

"Melissa…" Roderick said accusingly.

"Monster Lab?" Jacob asked. "Roderick, is that what you call your lab?"

Roderick grinned, and said, "It seemed to be the only thing I could think of. I never told her about it."

"About what?" Melissa asked.

He looked at Melissa. "That's the name of the play-lab your uncle and I had when we were children."

"We used to find dead animals," Jacob explained, "and sever their body parts and re-attach them to the bodies of other animals, hoping to create living monsters. Of course we never succeeded, the poor animals being, as they were, dead already."

"What a gruesome thing for two young boys to play at," Melissa commented. "But that's boys for you."

"We never actually killed the animals ourselves," Jacob said. "Roderick used to hike all around looking for ones that were already dead. I always marvelled at how he could find so many that'd been freshly killed. Still, I guess we entertained ourselves with pretty gruesome play! Luckily Mother and Father never found us out. We built the Monster Lab in a big oak tree way out in the woods, and as far as I know no one ever knew about it."

"It sounds like *you* haven't changed much," Melissa told Roderick in a mischievious tone.

"Are you *still* performing those macabre surgeries?" Jacob asked, amusement in his voice. "You haven't outgrown *that*, then."

"Quite the contrary," Roderick said. "The work I do now is *real*. Not play. Some day it shall revolutionize medicine. But…you'll see when I take you downstairs later."

"You won't need me…will you, Father?" Melissa asked.

He waved the question off. "Don't be silly, of course I will. Nob, too, for that matter."

Melissa lowered her gaze to her breakfast and didn't say anything else, nor did she eat any more. Roderick and Jacob finished breakfast in silence, too. The reunion of the brothers had apparently already lost its sheen of newness; they'd run out of things to talk about, or at least things either wished to speak of.

At the end of the meal, however, Roderick did speak.

"You are free to do as you wish with your body today, Jacob," he said. "Indulge yourself with drink, food, tobacco, or anything else you desire. I have plenty of everything in this house. We shall have an enormous feast for dinner, and then I'll take you down to the so-called Monster Lab and we can begin the procedure."

That ended breakfast. Roderick disappeared downstairs. Nob worked in the kitchen preparing for dinner. Jacob asked Melissa to accompany him for a walk outdoors.

Outside, the sun peeked through gray clouds. A cold wind blew across the grounds. Jacob remarked to Melissa how it made him feel good to take it all in, the place where he and Roderick had summered with their parents so long ago.

"A lifetime ago," he finished, wistfully.

He told Melissa her grandfather used to do a lot of fox hunting in the rolling countryside when they were here. Now the stables held only horses for the carriage. The walk enlivened Melissa at least, but Jacob looked worn and tired by the time they got back to the house. Melissa ran on ahead, up the stairs, and waited for her uncle at the front door.

As he slowly climbed the front stairs, Jacob paused, stood still for a moment, then collapsed.

"Uncle!" Melissa yelled, and rushed to his side.

Nob carried Jacob upstairs, led by Melissa. Jacob groaned and came to in the upstairs hallway, halfway to the guest room. "The nervous new husband carries the blushing bride to the bedroom," Melissa said, smiling.

"I fainted," Jacob told her. "Please fetch me some brandy."

"Yes, Uncle." She ran downstairs, got the bottle, and returned as Nob opened the door to Jacob's room.

"You can let me down," Jacob told the hunchback. "I'm fine." He felt Nob hesitate. "Really, I'll manage."

Ever so gently, Nob let Jacob down on his feet. Jacob had to place one hand against a wall for support, but other than that he seemed strong enough to stand.

"Thank you," he said to Nob.

Melissa handed the brandy to Jacob. He took it with his free hand. Then she looked at Nob.

The Monster Lab

"Don't you have to finish preparing dinner?" she asked. Without so much as a grunt in reply, Nob retreated downstairs. Melissa watched the hunchback go, then turned to face Jacob.

"You know it's strange," Jacob said, "but Nob reminds me of your mother. I watched him cutting the vegetables earlier, just before we left for our walk, and he did it just the way *she* used to."

Melissa felt the expression on her face harden almost automatically. Her vision seemed to cloud.

"Ridiculous," she said, tight-mouthed, "and I would thank you not to defile Mother's memory with such disrespectful comparisons in the future! Mother was a brilliant woman, well-educated, a wonderful chef; kind, noble, beautiful...Nob is an ugly, brainless animal who has learned certain tricks the way a smart dog might learn how to roll over or play...dead!" With that last word — *dead* — Melissa broke into tears and ran to her room, slamming the door shut behind her.

Roderick seemed lively enough at supper, but he looked haggard. Jacob came to the table drunk, bringing the now half empty bottle of brandy. Melissa felt better after a nap, and no one made mention of the dark circles under her eyes. She felt bad about her confrontation with Jacob earlier, and imagined leaving him there in the hall, bewildered and perhaps a little hurt by the razored tone in his niece's voice. She just could not face discussing her mother with him. It relieved her that Roderick chose not to mention her tirade, for she was certain he heard every word of it. Voices carried throughout the house with astounding clarity, especially when raised in anger.

Nob retired to the kitchen after serving the food, which filled the room with a rich aroma reminiscent of a holiday feast.

"Mmmm, thish'n *good*," Jacob slurred around a mouthful of roast pork, spitting bits of food with each word.

"I'm glad you like it," Roderick said, but he wasn't smiling. He sighed as his brother took a gulp of brandy straight from the bottle.

A moment later Jacob speared another mouthful with his fork, but as he raised it to his lips he paused, then dropped it, and slowly slid out of his chair and onto the floor.

"Finally," Roderick said. He looked at Melissa. "He never could hold his brandy, but I was beginning to wonder."

Melissa said nothing.

"Now what's the matter?" her father asked.

"Nothing."

"You should be happy, you know. You'll be living in Boston before long, with a substantial monthly allowance from your Uncle Jacob's holdings. I'll have enough money with *my* share to continue my work. And Jacob will be alive and *healthy* again. We should *all* be happy. I *am* happy, though I'd be happier if you were happy, too."

Melissa sighed.

"If it's all the same with you," she said, "I'd rather feel miserable for now."

"You were like this with your mother," Roderick said. That comment ignited a fire in her gut, but she didn't say anything to him. Roderick continued. "If only you knew how much your denial hurts her…but then you *do* know, don't you? She wrote you those letters, the ones you burned."

"She wrote those letters *before* she died!" Melissa practically screamed, her pent-up emotions bursting forth all at once. "*You* told Nob to slip them under my door after you buried her body! My mother's soul is in Heaven, not trapped in the body of that hunchback!"

Roderick sighed.

"How many times must I tell you, Melissa?" he asked. "The soul is housed in the *brain*, not the breast. The heart is merely a pump—"

"Then why when I feel sad does it ache *here*?" she said, hitting her chest with her fist. "Why, when I am happy, do I soar *here*!" She struck herself on the chest again. "Just because he knows what she knew doesn't mean he's *her*! When her heart stopped beating, her spirit left! Mother is *dead*, just like Uncle Jacob will be *dead*, and you're the one who's fooling himself, and that's why I can't take it anymore! *That's* why I want to go to Boston—"

Melissa broke down into sobs then, while Roderick silently watched her. Jacob groaned on the floor.

"I have to start," Roderick told his daughter. "My offer remains. If you help me this last time, you can go to Boston with no ill will, living off money from Jacob's holdings. If you refuse to help me, I will insist you remain here until you find a husband—"

"I'll help you," Melissa said. She regarded the place at the table where Jacob had been sitting. "He's dying anyway, isn't he?"

Roderick nodded.

"Then let's begin."

Roderick's so-called Monster Lab wasn't in the basement. It was *below* the basement. A massive iron door kept it sealed off from the rest of the sub-basement, most of which Roderick never used. The dust, cobwebs, and stale flavor of the air attested to that. By the dim glow of a gaslight, Melissa saw the iron door had a wooden sign glued to it, jagged-edged with the words MONSTER LAB written on it in uneven, childish script: the actual sign from the tree house Monster Lab years ago, Melissa's father explained.

Roderick pulled down a lever across the hall from the lab, and the iron door opened slowly. Its elaborate mechanism of pulleys, gears, and chains clanked and wheezed, echoing throughout the sub-basement. Melissa sneezed as the

The Monster Lab

door kicked up dust. The unmistakable stench of decay, mingled with the odor of the chemicals that kept it somewhat subdued, hit them like a sudden wind.

Nob carried Jacob's limp form in, draped over his deformed shoulder. Melissa followed, then Roderick, who flipped up another lever, igniting the electric lights he'd recently installed. They hummed loudly, filling the room with as much noise as light.

Though she knew what to expect, Melissa still recoiled at the sight of what Roderick had created in the Monster Lab: an actual, honest-to-God bloody mess. Red stains smeared the walls, rivulets dripped into pools from the operating tables, unidentifiable pieces of flesh rose in lumps from the puddles on the floor, entrails snaked around table legs, while in the corners sat piles of discarded pieces of human bone. Most of the torso of a body, half again as big as Roderick, lay on the main table.

Nob set Jacob on a table across the room.

A set of cabinets lined the wall opposite the door, the drawers marked with the names of various body parts, and designations whose humor apparently only Roderick could appreciate, such as *Warts and Hickeys*. Human brains floated in jars, each labelled, again utilizing a peculiar sense of humor: *Good, Bad, Sick, Twisted, Criminal*, and *Unimaginative*. Melissa, who'd visited the Lab a few times before, didn't remember seeing these odd labels.

"Father?" she asked.

Her expression must have given her thoughts away, because Roderick explained, "I made those for Jacob, to remind him of the Monster Lab from our childhood."

She wondered what the drawer marked *Fun Bits* held.

"Here," Roderick said, handing her a label with the phrase *My Name Is* on it, and just beneath that her own name scribbled in Roderick's barely legible handwriting. He had one for himself and one for Nob, too, although Nob's bore the name *Catherine*. Melissa's mother.

"What are these for?" Melissa asked.

"Everything must be labelled," Roderick replied. He didn't elaborate. Melissa noticed a certain wildness in his eyes, and decided not to pursue the issue.

Jacob groaned and came to, slowly sitting up. He blinked at the bright lights, then looked around, taking in his surroundings with a growing expression of disbelief and horror on his face.

"My *God*," he said. "Roderick...What have you done?"

"This is my Monster Lab, Jacob," Roderick told him, indicating the blood-soaked room around them with a sweep of his arm. "Remember when we were children? The cabinets for eyes and noses and warts and hickeys...Well, this is *it*."

"You weren't joking, then," Jacob practically whispered. He looked at the headless body on the operating table, then over at a severed head on another table. The top of the head had been removed, the brain and eyes scooped out.

"Like it?" Roderick asked. "That'll be you, when I'm finished. Your brain in that head, atop this body. You'll have your own eyes…I'll be attaching new feet, as this poor fellow had clubbed ones, and deformed hands, as well. You'll be as strong as an ox. A smaller, more aesthetically pleasing body I cannot provide, I fear, as I am not so adept at putting one together…yet. The more I do it, the better I get, and soon I'll have you in a body as thin and tightly wound as the one you have now, and I'll have Catherine in a delicate, petite woman's body instead of the one *she* now inhabits." He looked purposefully at Nob, then at Melissa.

"Catherine?" Jacob said, also looking at Nob and then at Melissa, as if expecting confirmation from one, or both, of them. Nob didn't react at all. Melissa's face burned, and she bit her lip, forcing herself not to speak. She lowered her head to stare at the red puddles on the floor.

"Melissa," Roderick said. "The syringe. We must begin at once. Time is not on our side."

"Syringe?" Jacob asked. Melissa walked over to another cabinet, opened it, and produced a big syringe with a long needle. It looked more suited for injecting a horse than a man.

"We must inject you with a compound that will render you unconscious so you will not feel any pain. I hope you won't mind being unconscious."

"Pain?"

"I highly recommend being unconscious while I remove your brain," Roderick explained patiently.

"Remove my brain?" Jacob looked around nervously, his eyes appealing to Melissa for support, or reason, or *something*.

"Don't be afraid," Roderick said. "The procedure *worked* on Catherine. She inhabits the body of Nob! Alas, I disposed of his brain. It had been damaged *in utero*, the same accident that rendered him a hunchback. But as you can see, she's fine. Oh, she can't talk because Nob didn't have a tongue, but I've been meaning to get her one soon. Maybe I'll give her yours. You won't be needing it…"

"Father," Melissa said, suddenly feeling ill, "please stop."

Oblivious to the effect his words had on her, Roderick continued without missing a beat, "…and besides, I've put a perfectly workable cow's tongue in your new head." He walked over to the severed head on the counter, near Melissa. "Would you like to see?"

As he turned the head around to give Jacob a good view inside its mouth, Melissa suddenly plunged the needle into his left buttock and pressed the plunger down about a third of the way with her thumb. A stunned expression played across Roderick's face. His eyes rolled up into his head, his lids fluttered closed, and he fell to the ground, soundly thwacking his skull on the floor and splashing gobs of thick blood onto Melissa's clothes.

The Monster Lab

"I'm sorry!" Melissa cried to her now unconscious father. Then she looked at Jacob. "I couldn't do it! He's...He's crazy, you see, and...With Mother, she was already dead, or she would have died soon enough, but I couldn't let him kill Nob because it wouldn't have worked! It wouldn't have!"

"Melissa," Jacob said. "What are you talking about?"

"Mother's brain is *not* in Nob's head," Melissa told him. "Father had Nob drugged, and was going to cut the top of his head off and remove his brain, and replace it with Mother's, but I injected him, just as I did now, and knocked him out before he started. When he awakened, I convinced him he'd succeeded, and he didn't remember because he'd been working in a delirium for several days.

"*I* taught Nob how to cook the way Mother did! *I* showed him how to write the way she did! Nob went along with my ruse, and continues to do so because I saved his life, and he knows no other world than this house and Father's employ. He killed Mother, and it was no *accident*. She hated him. She treated him like a slave, always beating him, even when he tried to help her clean the upstairs windows! So he pushed her out one day. She lingered for weeks, her body broken but her mind still active. She could open her eyes and see, but that was *all* she could do! So Father decided it was only fair for Nob to let Mother's brain inhabit his body. He'd been performing experiments for years, and had succeeded in switching the brains of two dogs, though they died less than a week later. But he determined he was ready to perform the operation on Mother and Nob.

"I knew he would fail if I let him proceed! I devised a plan to stop him. Then, for show, I rebelled against the idea of Mother's brain in Nob's head. It worked because I've always been contrary, so Father expected it of me! My refusal to accept his truth only reinforced his belief that he'd succeeded!"

"I think I understand," Jacob said. "But then that means his 'procedure' for curing me of my illness isn't real, am I right?"

Melissa nodded.

"And you were going to go along with him anyway, knowing he'd fail?"

Melissa nodded again.

"Why? In God's name, *why?*"

"Because, it would make him happy," Melissa answered. "And he and I had worked out a deal. You see, we'd have to declare you dead, and Father would be your beneficiary. He was going to give me enough of a monthly allowance to move to Boston — and leave this dreadful place once and for all."

Jacob considered this, then asked, "But what of our 'sister?' What of Dre?"

"Who?" Melissa asked, confused.

Jacob indicated the dinner dress he was still wearing. "Oh, *her*. Well...I suppose we'd have to say she decided to stay on with Father. Or maybe got married off again or something. I don't know. I'm sure Father had something figured out for you, or her, or...you know."

"Melissa, why didn't you just inject *me*, instead of Roderick, as you were supposed to?" Jacob asked.

"I couldn't!" she replied. "It's so horrible, to have your brain removed! I couldn't bear the thought of him doing that to you! Not after Mother."

"But I am *dying*," Jacob told her. "My strength is being sapped from my body by the moment. Soon I'll need a nurse to care for me, to feed me and help me with my toilet. I don't want that! That's no way for a *man* to end up!"

"Do you *want* Father to remove your brain and to try and put it in the head of this...*thing?*" Melissa asked.

"If it makes him happy," Jacob said, "then perhaps I do. And you will benefit from it, too. Even if the operation fails, if I know my brother you'll still get your wish. You'll be living in Boston in a month. And Roderick, well, he'll still have Nob as his success, so his failure with me will be bearable, right?"

"I suppose," Melissa said.

Roderick groaned on the floor.

"See to his head," Jacob said. "I think he hit it pretty hard. And inject me before he awakens. You can tell him he slipped in the blood and fell, hitting his head."

"This is what you want?" Melissa asked.

Jacob nodded.

"I'll miss you, Uncle Jacob," Melissa said, as she refilled the syringe.

"You never know," Jacob replied, "maybe he'll *succeed*."

This story holds a special place in my heart. For one thing, it is the only "swords and sorcery" story I've ever written. For another, the character of Shan was actually an old Dungeons & Dragons *character of mine from high school. (Yes, I know Shan is a woman. Don't ask.)*

"Be My Hero" was somewhat inspired by the song of the same name by the band October Project. I liked the idea of someone wanting someone else to be their hero. I also liked the idea of someone who actually was *a hero wanting someone to be their* hero *for a change.*

As with "Captain Asimov" I wanted to make this story "family friendly," something a parent would be happy to read to their kids, but which would also appeal to adult sensibilities. Daydreaming, I came up with the plot while listening to the October Project song. The song itself is very stirring, while I feel the story is more amusing in nature. Nice, is how I like to describe it, meant only to bring a smile to the face of the reader. I hope it works.

Be My Hero

THE RIDER WAS CLAD ALL in black armor, and his identity was concealed by a great helm, plumed with the black feathers of a gryphon. He sat atop a black steed that seemed to snort fire. They stood calmly still for three days until the Queen sent a messenger to ask what business they had in Cala.

When the messenger returned, he had this to say:

"The Black Rider is here to challenge Shan Lyera to fight to the death, or to choose a hero to fight for her if she is afraid."

daydreams undertaken

Stephen L. Antczak

Shan was given the message. She considered the challenge for a few quiet moments, and then sighed deeply.

"Illa," she said, "good Queen of Caladon, I have never asked anything of your people, have I?"

"This is true," Queen Illa replied. "All that you have received from Caladon has been given of our own accord, and indeed we are indebted to you far more than we could ever hope to repay."

"Then I would consider your kingdom's debt to me paid in full if you will grant me this request: Allow one of your gallant warriors to stand for me in combat against this Black Rider, for I know I cannot defeat him in battle."

The Queen was taken aback by this request. Here was someone that the great Shan Lyera *feared*? If Shan couldn't hope to defeat the Black Rider, how could one of Caladon's warriors, who to the last knew without a doubt that she was their better in combat? The answer was apparent: Whoever stood as Shan's hero in this fight would die, sacrificed so that she may live.

"The lives of many of our people would be forfeit were it not for you, Shan," Queen Illa said. "Therefore I decree that if there be any warrior in all of Caladon who would stand as your hero in this single combat, it will be with my blessing."

Shan bowed her thanks to the Queen, and criers were sent throughout the capitol, Cala, and to the surrounding towns and villages, to spread the news of Shan's request.

Anwer was busy wiping yet another pint of ale off his person when a royal crier arrived at the Dragon's Head tavern. The ale had been poured on Anwer by Fenwin Junna, one of the Junna triplets, the other two of which stood by laughing and shaking their heads in mock sympathy for Anwer.

"It really is amazing how your head seems to attract ale like that," Fenwin said.

"Yes, Anwer," Balwin Junna added, "almost as if t'were magic."

"No sooner do you set foot in a pub," Merwin Junna continued, "than *swoosh* a pint of ale rains down on you!" The three of them broke into loud, raucous laughter. The other patrons of the Dragon's Head grinned at this familiar exchange, when suddenly the crier called out.

"Hear ye! Hear ye! Shan Lyera requests one man to stand for her in single combat against he who is known only as the Black Rider! Know this: Queen Illa gives her blessing to whoever agrees to stand as Shan Lyera's hero!"

When the crier was finished he tacked a bulletin, reiterating what he'd just announced, on the pub wall.

"For Shan's favor," Balwin Junna said, "I'd slay a dragon!"

"I'd slay *ten* dragons!" Fenwin Junna boasted.

"And I'd let the two of you go off slaying dragons whilst I swept Shan Lyera right off her feet with my charm!" Merwin Junna said.

Be My Hero

"So, who is this Black Rider?" Fenwin Junna asked. "I've never heard of him! How can it be that Shan Lyera fears him?"

"Perhaps he doesn't pose enough of a challenge for her," someone else in the pub offered. "She's not afraid of him, she just wants a bit more sport!"

"Only one who has not felt the cold burn of battle in his gut would say such a thing," another, older, man said. All eyes turned towards him. He was a veteran of the days when the monster known as the Stith terrorized Caladon. He was missing an arm that had been hewn from his body by the Stith itself. "The killing of a man isn't about sport. If it has to be done then it is a grave deed that can only be undertaken with one's spirit properly prepared to either kill...or die."

"But Shan Lyera has killed many creatures that are far more dangerous than a mere man," said Fenwin Junna.

"She has been living an easy life since returning to Caladon," Merwin Junna said. "Perhaps she has grown soft..."

"Perhaps she knows she would lose," another man said. All eyes cast their gaze down to the floor. None wanted to think that, never mind say it aloud.

"Could it be she fears death enough to let someone else fight for her?" Balwin asked.

"If she cannot defeat this Black Rider," Fenwin said, "then how can any of us expect to?"

"Even great warriors may know fear in their day," the one-armed veteran said, nodding. "And defeat."

"Indeed," Fenwin said. "And someone like myself, who is no warrior, can I be blamed for not wishing to go to my certain death over some...point of honor? This Black Rider doesn't seem to be a threat to Caladon, does he? If so, why then there would be no question! I'd gladly go to my death in defense of my people!"

Anwer Fane listened to the conversation with growing despair. Like most men in Caladon, he believed himself to be in love with Shan. But he did not even pretend to hope that he could defeat a foe that she could not. He didn't even have the courage to fight back against the Junna triplets.

Conversations like the one in the Dragon's Head arose in pubs across the land, from the finest establishments in Cala to the smallest beer shacks in the tiniest hamlets. Young warriors-to-be talked themselves out of volunteering for what they saw as a suicide mission. Others said they would happily lay down their lives for the great Shan Lyera, if only they didn't have families, or good jobs with responsibilities. Older men who'd fought the Stith reckoned they'd already done their part and deserved their retirement; it was time for the younger generation to serve.

In short, no one came forth to be Shan Lyera's hero.

Later that night, Anwer Fane lay awake in bed, tossing and turning, imagining he could hear Shan's voice telling him she was disappointed in his people, in *him.* When he did find sleep he had nightmares of being cut down by the Black Rider, run through by his pronged sword, dying a painful death on the field while his countryfolk applauded. The next morning he awoke drenched in sweat, and he knew what he had to do.

He made the announcement in the Dragon's Head tavern.

"*You!?*" was the general reaction of the regulars.

Anwer stood as straight and tall as he could, which still put him a full head shorter than most men of Caladon. He was thin and wiry, and his hands and feet were so big they looked as if they belonged on a man half again Anwer's size. His experience with weapons was somewhat limited. He was a fair shot with a sling, which was great for knocking out squirrels from fifty paces but useless against a man in full armor!

He had used his father's sword once as a teenager, to chop wood when his axe handle had broken. When his father found out about it, he forbade Anwer to ever pick up a sword again. And Anwer had not.

When the pub regulars saw that Anwer was serious about being Shan's hero, the realization of what it meant sunk in. Anwer was going to sacrifice himself for her. He, alone of all of Caladon's men who'd professed their love for Shan, was willing to die for her.

"A toast!" Merwin Junna shouted then, raising his pint. "To Anwer Fane!" Each man and woman in the Dragon's Head raised a pint to him. They then proceeded to buy Anwer drink after drink after drink, until he wound up crawling home from the pub, his head spinning, his gut wrenching, but as happy as he'd ever been in his life.

The Kingdom of Caladon had been much the same then as it is now. It was a small kingdom as kingdoms go, proud yet peaceful with its neighbors. For most of Anwer Fane's youth, Caladon had paid tribute to a creature known only as the Stith.

The Stith was an eight-armed giant who'd come to the kingdom not long before Anwer's tenth birthday. The Stith laid waste to the capital city of Cala, killed most of the Royal Guard, and exacted a heavy price in return for not doing even *more* damage. After that, two or three times a year the Stith demanded vast quantities of treasure from the royal coffers, and barrels of wine, and whole cows for it to rip apart and eat. In a few years the demands grew more frequent, and started to include women and boys to entertain a growing army of ogres the Stith had gathered around it.

King Inwann reacted to the initial demands for women and boys by sending the Stith poisoned cows, and attacking his camp of ogres after their feast. His warriors managed to kill half the ogres before being defeated by the Stith, on whom the poison cows had no effect. King Inwann was executed and eaten by the remaining ogres, as were most of the royal family, along with many of the warriors who survived the battle. Thereafter, the Stith and its ogres had the run of the kingdom…until Shan Lyera showed up. She had come to fight the Stith on her own terms, one-on-one, single combat to the death.

Shan Lyera. The name carried with it the legend of a young woman borne of a warrior culture far to the south of Caladon. She rose through the ranks of its sword fighters during a round of contests, duels to the death, the winner of each absorbing the skill of his, or her, opponent. It was said she now possessed the combined abilities of one hundred of the greatest sword fighters known. It was her duty then, as the shining example of her culture's warrior class, to travel the world and meet in combat any creatures who dared use their strength, or skill in battle, to terrorize those weaker or less skilled. Such was the nature of her people, such was their code of life, and they wished other nations to know it by the deeds of their greatest warrior.

Shan arrived incognito, and proceeded to kill the ogres, one by one, as they wandered through the city of Cala seeking their foul entertainment. Twenty of them were dead before the Stith realized someone was picking them off. It organized the two hundred or so who were left, determined to raze Cala and leave it in ashes. Even without the capital city, the Stith could continue to exact tribute from the rest of Caladon for years to come.

It was then that Shan stepped forth and challenged the Stith to single combat. She knew the ogres he led would expect it to accept, and would await the outcome of the contest. If the Stith refused her challenge, the ogres would abandon it, as it was their nature not to follow one whom they perceived to be a coward.

The Stith met Shan on the tournament field north of Cala. Caladonians came from far across the kingdom to bear witness, as did the Stith's ogres, who now mingled with the citizenry with nary a thought of murder in their heads. Shan wielded her one sword, rumored to be an ancient, enchanted blade. The Stith held a wickedly curved blade in each of its eight hands. It swung these blades in such a manner that it seemed to create a tornado of steel all around it, a familiar and terrible sight to those Caladonians who'd lost loved ones, or limbs, in battle with the Stith.

The song of steel striking steel, as if dozens of warriors clashed together in quick thrusts and parries, rose over the field. The Stith spun at Shan and she stood her ground, sparks flying as she fended off blow after blow. Suddenly one of the Stith's arms flew out of the whirlwind! The Stith cried out, and Shan pressed her attack. Another arm was severed, and then another, and the Stith staggered back, no longer whirling and spinning. It howled as Shan's ancient sword cut into its flesh, until all but one arm lay severed on the ground. Then Shan moved in for the *coup de grace*, a swift thrust into the thing's heart, and then a sudden slash up and she beheaded the monster.

Stephen L. Antczak

A cheer went up as the headless body fell. The people of Caladon took heart in Shan's victory and quickly cut the ogres down to the last, returning their kingdom to peace.

Shan Lyera stayed in Caladon long enough to help train a new Royal Guard. She took no payment, no reward for her great deed. A few months after the death of the Stith, Shan left Caladon to continue her journeys, promising to someday return. Dozens of young men swooned after her, offering marriage and vows of eternal love...It was said Shan could have kept a castle full of young men as happy servants to fulfill her every need, had she so desired.

Anwer Fane was one of those young men Shan could have had. Her golden hair, azure eyes, finely muscled yet womanly figure...How many men of Caladon had dreamed of holding her close? How many had dreamed of kissing those full lips and gazing into those fiercely proud eyes? All of them, probably.

Shan did return, nearly a decade later. Just as beautiful as ever, unscathed from her countless escapades during her absence. Tales were told of her deeds since leaving Caladon, that she'd defeated dozens of monsters as powerful as the Stith, from a fire-breathing dragon to an army of zombies.

Upon her return, Queen Illa, niece of the doomed King Inwann, ordered several days of feasting. For a year Shan Lyera lived in the royal palace. It was said that the florists of Cala couldn't grow enough fragrant blossoms to meet the needs of the young men of Cala who sent them to Shan daily. The scribes couldn't write fast enough as they scribbled down line after line of poetry dedicated to Shan, dipping their quills into ink pots while young aristocrats excitedly dictated their verse.

Just over a year into her stay in Cala, when she had become the darling of society, the Black Rider appeared on the field of her battle with the Stith.

Anwer's arrival at the palace was unspectacular. There were no horns trumpeting, no banners unfurling, no flags waving in the breeze, no ceremonies. In fact, he had trouble convincing the gatekeeper that he was indeed there to offer his services as Shan Lyera's hero. When he was finally let in, he stood there gaping at the stained-glass windows that cast an otherworldly glow across the main hall. A rainbow arched across the room, passing through the mist of a fountain at the center.

A feast had been laid out on a table that stretched across the room like a serpent, meandering around the fountain and finally ending at the royal throne, presently empty. Anwer had heard about the neverending banquet, always kept ready and available to anyone admitted to the palace, continuously tended to by servants. He approached the table cautiously, fearing someone might decide he did not belong there and usher him out before he could explain himself. A servant came over and pulled a chair from the table, offering it to Anwer.

Be My Hero

"All that you see before you is yours," the servant, a very pretty young woman, said. She filled a goblet with golden wine and set it before Anwer. At first he picked at the food near him, only taking small portions of roast duck, baked apples, stuffed mushrooms as big as his fist, and honey-glazed venison. He felt exceedingly conspicuous as he was presently the only diner at the table. The food tasted so good, though, that he soon forgot he was alone. He dug in with gusto, piling his plate high with another round of what he had just eaten before, and adding peppers roasted and stuffed with nuts and seasoned meats, small pies filled with minced vegetables and fruit, warm bread lathered with butter…It was all so delicious he wanted to keep eating even after filling himself, to enjoy the subtle nuances of flavor in every bite.

So much did he eat and drink that soon he started nodding off over his plate. Lower and lower his head bowed, until he wound up snoozing face down in the food…and none other than Queen Illa herself, accompanied by her court *and* Shan Lyera, made her appearance in the great hall. When the trumpets sounded announcing the Queen's arrival, Anwer sat up suddenly, his face covered in food. The court erupted into laughter while Anwer hastily wiped his face clean. The Queen, seated at the head of the table, bade him come forth.

"You are Anwer Fane," she said, "son of Orrin Fane, soldier and husbander, and Milla Fane, mid-wife. I am told that in all of Caladon you are the only man come forth to fight the Black Rider as Shan's hero."

Anwer bowed deeply, then said, "I know only that I am willing to face the Black Rider in single combat in Shan Lyera's name. She has done much for our — for *your* kingdom, my Queen, and I believe it is just and right for her to ask of us this small thing."

Queen Illa looked at Shan.

"Do you accept this brave subject's offer, Shan Lyera?"

Shan! Anwer had not actually looked directly at her yet. He feared his desire for her would be too painfully obvious. He feared she would laugh at the pathetic spectacle he was now positive he must seem to them.

"Raise your eyes," Shan said, her voice soft and her tone respectful. "Raise your eyes, Anwer Fane, and look at me. Let our eyes probe one another and glimpse each other's true self. It is said the eyes are like windows, through which true selves are observed and cannot hide."

Anwer raised his eyes, and mustering all of his courage, looked into Shan's azure windows and saw her true self. He saw her famed courage and knew that no creature spawned of evil could ever face her and live. He saw supreme confidence and knew she would accomplish everything she set out to. He also saw a weariness there. She had grown tired of fighting and longed for rest, peace, and place to call home.

She smiled. "I accept you, Anwer Fane, as my hero."

Stephen L. Antczak

It took a while for what Shan said to sink in. Anwer stood there, still gazing into her eyes for several seconds, while Queen Illa and her court looked on. Then he suddenly realized what Shan had said, what it meant, and he fainted.

When Anwer awoke, he found himself in a lavish bed softer than anything he'd ever felt. The room was decorated with finely embroidered draperies that hung down from all four walls, and it smelled of roses. A silver bowl containing fruit had been placed on a stand by his bed. He sat up and considered eating, but felt rather queasy from his overindulgence the day before.

He remembered what happened the evening before. Fainted! In front of the Queen! In front of *Shan*! They were going to laugh him out of the palace, right out of Cala, out of the entire kingdom when word of his foolishness spread. He'd have to move somewhere far, far away where no one had ever heard the name Anwer Fane!

Someone knocked on his door, and then it opened. A young man entered, dressed in the red finery of a palace servant, and bowed.

"Your grace," the young man said, "Queen Illa requests your presence at breakfast."

The thought of eating anything, never mind the thought of having to see the Queen again after last night, made his stomach flip-flop. One did not, however, refuse a request to appear before one's sovereign.

His clothes had been cleaned and laid out for him, so he washed, dressed, and went down to breakfast. Illa was engaged in conversation with a man Anwer took to be one of Cala's wealthy merchants, judging by the bright plumage of his hat, which Cala's merchant class were known to favor. The Queen nodded briefly in Anwer's direction as he took his seat, then went on with her conversation.

The table was now laden with seasoned sausages, cheese, dense bread stuffed with pieces of fruit and nuts, pastries filled with cream, and spiced cider to drink. Despite his hang-over and nervous stomach, Anwer managed to eat a bit. Again, the food was so delicious he didn't want to stop eating, but this time he was determined *not* to overdo it.

"Is Shan's hero ready to face his destiny?" the Queen asked. It took a moment for Anwer to realize she'd spoken to him.

His destiny. The Black Rider. Anwer's appetite rapidly diminished.

During the rest of the morning Anwer could only sip the cider. A servant told him to meet Shan on the south lawn. He found her throwing daggers at a man-shaped target made of wood and straw. She'd just thrown four daggers at once, two per hand, and hit the target once in the head, once in the throat, once in the chest, and once in the stomach. *This* woman feared the Black Rider?

"Ah, Sir Fane," Shan greeted him. "How are you today?"

Be My Hero

"Okay, I guess," Anwer answered her. He warily eyed the large pile of gear on the ground behind her.

"I bought some armor for you to wear." She lifted up a padded leather jerkin. "This you wear underneath the actual armor. I hope I got your size right…"

Anwer put it on, then various pieces of armor until it entirely encased him. The armor felt several sizes too large. He wondered if he looked like a giant turtle. Then she put a great helm on his head, almost completely blinding him except for a thin line of sight directly ahead, and even that was partially obscured because the helm was too big.

"Can you see me all right?" she asked. He had no idea where she stood.

"Umm…" He didn't have the heart to tell her she'd purchased armor for someone fifty pounds heavier and half a head taller than him.

"Good. Now I have something special for you." He twisted his head around inside the helm, following the sound of Shan's voice, until he finally saw her. She walked over to a small pile of gear lying on the grass, and picked up a sword and scabbard. She held them out to him. "I want you to use my sword against the Black Rider."

It was a big sword, a weapon he'd have to wield with two hands, no doubt. Anwer took the sheathed weapon, holding it awkwardly by the scabbard's belted strap. It surprised him to find the sword didn't weigh nearly as much as he'd expected.

"We need to determine how best to position this on you," she said. "For instance, I prefer to wear it on my back. Some people like their sword at their hip. What about you?"

"Um, well…I, um…"

"We'll try it on your back first, see how that works. Okay?"

Anwer nodded. When Shan had strapped the scabbard onto his back, he tried to grab the hilt of the sword. In the armor he couldn't reach back far enough. Then they tried it at his hip, but he couldn't pull it out enough to totally clear the scabbard and kept getting the tip caught in it.

"I have an idea," Shan said. She unbuckled the scabbard and drew the sword. Then she handed it to Anwer. "There. Now you won't have to worry about the scabbard at all. Let's go."

"Let's go?"

"Yes. The Black Rider awaits, remember?"

"You mean…*now*?"

"Not *right* now," Shan said. "It could be another hour or so before the Queen and the cream of Cala's aristocracy take their places around the field to watch. But we should head that way so you're already there, face-to-face with the Black Rider. It'll give you a psychological edge to see the crowd grow around you, knowing they're on your side."

Anwer trundled along behind her, keeping her in sight with extreme difficulty, while his armor seemed to get heavier with each step. And it seemed a lot hotter outside now, *unseasonably* hot. He could feel the sweat running in rivulets down his skin. Then he got an itch, on his knee, and another on the very tip of his nose. These things kept him from dwelling on a thought that flitted around in his mind, refusing to go away. He was going to die. He was marching towards his grave behind a woman he had foolishly sought to impress, and who was now leading him to his doom. He was so distracted by this thought that he almost ran into Shan's back, not realizing she'd stopped.

"This brave Caladonian," she was saying, "will fight for me today. What say you to this?"

Anwer was about to ask who she was talking to, when he heard another voice, this one deep, dark, and foreboding. It reminded him of the distant rumblings of thunder that he used to imagine, as a child, were actually the angry murmurs of dragons.

"So be it, Shan Lyera. It is your right to choose a hero, by the laws of the duel." The voice, Anwer presumed, belonged to the Black Rider. "What is the hero's name?"

"His name is Sir Anwer Fane," Shan said. Anwer turned until he could see past her, and saw the Black Rider standing beside his mount: he was a pillar of black iron, atop which rested a black helm vaguely shaped like a dragon's head, inside of which glowed red eyes.

"Know this, Anwer Fane," the Black Rider said, "I have no hatred of you, nor of Shan. This is a duel to settle a debt of honor. Do you understand?"

He didn't, but answered, "Yes, I do." He surprised himself at how clear and steady his own voice sounded, considering that his insides felt like they were being churned into butter.

"Good. We shall begin when your Queen gives her signal."

Then Shan placed herself between them, smiling at Anwer.

"I thank you, Anwer. Now...look around you."

He did, and saw the field was filled with colorful plumage and finery. All the upper crust of Cala's high society seemed to be there. And whichever way he turned to look, a cheer went up. They were there for him, the people of Cala, and he imagined all over the countryside the subjects of Caladon thinking about him, wishing him good fortune in his battle with the Black Rider.

"Anmar Dane!" someone shouted, and other voices picked it up, until the whole crowd chanted it over and over again. "Anmar Dane! Anmar Dane!"

It took Anwer a moment to realize they'd gotten his name wrong, but he didn't care. It was *him* they'd come to support.

Then he saw Queen Illa, and Shan now sat beside her. Illa nodded in his direction, and he attempted a bow, only barely able to bend at the waist. She raised her hand, in which she held a rare Rainbow bird. She waited until the

Be My Hero

crowd stopped cheering, until it was absolutely silent, and then she let the bird go. It flew into the wind, rising above the field, and soared over Anwer's head.

"Now, then," the Black Rider said, drawing his sword, a blackened version of the one Anwer held. He came at Anwer in a sudden, lightning quick attack. The black sword arched through the air, and before he even realized what was happening Anwer had brought his sword up to parry the blow. The clang of steel on steel rang out across the field. The Black Rider pressed his attack, moving in and thrusting toward Anwer's gut with the black sword, and again, before he even knew he'd done anything, Anwer brought his sword down and deflected that attempt to disembowel him.

Still the Black Rider kept at it, whirling the black sword over his head and bringing it around to decapitate Anwer. But again, Anwer's sword moved to block the attempt, almost as if it had a mind of its own. The Black Rider growled with rage, then came at Anwer with a two-handed swing, which once again was stopped short. This time, however, the very force of the blow knocked Anwer off his feet. He fell to the ground, his helm rolling off his head. Somehow he managed to hold on to his sword.

The Black Rider brought his sword down again, intending to impale Anwer to the ground, but somehow Anwer managed to knock that blow aside while struggling to his knees. The black sword got stuck in the ground, halfway to the hilt. Anwer stuck one leg out for balance, to try and get back to his feet, and accidentally kicked the Black Rider in the shin. The Black Rider stumbled, losing his grip on his sword, while Anwer got to his feet.

Anwer went for him, swinging the sword in what he hoped was the appropriate fashion for a killing blow, but it was a wild and untrained strike that the Black Rider was able to knock aside with his armored forearm. Anwer suddenly realize something. He now had the advantage over the Black Rider! He knew if he pressed the attack he would, sooner or later, find a target and hurt the Black Rider, enabling Anwer to finish him off with one last death-strike.

Then *he*, Anwer, would be the victor!

He, Anwer would defeat the Black Rider!

He. Anwer.

"Wait!" Anwer yelled, pulling his sword back from the Black Rider's armored chest. "Can I call a temporary halt to the duel?"

"It is permissible, yes," the Black Rider answered.

"Then I do, for I believe I possess an unfair advantage in this fight."

"In what way?"

"I believe this sword…is enchanted."

The Black Rider laughed, a thunderous, quaking sound that caused Anwer to shiver.

"How else would you explain the way I was able to fend off your attacks?" Anwer asked. "This sword is magical. I should be using a normal sword, like you."

Again the Black Rider laughed. "What makes you think *mine* isn't enchanted, too?"

Anwer considered that.

"If you had an enchanted sword as well," he said, "then I would be dead. We both know that."

"Perhaps," the Black Rider, said, nodding. "However, it is not against the rules of the duel to use an enchanted sword. You would be perfectly within the realm of law to run me through right now, and I might add that if you strike true, your sword will pass right through my armor. As you have disarmed me, it is your right to kill me where I stand."

All things considered, Anwer didn't really want to run anyone through. He didn't have it in his blood to spill someone else's.

"If I spare you," Anwer said, "what then?"

"You would have to require some service of me, to preserve my honor."

Anwer thought this over for a moment, but already knew he had the perfect service to require of someone like the Black Rider.

"Then I spare your life, Black Rider," he said, "and require this service of you: to travel throughout the world fighting evil and helping those weaker than yourself, as Shan has done in the past. It is my belief that she has grown weary and desires to cease wandering. Therefore you must take her place and perform such tasks as she herself would undertake."

The Black Rider stood silently for a moment, then bowed deeply to Anwer.

"So be it." With that, the Black Rider retrieved his sword, mounted his steed, which had stood patiently by the whole time, and rode away. The wall of Caladonians parted for him, and then closed up again. A cheer went up.

"I am indebted to you," Shan said, then leaned in close, and whispered, "and I have something I must tell you. I hope you will not be too angry with me..."

Angry? At that moment, Anwer couldn't begin to imagine being angry with anyone ever again.

Shan closed the door behind them. Anwer wore a golden pendant around his neck, his gift from Queen Illa. They'd been feasting and partying all night, and while Anwer had stayed away from drink for the most part, Shan hadn't. At one point during the festivities she grabbed him by the arm and led him away from the great hall. He now found himself alone with her in her room.

"At last," she said. "I have you all to myself!"

Before he could respond, Shan grabbed Anwer by the shoulders, drew him to her, and kissed him. Passionately. When she finished, she let him go and stepped back, smiling shyly. He just stood there, flabbergasted.

Be My Hero

"Sorry," she said. "I should have asked, but...I just couldn't help myself. After what you did out there...Well, after I tell you the truth, we'll see what happens."

"The truth?" Answer asked.

"The truth about the Black Rider," she said. "The truth about why I wanted a hero to fight for me today. You better sit down for this." She shoved him into a chair, so he sat.

"You see," she began, "the Black Rider isn't what he appeared to be. He's my brother."

"How can that be?" Answer asked. "I saw his eyes...they were red, and they glowed. He—"

"A trick of the dragon helm he wore," Shan explained. "No more."

"Your brother?" He understood, now, what that meant. "No wonder you wouldn't fight him. I wouldn't fight my own brother in a duel to the death, either."

Shan was shaking her head.

"We've fought lots of times," she said. "And once I almost *did* kill him, but that was years ago. We've come to be good friends as adults. That's why he was willing to do me this favor."

"Favor?"

Shan sighed. "I'm not exactly proud of what I did. But now that it's over...I will say this, that you exceeded my every expectation, Answer Fane. You see, I was looking for a man who possessed the traits of bravery and honesty, who knew mercy, and who was just."

"Just what?

"Just *just.*"

Answer blinked. Was she talking about *him*? Did he really possess all those traits? Bravery? He didn't feel very brave at all. Honesty? Well, sure, but that was the way his mother and father had raised him. Mercy? Why, because the mere thought of killing made him sick to his stomach? And just? Again, he'd been raised to be fair in all things.

"Why?" Answer asked.

"Because...I wanted that man as my husband."

"Husband?"

"Yes, Answer. I asked Dagan to help—"

"Dagan?"

"My brother. He agreed to help, to pose as the Black Rider. And the sword you used *is* enchanted. Legend has it the sword was forged for a king who wanted to make sure his son learned all the best defensive moves. The sword magically blocks and parries to teach you the motions first-hand. So there was no way Dagan could hurt you, even if he'd wanted to." Shan sighed again. "Oh, you would have *died* for me, Answer! How can I tell you this and not expect you to be angry with me."

"I'm not angry," Anwer said, surprising himself because he *did* feel a little perturbed at being manipulated so thoroughly, like a marionette. "I'm just curious."

"About?" Shan asked.

"You said you wanted a husband, right?" Anwer asked. She nodded. "Surely you must have thought that one of Caladon's soldiers would fight for you. You were probably expecting someone tall and handsome and full of muscles—"

Shan shushed him by placing her fingers to his lips. Then she got down on one knee before him.

"Anwer Fane," she said, "will you be my husband?"

He looked into her eyes....

To her, he realized, he was more than tall, and more than handsome.

...and said yes.

I began this story years ago under the title "Firecall." My pal James C. Bassett had come up with, but never used it for a story. The title fit with an idea I had about orbital laser platforms controlled by a single person on the ground, giving her absolute power. I wanted to set it on a world with a single city that had succumbed to anarchy and was falling apart. I wanted to turn the city into a cargo culture of religions, a mishmash of belief systems from Christianity to Wicca to Hinduism. I was inspired by the novels Nightside City *by Lawrence Watt-Evans,* Dream Park *by Larry Niven and Jerry Pournelle, and the* Gaea *trilogy by John Varley. I started it, but soon ran out of steam and set it aside.*

Years later, I was inspired to add elements of Buddhism. I changed the title of the story to "Digital Buddha" to reflect this new element. I finished a rough draft, but was not very happy with it, mainly because I could not come up with a solid ending. A year later I was daydreaming in my chair, and this story sprang into my head... the main character, who didn't fit in, who felt so isolated...what did he ultimately want? With that question, the ending became clear.

The Deity Effect

DANE TRIED TO CONVINCE HIMSELF he was making the right decision. He'd heard that they were looking for him. He did not know why. With no reason to keep living the way he'd been living he decided to take a chance and go. He went with mixed emotions, because he was going back to the place from whence he'd come so long ago.

He walked the whole way, from the edge of the sprawling city to its center. As he walked it got colder and colder, reminding him of why he'd

daydreams undertaken

moved in the first place. He didn't have what it took to stay in the cold heart of the city.

The center of the city was always cold…the edges were warmer, but lacked everything else that the center had going for it. The arcades, the malls, the high rises, the clubs. The warm edges were a wilderness broken up by farms. These were tended by people for whom the simple life beckoned.

And now he was back, seeing his breath in the air as he huffed and struggled to keep going as it got colder and colder. He found an abandoned house that looked like everyone had suddenly vanished from it without warning. There was no heat, of course, but there were blankets.

Dane wrapped himself up and tried to convince himself it wasn't *that* cold, and it just *seemed* like he might be freezing to death.

The city had once been called Gem, a name glistening with hope and promise. The other cities that dotted the inner surface of the Ring had been similarly named: Jewel, Shine, Dazzle, Luster. The other cities had died over time, and the city once called Gem was no longer called anything. The people all lived within the confines of one city. Why give it a name?

It had lost more than its name. The artificial sun that had been constructed at the center of the Ring had long since begun to die, until it provided barely enough light, never mind heat. And to make matters worse, the inner ring of nighttime panels had ceased rotating…it had stopped with one of the panels right over the heart of the city, forever locking it in night.

The Ring and its sun were products of the forgotten technology of the Ring inhabitants' ancestors, part of a far-flung interstellar civilization that had crumbled, fractured, broken apart. The Ring was forgotten, an orphan. Whatever fuel the artificial sun had devoured had been all but depleted. Some day, everyone knew, it would finally die; and then, so would they.

"There's nobody here," Dane heard a deep voice say. Sudden panic: there was somebody *inside* the house?

"Check the bedroom, Linx," a woman's voice said with authority.

Dane heard the wood floor creak under heavy footsteps as someone came into the bedroom. There was no bed; Dane huddled on the floor wrapped up in every blanket he could find, trying to stay warm. He knew the name Linx. He had reason to be afraid, but he was too cold for that.

"Come on, kid." Strong hands grabbed Dane's arm and lifted him up with ease.

"Where are we going?" Dane asked, shivering. "It's warm?"

Linx grunted. "Yeah, it's warm. Let's go." Despite Linx guiding him, Dane stumbled through the darkness — the entire house was dark. Dane knew Linx had infrared.

"Kitten," Linx said. "I got him."

The Deity Effect

Dane's heart pounded harder at the mention of her name. Kitten was a major celebrity. Despite the cold he was excited that she was there, and he was in her presence.

"Good Linx," she said. Linx actually purred in response. Dane still couldn't see anything, but felt her nearby. Then fingers touched his face, traced from his cheekbone down and around his jaw. "Shall we?"

"The sooner we get back, the better," Linx said. "We may wind up having to amputate a few of the smaller extremities."

Amputate?

"Oh, that wouldn't do at all," Kitten said. "Can't damage the merchandise."

Merchandise?

Linx led Dane out of the house. The night wind bit him through the comforter with Jack Frost's fangs. They started down the street on foot.

In the faint glow of half-powered streetlights, Dane saw that neither Kitten nor Linx wore what might be considered winter wear. Linx wore practically nothing at all — a loin cloth, and a vest. Of course, he was also covered with fur, brown with white and black spots. Kitten wore a black mini-skirt and halter top. Fur also covered her body, black, white, and rust-colored stripes, tiger-like. She and Linx walked along barefoot, stepping on ice patches without hesitation. They had nanotech — commonly called mites — which regulated their body temperatures and kept them warm. The fur helped, obviously. Fur was the latest thing, and very expensive. *The rich get warmer while the poor stay cold.* Mites good enough to keep a person warm in the freezing cold were expensive, too.

Dane had been brought up as a purist, a Natural. Not having mites inhabiting his body was as much a matter of principle as anything. Even the poorest of the poor had basic mites to keep them healthy.

Dane stumbled several times, but Linx held him up and kept him going so he didn't slow them down at all. Can't damage the merchandise. At least that probably meant they wouldn't kill him. If warmth was in the immediate future, then Dane didn't mind being merchandise.

Four or five empty intersections later they found their way blocked by Jaffe and his crew. Dane recognized Jaffe, of course. Another celebrity. Jaffe's garb made him the Fool of Tarot. Jaffe was to Matsya what Kitten was to Vishnu.

"I'm not in the mood for this," Kitten said to Jaffe.

The bells in his hat jingled as he tilted his head back, then threw it forward and fixed his trademark, a wide-eyed crazy stare, on Kitten. The trademark Jaffe-laugh echoed off the surrounding concrete.

Jaffe said, in a mocking whine, "You're *never* in the mood, Kitty-cat!"

"Linx," Kitten commanded. Linx let go of Dane, then stepped forward, emitting a low growl. Dane slumped to ground, no strength in his legs to keep him standing.

Jaffe held his hand up, gesturing time-out for the moment. "I know what you're doing, Kitten," he said in an accusatory tone. "Do *you?*"

Kitten didn't answer right away, thought about it for a second, then said, "I *always* know what I'm doing, Jaff. I *always* know what *you're* doing, too."

A flicker of doubt clouded Jaffe's face, but only for an instant. "Take him back, Kitten. You'll upset the balance if you go through with it. Matsya wants you to take him back."

Kitten laughed. "You need a better deity, Jaffe. Matsya's all wet. Skip the avatars and go straight for the source."

"Vishnu," Linx said with a grin, as if Jaffe needed the hint. That wasn't quite true, Dane thought to himself. Vishnu wasn't exactly the source, just the most powerful of the gods, although he didn't like to think of them as gods…because they weren't. Not that it mattered, since they might just as well have been.

Dane couldn't get over how foolish the man looked up close and personal. Jaffe's crew were also dressed outrageously, giggling to themselves. The giggles were too practiced, too artificial.

"Well?" Kitten asked.

"Well what?"

"Get out of the way. Now." The giggling stopped, except for one of the crew who stopped a half second later. "Tell you what Jaffe. This one dies first." Jaffe and the others held their ground, although the targeted one was now visibly shaking.

"We got our orders—" That was all Jaffe got out before Kitten hissed her command. Linx lashed out so quickly it was over before Dane knew something had happened. Linx was back in position before the man fell in a heap on the pavement.

"That wasn't very nice, Kitten!" Jaffe yelled, his voice shaking. It was that edge he was supposed to have. The insanity was there. It sounded real, at least to Dane.

Linx noticed it, too. "I think he's going over," he said. The remaining members of Jaffe's crew were probably triggering hoppers in their blood, just to keep up with their leader. "I won't be able to take 'em all without some damage to the kid."

"Shit," Kitten muttered under her breath. "Okay."

She closed her eyes and held out her hands, palms up, and began to chant towards the sky. Psychobabble, as it was known to Dane and most other people who didn't understand. One of Jaffe's crew broke toward Linx, who defended himself with a roundhouse kick that broke the man's neck in one fluid motion.

"Two down," Linx said.

Right then, it happened. From the sky, a red beam of light flashed down, seemed to hang in the air like a solid object, but was gone in an instant. Where

Jaffe had been standing was now just a black spot on the pavement. The air smelled of burnt ozone.

No scream. Jaffe's crew didn't notice right away what had happened, but when they did, they wasted no time in scattering.

"Jesus," Dane whispered.

Kitten heard. "What'd he say?" she asked Linx.

"I believe he said Jesus," Linx told her.

"Why would he say that?" Kitten asked.

"What did you *do* to him?" Dane asked her.

"I killed him," Kitten said, for the first time addressing him directly. "No worse than what Linx did to the other two, right?"

Dane shook his head. "Uh uh. A red light from the sky...what was it, a laser? How can you control an orbiting laser from *here*?"

Kitten laughed. "You'll find out."

The rest of the journey was uneventful. Not even the stoplights were against them, and then Dane realized that the lights had been with them all along. It was one of those little characteristics Kitten had that added to her eclat. Security doors opened for her when she approached, elevators waited for her, autocabs came to her without her having to wave one down, and everything was always free. Of course, most of the elevators no longer worked, and the autocabs were breaking down all the time. It wasn't uncommon to see abandoned autocabs sitting idle on the side the road, rusting away.

The city was at Kitten's beck and call. Of course, Vishnu didn't control the entire city. Avatars had managed to take over different neighborhoods and districts. Still, most of them paid homage to Vishnu.

They reached a tenement building and turned to go inside. From within the entranceway stepped two massively muscled, dreadlocked guards.

"An' where d'ye think ye're goin', Missy?" one of them asked, staring down at Kitten with dulled yellow eyes. The other kept his glazed over eyes focused on Linx. They ignored Dane.

"I'm here to see Alliette," Kitten said.

The yellow eyes dimmed slightly, then the man smiled, revealing equally yellowed teeth. "Enter," he said, "and welcome, Miss Kitt-onn."

They climbed the stairs all the way to the top floor, the seventh story, where there was only one door at the end of the hallway, standing open. The hallway was grimly decorated with skulls mounted on the walls, smokey, candles flickering in the open air, and elaborate designs along the floor and ceiling. Dane bumped Kitten, then shrank back when she looked at him, bumping into Linx. Linx gave him a gentle shove forward.

"Quit fooling around," Linx said. His voice was barely above a whisper.

The designs were for the most part unfamiliar to Dane, save for a few. One he recognized was the Egyptian *Udjat*, looking down over them from the ceiling, and another ancient Egyptian symbol, the *Ankh*, on the floor. He could have sworn that the eye had blinked when he looked up at it, and that it was watching *him* specifically. There were forces at work greater than he, and whether they were cybernetic, genetic, or true magick didn't matter. The rules were the same. If he did the wrong thing, maybe even if he just *said* the wrong thing, those forces could do to him what they had done to poor, crazed Jaffe.

They entered the apartment. It was hazy inside, from incense. Dane frowned, wrinkling his nose. The odor was pleasant enough, but unfamiliar.

"Black poppy," said a woman's voice from behind a wicker divider. "Saint John's wort, henbane, calamus root, fennel root, camphor, flax, and hemp." She came around from behind the divider. She was striking, deeply black, tall and slender with wide white eyes and giant black pupils. Her hair hung long and straight down to her waist, and she wore a white t-shirt bearing the Udjat design, and a long skirt patterned in shades of red. Her feet were bare. "It's one of my special mixtures," she said.

"Alliette," Kitten said, "This is the one."

Alliette regarded Dane silently for a moment. "I know."

For the first time, Dane had a chance to really see Kitten. He'd never actually gotten close enough, long enough, to get a real good look at her. She was really petite, and looked almost too much like the girl-next-door, except for the fur. Her eyes had been replaced with solid white orbs. Linx, Dane had noticed before, had his own eyes, but they were tinted red from the infrared nanosensors in them.

Dane kept his gaze on Kitten. Her body was taut, athletic; her cheekbones were high, and her eyes only added to the overall effect. She was a predator. She turned around, he looked away, but she caught him.

"Never seen a celeb up close?" she asked.

Dane shrugged.

"Cat got his tongue," Linx said, then asked, "How about some tea?"

Alliette snorted. "You know where it is, Prince Charming. And make some for me, while you're at it…and the boy."

"And me," Kitten added.

"Your wish is my command," Linx said, sighing.

"We know," Kitten and Alliette replied in unison. Then Alliette fixed her gaze on Dane again. It him uncomfortable.

"You should relax," Alliette said. She waved her hand toward a stone fireplace against the far wall, and flames rose from the kindling. "Do you know how to firegaze?"

Dane shook his head.

"Look into the fire, and when you see an image, no matter what it is, say it out loud." She closed her eyes for a moment, breathed in deeply. "My grandfather taught me how. It always made me feel good. It's kind of like a game." She nodded toward the fire. "Try."

The Deity Effect

Dane walked over to the fire and knelt before it. He looked, but could see only the flames, no images.

"You will see only good things, I promise."

Dane liked the warmth from the fire. He closed his eyes for a second, then opened them. In the flames he saw something, a shape swirling and gyrating. The shape took form, became human, became a woman. Then he realized it was Kitten, a flickering firebrand, nude, dancing just for him. He turned to look at her now. "I see you," he said. He looked back at the fire. "You're dancing...."

The flames changed. Now he saw a swirling grid, pretending to be a flame but obviously not one. He frowned. What *was* it? It looked vaguely familiar. "Uh, I *think* it's something from cyberspace," he said. "But I'm not sure."

Abruptly it disappeared, and amid the flames arose his own face, life-size. Dane fell back onto his rear.

"What is it?" Kitten asked, and Dane heard Alliette shush her.

The Dane-face was smiling almost beatifically, and it too was formed by a warped, flame-grid. The eyes were gone, too, replaced by fire.

"It's me," Dane said. "My face."

"That's all," Alliette said. "Three things. Three visions, that is enough. The flames won't offer anymore, anyway." She helped Dane up, then lead him to a rattan sofa. Linx came out then with a silver tray, upon which were four earthenware mugs filled with steaming tea.

"What did you see?" Kitten asked Dane.

"I told you what I saw."

"No," Kitten said. "*Describe* what you saw. In detail."

"You didn't see anything?" Dane asked. Kitten shook her head.

"Only you saw what you saw," Alliette explained.

Dane described everything he saw, even the part about Kitten appearing to him nude.

"What does it mean?" he then asked.

"I think it's gonna work," Linx said. "Seems pretty obvious to me."

Alliette shook her head. "You would have thought that no matter what he saw," she said. "I've known you too long, Linx. If anything, you are never unsure of success."

"Tell me, Dane," Kitten said. "When you saw me naked...what did you think?"

Now Dane couldn't look her in the face. He was suddenly too aware of himself, his own pathetic body. He was skinny, his hands and feet were too big, his face was too angular, he was too tall, too gangly. The others watched him for a response. Instead of answering, he sipped his tea. It was hot, and good, and it immediately affected him. He suddenly felt stronger, and moments later he felt totally restored.

He set the cup down. "Mites?" he asked. Linx grinned.

"Special ones," Alliette told him. "Timed. They'll die soon, and your system will expel them. No need to worry."

"I don't do mites."

"We know," Kitten said. "That's why we wanted you."

"I don't understand."

"You will," Kitten said, then to Alliette, "Shouldn't we do his reading?"

Alliette nodded, reached her hand lazily up into the air, and snapped her long fingers twice. The wall above the fireplace shimmered and crackled, then the image of a Tarot seven-card spread appeared. The cards were turned over, the backs were each decorated with the *yin yang* symbol.

"A computerized Tarot reading?" Dane asked, incredulous.

"You do not believe in Tarot?" Alliette asked.

"I don't know. Doesn't it kill the whole purpose of the Tarot to have the computer controlling it?"

Alliette shook her head. "This is just another form of *expression*," she said. "No different than the cards you can hold in your hand. Vishnu generates each card from a constantly shuffling pool of electronic analogs as it is turned over…he cannot cheat, if that is what you are worried about."

"What, me worry?" They were all luminaries of the arcane junk culture Dane tried so hard to deny…they didn't think it ridiculous, a patchwork of Hinduism, witchcraft, Artificial Intelligence, mysticism, sleight of hand, and anything else that fit the mosaic.

"Roll the cards," he said, trying to sound as if he were resigned to his fate. Alliette snapped her fingers once more, and suddenly the seven cards were facing up.

They were, in order from left to right, the Devil, the Hanged Man, the Tower reversed, Queen of Pentacles reversed, the Hierophant, Six of Cups, and the World. Dane knew enough about Tarot that even at first glance he could tell the cards corresponded exactly with his life, except for the future which he didn't pretend to know. It was all too perfect for him, though.

He must have let it show in his expression, because Alliette said, "You think this is set up, eh?"

"Well," Dane didn't quite know what to say, but he figured he might as well put all his cards on the table, so to speak. "Something like that. I'm sure Vishnu has enough of my history…even if I wasn't barcoded the day I was born, like everyone else."

"True," Kitten said. "We know all about you, actually. The cards just confirm what we hoped."

"Which is?"

"That you are the right choice. We're offering you something better than you could ever hope to attain on your own," she told him. She gestured up at

The Deity Effect

the cards. "I'm no expert, but I think if the cards say there's wholeness in your future, the World, then…." She shrugged.

"It's all up there," Alliette confirmed. "Your current state of disillusionment. Being raised one of the last Naturals, your rejection of nanotechnology. You are one hundred and ten percent *human*."

"This is precisely why we need you," Kitten told him. "Remember what I did to Jaffe? The fire from the sky?"

Dane repressed a shudder. "You mean the high intensity laser from one of the orbital space platforms? Yeah."

"Well, I can't do that again anytime soon. That was a one-time deal I had with Vishnu. Vishnu controls the satellites that orbit the Ring just inside the night panels, but most of them are broken down, non-functioning. The one I used burned out its power supply with that beam. I wouldn't have used it at all if I'd thought there was a choice."

"We couldn't let them damage you," Linx added.

"Luckily no one tougher than Jaffe was after us. The other deities and avatars have made a pact to let Vishnu do this one thing. If it works, we'll all be better off for it."

Dane preferred to refer to those so-called deities and avatars as A.I.s and sub-programs, which was what they were, but he didn't bring that up.

"What if it doesn't work?" Dane asked.

"I don't know," Kitten answered.

"If it does not work," Alliette said gravely, "Vishnu will die, and the deities and avatars will descend even further into madness striving to take its place as the supreme deity. They cannot, because by their very nature one is not more than the other. Only Vishnu can do this one thing."

"What *is* this one thing?" Dane asked.

"You," Linx piped up suddenly. "Lucky devil."

"I'm lost."

"No," Kitten said, shaking her head slowly. "You are definitely found. Fate told us about you, that you were lost, and it was up to us to show you the way home."

Fate. Another one of the celebs of his world. Fate was a woman tapped into every A.I., every god and demi-god, driven insane by the onslaught of information. It was said she told futures in riddles and rhymes. She'd know what Kitten had in store for Dane, and she'd tell him. That was the rule. If you could get to her, no one could prevent her from telling you your future. *If* you could get to her. She'd tell you your future in riddle and then you had to figure it out. It was said that those who did manage to figure it out attained riches beyond imagination. Getting to her was the trick, though. She was guarded by zealous family members who wished to preserve what little sanity she had left, and used lethal force to keep just anyone from getting to her. Obviously Kitten wasn't just anyone.

Alliette checked her watch. "We have time to kill. Why don't you tell us why you were letting yourself freeze to death in that old house, Dane?"

"No heat." Which was the truth, at least in that house.

"You could have gone somewhere that *has* heat," Linx said.

"Yeah, I wish." Alliette's was the first apartment Dane had seen in a long time that had a fire in a real fire place. No one needed heat anymore when they had mites, fur, or both. Most buildings had lost their central heating systems. So that left Dane, well, out in the cold.

His father had been a Natural, had refused to allow mites inside his body. Got regular inoculations against them even though the conventional wisdom said if you didn't accept them, emotionally, mentally, spiritually, then they died off anyway and you expelled them with the rest of your waste. Dane always figured the inoculations were an expensive scam.

But his father died from food poisoning, something that never would have happened if he'd had mites in him. Dane's mother gave in after that, accepted them, as did his sister. Dane, however, couldn't do it. His sister's body rejected the mites, and tried to bleed them out. That happened sometimes, the mites and a person's body just couldn't seem to work out a mutually satisfactory arrangement. Their eyes bled, or their skin boiled, or the mites fed on their innards and devoured them from within. Dane's sister bled to death. His mother left, and he never heard from her again.

"How you been feeling lately?" Linx asked Dane. "You been sick lately?"

"*Linx,*" Kitten warned.

"Just makin' small talk," Linx said.

"Been okay, I guess," Dane told him. "Had a cold a week or so ago. Other than that...." He shrugged.

"That's good." Linx nodded and grinned at Kitten. "So, you ever, ah, been with a woman before?"

"*Huh?*"

"You a virgin?"

"*Linx!!*" Kitten and Alliette yelled in unison.

"If you don't shut up I'm putting you outside," Kitten said sternly. "I'm not kidding."

"I was just making conversation," Linx said, sounding hurt.

"He is a virgin," Alliette said. "Now, Linx, leave the boy alone."

"I'm not a virgin," Dane said, somewhat indignant.

"It's nothing to be ashamed of," Kitten said.

Dane simmered for a moment, then sighed. "Is it that obvious?" he asked Alliette.

She shook her head. "Only to a witch like me."

"You're not really a witch," Dane said, feeling bold all of a sudden. "It's all technology, not magic."

The Deity Effect

She shrugged. "What's the difference? The effect is the same, no?"

The idea of either, true magic or technology that might as well be magic, scared him because of the power they could give into the hands of an individual like Kitten. Fire from the sky. If she could do that at will, no one could stand against her. If she were a good person, maybe that would be okay. Was she a good person? Was anyone?

He felt suddenly tired, and suppressed a yawn.

"It is almost time," Alliette said.

"Time for what?" Dane asked sleepily.

"Time to get lucky," Linx said with a grin, drumming on his chest. "Time to glimpse Paradise, my man."

"Linx, shut up," Kitten said, fuming. "I swear I am going to wrap you in duct tape, spin you like a top, and watch all your fur come off in clumps."

Linx winced. "*Ouch!*" He looked Dane. "She did that to her cousin Jag once. It wasn't pretty."

These people are insane, Dane thought.

"We are not crazy," Alliette said to him. "We think a certain way, and you think a certain way." Alliette smiled as Dane started to deny thinking anything. "I saw it in your face, boy. However, we are not offended."

Dane really did feel sleepy. He could barely keep his eyes open. He was unable to suppress a yawn.

"You want to lie down for a while?" Alliette asked him.

Dane nodded.

"You're gonna love this," he heard Linx say, also sounding far, far away.

"Ah, the mites are transmitting," Alliette said. "Are you ready?"

"I'm ready," Kitten replied.

"Try not to drool too much," Linx told her.

"He's very cute," Kitten replied. "I don't think he realizes how cute he is."

"Not cuter than me, though," Linx said. "Right?"

Dane felt himself slipping into a pool of warm water, being submerged, sinking down, down, down. Somehow he could still breathe. There were lights in the distance blinking on and off, slowly at first, then rapidly. After a while he realized it was a code. The blinking lights swirled around, seemed to be pulling him down like a whirlpool. As he got closer he began to hear words, or rather to feel them in his head, to sense them, and understand.

Open, it said.

Accept.

Welcome.

Tendrils sprang forth from the lights and came toward him, like ten thousand arms issuing forth from the god of jellyfishes, and they pierced his body. He felt them inside, tracing the routes of his nerves to his spine and brain.

Open your eyes, a voice told him.

He did.

A thought came to him. A name. *Vishnu.* And he was staring into the face of the owner of that name. Rather, he *was* the face of the owner of that name. Dane looked into his own eyes, except the eyes weren't his, they were golden orbs. The eyes of Vishnu. He frowned, and the reflection of his face frowned back at him.

Upon closer inspection, he noticed that the reflection of his face was made up of millions, *billions*, of tiny 1s and 0s constantly swirling around in minute patterns. Awareness of his Self blurred. He saw himself from the outside as well as the inside. *Who am I?*

Vishnu.

I'm Dane, he thought.

The face of 1s and 0s smiled, the information changed. Vishnu was pleased. Dane was pleased. He didn't know why.

A stream of photons pulsed out from Vishnu's mouth towards Dane. They splashed over him and he realized it was a program. The program started, and in an instant Dane knew.

He knew that Vishnu loved Kitten.

Love to Vishnu was not something it *felt*. Vishnu experienced love as logical data. Love, logical? Externally, love was expressed in the way you behaved towards somebody. Somewhere along the line in its relationship with Kitten, Vishnu figured this out, and determined that because of the way it acted towards Kitten, it must love her. But *why* did Vishnu act in such a way towards Kitten? Vishnu was a deity. Deities weren't supposed to be able to experience human emotions.

If you loved someone, then you wanted to make love to her. More logical data.

Vishnu decided to 'want' to make love to Kitten, because that was what you were supposed to want if you loved a woman. How could a non-corporeal deity make love to a mortal, very corporeal woman? It would require a body. Vishnu knew it could transfer its Awareness to a human body using millions of microscopic super-mites, each carrying a small copy of Vishnu in its memory. It had to be a human body without any of its own mites, because the combination of Vishnu's with the ones most people already had in their bodies would overload the nervous system, resulting in the death of the host.

It had to be a Natural. There weren't many people like that anymore, and they were hard to find.

Even with Alliette's help it had taken Kitten three weeks to find Dane. Alliette, like Fate, could use her "magic" to traverse the domains of the different A.I. godlings. Vishnu could not.

He saw the Big Picture. He saw the reality of Vishnu. Everyone knew the truth, even if they wouldn't admit it to themselves. But no one understood what it meant. Vishnu was an Artificial Intelligence of the highest order, but even that didn't explain Vishnu's true nature.

A virus, however, did. At one time, Vishnu did not exist as a separate entity; rather it was part of an even greater whole, a global A.I. unified in purpose and process. A virus split the A.I.'s personality, fractured it, colored each section differently, and created a stained glass window. The virus was called the Deity Virus, and aside from splitting the A.I. into its multiple selves, it gave them the divine personas by which they were now identified.

Vishnu, Wodin, Zeus, Jehova, Rama…a potpourri of gods from different mythologies were represented as subroutines of the A.I. that, collectively, was now called Deity. Just as Deity was divided into these "gods," so too were the gods further divided into the individual lesser gods, heroes, avatars, and saints of their respective pantheons. Thus was created the world that Dane had known all his life. The deities controlled almost everything. Nature and Chaos were all that prevented them from being in complete control of every aspect of every person's life, prevented them from being true gods.

Dane had known some of this, and a lot of it was new to him. But now he experienced it the way Vishnu did. He *felt* it, felt his Self fractured, splintered into Vishnu's avatars. It was maddening — he needed something to focus on, something to center him, something to become the center of his universe.

Out of the blue, the wild blue of her original eyes, Vishnu found Kitten. She'd been like Dane, free of embedded mites that infested the population for their own good, a near-feral child inhabiting abandoned suburbs with her techno-phobic grandfather, who'd stolen her away and then died when she was just eight years old. But his fear had become instilled inside her, and she stayed away from civilization for as long as she could.

Then she hit puberty, and the lure of boys drew her into the world again. She was more than beautiful. She possessed a wildness below the surface that attracted and frightened both men and women. She knew most of them desired her, and she used it. In the city there was generally only one goal, which every inhabitant shared. To become a celebrity.

Before long Kitten became a minor celeb. Celebs attracted followers, and the various gods tracked their popularity. When celebs were popular enough, gods and avatars would align with them to add to the base of their faith and increase their power in a never-ending contest against rival gods and avatars. This made celebs the haves and everyone else the have-nots, and that was the reality of Dane's world.

A flash of light, burning skin, hot breath in his ear. Dane slowly became of aware of another reality. He was inside Deity, but he remembered too that he had a body, flesh and blood and bones and chemistry, life, thoughts, dreams, desires.

"Oh, yes," Kitten whispered.

Dane blinked, felt her all around him, her hands on his back, kissing his face. He couldn't see her. All he could see was a spiral of 1s and 0s, spinning and fluctuating like the surface of an ocean. His mind was separate from his brain, and he was aware of each individual neuron, could feel each synapse firing, and the neurotransmitters flitting about to their individual destinations.

A force stronger than anything he'd ever felt grabbed his mind and propelled him towards a fountain of rapidly blinking lights. It plunged him into the fountain, and he exploded into a billion 1s and 0s himself, became one with Deity and Kitten.

Kitten moaned, her nails scratching deep furrows into Dane's back, her arms and legs encircling him like serpents, squeezing, holding him to her until he felt as if her body and his would merge as their minds had. It was too much. He whirled about like a small boat lost at sea, tossed on a storm. Waves crashed down on him, water choked him and stung his eyes.

Dane blacked out.

Hot.

Each thought seemed to generate more heat. He needed to stop thinking, he was burning up. But just the thought that he needed to stop thinking generated even more heat. He feared he might burn up, burst into flames and float away like a spirit of smoke. The smoke was still information, though, and information was heat.

The heat was driving him crazy. How could he cool off? How had he done it before? A glass of sweet iced tea, a wedge of lemon. But he couldn't drink a glass of sweet tea now. He didn't have lips, he didn't have a mouth. Then he remembered, he'd never been hot before, in his whole life. He'd always been cold. He'd imagined being hot. He'd imagined drinking sweet iced tea. Imagined.

"Hey, lover, wake up."

Dane opened his eyes and found Kitten lying beside him, smiling.

"You were dreaming."

"Was I?"

Kitten nodded.

"It doesn't mean anything," Dane told her.

"I know."

"I mean, it really doesn't. I don't want to go back to that place."

Place? A solid state of mind. Electric sheep.

"I got a taste of it, too," Kitten said. "I can imagine what it must have been like for you. For a brief, eternal moment you *were* Deity."

"And Deity was me."

He touched her belly, miraculously swollen with six months' worth of pregnancy in only a few weeks. Although they had not made love again, Kitten had

The Deity Effect

stayed with him. Kitten purred. His baby? Vishnu's? Deity's? The mites in his body had exited with his semen, making sure Kitten became pregnant, and now they were an integral part of the developing fetus, accelerating the process. The baby would be perfect, of course, Dane realized. He also realized that the baby was their only hope.

That's what scared him.

"He wants his breast milk," Dane told Kitten. She sighed and held a glass to her left nipple, then filled it with breast milk. She could do it at will, with the help of her mites. He brought it out to Tama, who sat lotus-style in the front yard of their house, at the outskirts of the city. My son, Dane reminded himself as he watched the fat, bald child slurp down the breast milk, then wipe his mouth on his naked arm. Six months after conception Tama had grown rapidly. He was still growing before their very eyes.

Tama held out his right hand, and a nearby cardinal, bright red, flew over to land on his wrist. He held out his left hand and a large crow flew from the roof of the house to land on that wrist.

"Crow," said Tama, "I want you to fly into the city and give a message to Alliette. Tell her to come to me so we can play checkers." The crow, without hesitation, took off with a flurry of beating wings and headed towards the city.

"Cardinal," said Tama, "I want you to fly as fast as you can into a window—"

"Tama," Dane said sternly.

Tama giggled. "I know, Father."

"I wish you wouldn't do that."

"I know, Father."

"Then why—?"

"Because it must be done. Because it is the Will of Gautama."

"What is? To make fun of me?"

Tama smiled playfully. "Sometimes, yes." He let the cardinal fly away, unharmed. He then closed his eyes and let out a long, deep sigh. The conversation was over. Dane stood there and watched his son. He didn't really feel any kinship to the boy. Tama was more closely related to Vishnu than to Dane. It was Vishnu who had made love to Kitten, using Dane's body. Vishnu's mites lived inside Tama, defined who Tama was as much as Dane's genes did. More, perhaps, because they manipulated the genes.

When Alliette arrived several days later, Tama was still sitting there, eyes closed, legs crossed in the lotus position, breathing evenly. Dane sat in the porch swing, sipping hot tea. It was still mostly cold outside, although supposedly it was getting warmer every day. Dane could not tell, although others swore they felt it. Linx leaned against the rail on the front porch, looking as much the part of the ne'er-do-well tomcat as he ever had before. Alliette greeted him with a smile.

"How long has it been?" she asked.

"He's been sitting there for seventy-two hours straight," Linx replied. "He hasn't moved once."

"Not at all?"

"Not a millimeter," Linx said.

Alliette walked around Tama. She got on her hands and knees and bent down to peer under Tama's backside. She softly placed her hand on Tama's back and gently pushed him forward just a little bit.

"What are you looking for?" Linx asked.

Alliette stood. "I am not looking for anything," she said. "I have found it."

Linx waited for her to elaborate. She didn't. Instead, she went into the house where she found Kitten doing Tai Chi.

"What's happening to Tama?" Kitten asked as she stood up straight on one leg and brought the knee of the other to her chin.

"His destiny," Alliette answered.

"Could you be more specific?"

Alliette only smiled, and Kitten sighed.

"Kitten, you need not worry about the boy," Alliette said.

"I can't help it. He's my son, no matter what else he might be."

"What else he *is*," Alliette corrected her. "He is your son and more."

"What if I don't want him to be more?" Kitten asked. "What if I just want him to be my son?"

"You know it is too late for that," Alliette replied.

"Alliette, Kitten!" Linx called from outside.

Hurriedly, Kitten went out, followed more calmly by Alliette.

"What happened?" Kitten asked urgently.

"He moved," Linx said. "He blinked. Once. I saw it."

"I didn't see anything," Dane said when Kitten looked to him for confirmation. Dane stood back as Alliette and Kitten approached the boy.

"Tama?" Kitten inquired hesitantly.

His eyelids opened. Tama's eyes were gone, and had been replaced by golden orbs. The eyes of Vishnu.

"Don't be afraid," he said. His voice carried an electronic buzz within it.

"What's happening?" Kitten asked.

"I'm one again," Tama said. "I'm whole."

Dane frowned. "Vishnu?" he asked.

"There is no Vishnu," Tama said. "There is just one Deity, and that…is me." He smiled.

"How is that possible?" Dane asked. "You're a child."

"Yes, I am a child, as are you, as are we all. The oldest being in the universe is but a child of time," Tama said.

"What's happening to you, Tama?" Kitten asked.

"I am fulfilling my destiny," he answered.

"Damn it, why can't anyone around here give me a straight answer?" Kitten asked angrily.

"There are no straight answers," Alliette said behind her.

"Time will tell all," Tama said. "I can tell you this, now. Kitten...Mother, you shall have what you most desire, although you don't know you desire it yet."

"Another riddle," Kitten murmured.

"Dane...Father, you too shall have what you most desire. And now, I must go. I shall never see you again with these eyes. I shall never call you Mother and Father again. But I shall always be with you, for as long as you live, and after you die...you shall be with me forever."

With that, he closed his eyes.

"Tama!" Kitten yelled. "Tama, wait! I just wanted to say I love you!"

Even though his eyes were closed, he grinned. "I know," he said, his voice metallic and echoing.

Dane was sure about one thing. If what Tama said was true, he would never be cold again. It was what he most desired.

No one recognized Kitten and Linx as they exited the autocab and walked up the steps to the Emigration Building. It turned out that the star-faring human civilization, of which the Ring had once been so proud a part, had not forgotten them. Although the Ring had been quarantined for over a century, for fear of the Deity virus being spread to the A.I.s that controlled everything from interstellar travel to galactic financial markets, monitoring had never ceased. When Tama had control of Deity, he made contact, allowed a remote diagnostic check, and the Ring began the slow indoctrination back into human civilization.

Kitten was now anonymous, just another person with creamy white skin, shoulder-length dirty blonde hair, and sky blue eyes. Linx was just as anonymous, with dark brown skin, brown eyes, and his head shaved. They still had their mites, of course, to protect them against the cold. And it was still cold most of the time, although not as bad as it had been. The city's other services had been gradually coming back online.

They made their way through the Emigration Building, until they found the door to Dane's new, temporary flat. Kitten knocked. A moment later the door opened.

"Hi," Dane said, smiling, and hugged her.

"Good to see you," Linx said, as he and Dane shook hands.

"So you're really going?" Kitten asked Dane.

He nodded.

"It's kind of ironic, don't you think?" she asked.

"What is?"

"That you, of all people, are going to be frozen solid for the next two hundred years."

Linx shivered as if for effect.

"I'll be warm in my dreams, though," he said. "At least, that's what they tell me."

Kitten looked away. "You'll be gone. Just like Tama."

"I'm sorry, Kitten," Dane said. What else could he say that he hadn't said before?

"There wasn't enough time to get to know him," Kitten continued, shaking her head. "I guess it's silly. I mean, he did save us all. But still."

"Are you happy?" Dane asked her, surprising himself with the question. After asking it, though, he discovered that it was the one thing he truly wanted to know, to be sure of, before he left.

"Happy?" Kitten asked.

"Yeah. I mean, ultimately, the way things worked out."

"Yes, I'm happy, in spite of things," Kitten said. "I never thought I'd like not being a celeb, but I do. I like people not knowing who I am."

"I know who you are," Dane said.

"Yeah, you do."

"That's the whole point, though," Dane went on. "Tama wants us all to be happy, not to suffer, not to want for anything."

"I don't think that's possible," Kitten said. "We can't all be happy. Not all of us. Some of us have to suffer, sometimes, don't we?"

Dane shrugged. "I don't know. I guess so, but we can't all be miserable, either."

"No, we can't." Kitten agreed.

"I think that's what Tama's here for," Dane said. "To make sure we all at least have a chance at happiness, at not suffering."

"Then why are you leaving?" Kitten asked.

"I want to see what people on other worlds are like," Dane said. "I want to know if we really did get it right, here. The Ring has been cut off for so long. Are we still really human?"

Kitten smiled. "We're human."

"Then I guess my only other excuse is that…I never felt like I belonged here, you know?"

She knew he was right about that. It was why Vishnu had chosen him in the first place.

"So where do you belong?" Linx asked, breaking the awkward silence.

Dane turned to look up, out the skylight and into the sky beyond. "Out there, somewhere."

There seemed to be nothing more to say. Anything else, 'take care of yourself' or 'be careful,' would be too mundane. They'd never see him again.

The Deity Effect

Linx opened his mouth to say something, but merely winked at Dane. With that, Linx and Kitten turned to leave. Dane watched as they walked down the hall to exit the dormitory that temporarily housed people who, like himself, belonged elsewhere.

I originally wrote this story for an anthology that rejected it. They were looking for stories inspired by the headlines of the tabloids like National Enquirer *and* Weekly World News. *I'd long had the title, "Space Aliens Ate My Head," in mind for a humorous science fiction story, and had a vague idea of what it would be about. When I started writing it, thinking in terms of those tabloids is what helped me figure the story out while daydreaming.*

It was while daydreaming that I came up with the idea of the biker gang. That made the story fun for me, to play with this idea of bikers vs. aliens, more or less. It also made it easy for me to find the sort of loose voice I used in the story.

"Space Aliens Ate My Head" was eventually published by John Benson, the editor and publisher of Not One of Us, *in a chapbook anthology called* In Your Face *in 1996. It was the cover story.*

Space Aliens Ate My Head

THE ALIENS HAD ME TRAPPED in some sort of restraining field. I couldn't move at all, but there was nothing holding me there, or nothing *visible*. It was a force field. All I could move were my eyes, which I did, and saw one of them approach me with a tool in one of its long-fingered hands...The tool emitted a bright, blue light, long and thin like a blade.

I watched as it came closer, bringing the glowing blade around to my head. I wanted to scream, but my vocal chords were locked up by the force field, too.

daydreams undertaken

Space Aliens Ate My Head

And then I felt the blade's bite as it penetrated my skull and sliced hotly into my brain.

FLASHBACK

The Outcasts, the local *hawg*-riding outlaw biker gang, showed up the other night at our party, uninvited, and announced only by the roar of their chrome and leather covered Harley-Davidsons. Led by Zeke Manning, the Outcasts had become a real bold enterprise lately, riding through the center of town at all hours, hooting and hollering drunkenly. They crashed high school parties, the Independence Day and Thanksgiving Day parades, bake sales for the Alzheimer's and Cancer Societies, and even knocked over the newsstand in the town square because Mr. Hopper, the owner, wouldn't stock magazines like *Biker Juggs* and *Chopper Chix*.

Squirrel Junction, a small town in the mountains of north Georgia, was not used to this kind of behavior. Our three-man police department didn't know what to do. They tried to get the state involved, but never got their messages returned by the Governor's office (he was too busy campaigning for the upcoming election, Squirrel Junctionites decided with understanding resignation).

The party was for my girlfriend, Nadine, who'd just graduated with an art degree from the community college, and we decided to have an honest-to-God wine and cheese art gallery showing of her work, just like down in Atlanta, or up in New York City. We had Kraft slices on Wheat Thins, grapes, sliced pepperoni, and pecan log rolls…a real classy affair, if you ask me. Everyone was there, all our friends and family, the Mayor, and Nadine's art teacher. Nadine was happy as she could be, and the folks seemed to genuinely like her art, especially one of the local First Baptist Church done with the shadow of a cross falling over it.

"No one understands it, William," she whispered to me once during the evening as we stood before it, but I didn't know what she meant. I wasn't quite sure what there was to understand. Still, she seemed pleased when the Right Reverend Archer bent over to get a better look at it.

"I may dip into the church coffers to purchase this piece," he declared. "You have surely been blessed with a gift from God!"

Nadine smiled pleasantly, and thanked the Reverend.

I was awake and aware the entire time while the aliens sliced my brain up with their laser scalpel. There was pain, but not as much as I would have expected. Somehow, I could almost see what they were doing as they removed the top of my head, pulled my brain out, and proceeded to cut it up into bite-sized portions. And then another alien scooped up the portions and inserted them into tubes that formed out of the wall of the space ship (what else could it be?).

I was still totally aware, and felt myself divided and compartmentalized in the tubes. I was getting panicky and claustrophobic until things started to heat up. They were melting me!

Stephen L. Antczak

Each small section of my brain melted, then slid down the tube, and into the mouth of another alien that was connected to the tube. These aliens were kept in pods. I slid right into their stomach sacs, realizing finally what was happening.

The aliens were eating my brain.

FLASHBACK

We heard a loud, rumbling, thunderous roar outside after the Reverend made his declaration. Everyone crowded to the plate glass window to see what it was. A light bright enough to be seen even during mid-day flashed overhead, and something streaked through the sky like a meteor. It went right over the town, burning brightly, but there was no smoke trailing behind it.

"Lord Jesus!" Reverend Archer shouted.

Then the meteor, or whatever it was, was gone, but there was still a rumbling, growling sound vibrating the walls of the gallery so that one of the paintings actually fell off the wall.

"It's an earthquake!" someone screamed.

"It's the Apocalypse!" Reverend Archer retorted. "Pray with me!" And he and a few of his more fervent followers bowed their heads and started praying aloud.

The rest of us continued looking out the window and saw the Outcasts ride into view, led by Zeke. They rode up to the sidewalk and lined their Harleys along the curb, seventeen of them, including one with a sidecar, then revved their engines even louder. Another one of Nadine's paintings fell off the wall, but she didn't notice. She was too busy watching Zeke as he climbed off his *hawg*.

"Great," I muttered under my breath.

"Aren't they?" Nadine added, apparently missing the sarcastic tone in my voice. She'd always had a fascination with motorcycles, especially Harleys, and with the outlaw image of bikers. She told me once she sometimes daydreamed of being a biker gang "old lady" who got passed around among the guys, then assured me she'd never *really* want to....

In the bellies of the aliens my brain-fluid was absorbed into their systems. All of them, fifty cousins of ET, were fed my brain, and I experienced the entire process consciously. I felt my essence enter their bodies like water being sucked up by a sponge. I felt my sense of identity, my sense of *self*, assimilate to the aliens' anatomy.

Then I lay there, times fifty, and opened my eyes....

FLASHBACK

Nadine had a wild side. She was the first one to go outside as the rest of the Outcasts got off their bikes, removed their spiked German helmets, goggles, leather hats with ear flaps, and other assorted biker wardrobe accessories. I went out and stood by Nadine's side. Zeke walked up, looked her up and down, head to toe, then at me.

"Heard there was a party," he said, "and the Outcasts weren't invited. How can that be?"

"It's not so much a party," I told him, "it's an art show."

"How about if I invite you now?" Nadine suddenly said.

"Just me?" Zeke asked.

Nadine nodded.

He looked back at his biker buddies, then shook his head.

"How about all of us?" he asked. "We all appreciate *art*, don't we guys?"

"Yeah!" a couple of them shouted, fists raised in the air.

"Dig it! Art, man!" another howled.

Nadine grinned, then said, "Okay, but then someone has to give me a ride on a Harley."

Zeke laughed. "All right!"

"*Nadine*," I said, and she looked at me. Her expression went from one of mischievous delight to concern.

"Umm, he wants a ride, too," she said, pointing at me.

Zeke looked at me with a sour expression, like someone had just given him a flat beer.

"Okay, no problem," he said, and my heart sank.

The Outcasts piled into our makeshift gallery, where the Reverend had finished his praying and was rehanging the paintings that had fallen. When he saw the Outcasts entering, he dropped one of the paintings, a rendition of Hatty Jones' boiled peanut shack on Route 7. Zeke smiled at him, and then they were all in there among our friends and family. They dutifully paused at each painting, emitting a few genuine-sounding remarks like "Far out!" and "Goddamn!"

Zeke started passing out the wine, screwing the tops off the bottles and sending them around, and it wasn't long before the entire stock of three cases was gone. One of the Outcasts downed an entire bottle in one long series of gulps, then chucked the empty back over his shoulder. It nearly hit the Reverend, but he ducked, and it smashed through the plate glass window. The place erupted with laughter and the sound of breaking glass as other empty wine bottles were shattered. The makeshift gallery began to stink of wine and bad biker breath from all the belching. The drunken bikers spilled out into the street. Someone produced a boom box and then loud rock music got them dancing and winging the remaining empty wine bottles through the air. Other windows on the street shattered as these 'dead soldiers' were transformed into missiles.

And Nadine was out there in the middle of the street, dancing to 'Slow Ride' by Foghat with Zeke, grinding their hips together, running their hands over each other's body....

I stared with fifty pairs of eyes. I breathed through fifty nostril-like slits with fifty sets of lungs. Fifty versions of me climbed from the coffin-like pods I suddenly, somehow, knew were stasis field chambers to prevent aging during interstellar travel. My body...My *bodies* were strong and dexterous, meant for exploring rough terrain, surviving long periods stranded in hostile environments, and fighting alien menaces.

Each of my fifty selves moved in unison, because although I could feel them as fifty distinct entities, I could not divide my consciousness enough to allow each one to act independently of the others. A lot of bumping into walls went on. A lot of just standing around motionless while I tried to split my personality into fifty separate individuals....

FLASHBACK

Zeke saw me watching him dance with Nadine. He kept grinning over at me, especially when he ran his hands over her absolutely perfect, soft, round butt. And she apparently *enjoyed* it! She threw her head back and closed her eyes while he thrust his pelvis into her, like some dancing Elvis from Hell.

Before the song was over, I made a bold move and went over to the boom box and hit *STOP*. The music went dead, the dancing ended in mid-motion. Zeke and his filthy Outcasts gathered around me.

"Um, what about that ride, huh Zeke?" Nadine asked nervously.

"Yeah," he said. "Yeah, sure." He turned around to face his troops. "Let's *ride*!"

Two burly bikers grabbed me by either arm and hauled me over to a *hawg*, roughly lifting me up and setting me on the seat behind another Outcast, this one a tall, lanky, wiry guy I heard one of the others call Cooter.

"Hang on, boy!" Cooter yelled as he started his Harley. He rode straight over the curb and onto the sidewalk, and knocked several of his fellow Outcasts through what remained of a plate glass window as they continued laughing their drunken heads off. "Yeeeeoooooowww!!"

A group of seven or eight bikers followed Zeke, and Nadine with her arms wrapped tightly around his lean frame, out of town. We roared through the suburbs, into unincorporated territory where huge tracts of land were nothing but wilderness and where Dead Man's Gulch on old Harvey Dean's land was. It was at this point Zeke pulled to a halt at the lip of the gulch, grabbed Nadine, and kissed her hard as Cooter rode up, offering me a full view. I saw all right, I saw Nadine try to push Zeke away, but he held her close anyway.

"Get your damn hands off her!" I screamed as Cooter coasted to a stop. Before anyone could react I jumped off his Harley and ran up to Zeke. He barely had time to push Nadine away, and I punched him right in chops. He stumbled back and fell right on his rear.

"Get 'im!" one of the other Outcasts shouted, and before I knew it, they had me by either arm again. Zeke stood up, wiping blood from his lip. He smiled wickedly at me. He smelled like stale wine and old leather.

"You know," he said, "I was gettin' to like you." With that, he socked me one in the gut, knocking the wind out of me. Suddenly I had this bitter taste in the back of my throat of cheap wine and imitation cheese. "*That* was payback!"

"William!" Nadine cried. She tried to hit Zeke, but no one had ever taught her how to throw a good punch, and she missed, twirling around and falling in the road.

"And this one's 'cause I'm *mean*," he said, then pulled his fist back. He slammed his fist right into my mouth, the force of the blow actually knocking me partly out of his followers' grasp. I tasted a mixture of blood, and hairy, sweaty knuckles in my mouth.

"Toss him over the side," Zeke ordered his men.

"No!" Nadine screamed. "Don't! I'll do anything!"

I wish I'd gotten my wind back enough to say something then, but I couldn't utter one word.

"I ain't interested in *you* anymore," he said to her. "But maybe one of the boys is. We'll take you back and see who wants you. But him..." He kicked dirt at me. "Over the side."

And someone, I didn't see who, grabbed me under the arms, lifted me to my feet, and brought me to the very edge of the gulch. I dragged my feet, let my body sag, anything within my power to hinder their efforts, but to no avail. With one good, solid push, I went over the edge into Dead Man's Gulch....

I got all fifty alien bodies standing in a circle so I could see them, so I could see *me*, myself, and I...and I, and I, and I...I could feel the strength in those unEarthly bodies, and I could feel something else. An emptiness, a void, a black hole in the multiple consciousness that I'd become. In the spaceship was one other alien body, and this one was different. I found it, sitting in a cockpit-like pod, with a larger head than the others, and practically nothing of a body. I knew this had to have been the controller, the brain that was *supposed* to occupy the fifty alien skulls I now found myself in. A tube went from the top of that massive head into the ceiling, and I knew that must have been how it activated the "drones," by feeding them parts of its brain.

Something had happened, somewhere in space not far from Earth, that had resulted in the ship crashing, and killing the controller. Emergency measures had been undertaken automatically, probably controlled by some back-up controller with limited ability, that resulted in *me* becoming the new controller. Except, my brain had been entirely consumed. What did that mean? Did I have a limited time only before they used my consciousness up? There were no answers in my head, or heads, at all.

However, I decided that if I did have only a limited amount of time left, I knew what to do with it.

I decided to head back into Squirrel Junction and crash the Outcasts' party.

Stephen L. Antczak

FLASHBACK

I fell. I crashed through trees, smashing against branches that ripped through my clothes, and my flesh, until the ground hit me like a sledge hammer. I could tell my body was broken, my legs, my right arm, a few ribs, and from the feel of it, my back, too. I lay there waiting to die, and as my eyes gradually lost focus, I saw them for the first time.

The aliens. Their pale, hairless heads, and big, red, pupilless eyes. They were taller than I'd ever imagined aliens would be. They hunched over me, silently gazing into my eyes, and I got the distinct impression they were looking for something there, something like intelligence.

I convinced myself they were angels, and then thought I was hallucinating and death was near. I even felt its icy grip touch on my skin as spirits lifted me into the air, and I floated in oblivion.

When next I was aware, the glowing knife of blue light was fragmenting my Self.

The alien bodies were tireless as they trudged through the wilderness of the gulch. It was night, with the lunar crescent obscured by clouds. I could see perfectly well with my alien eyes and made good time as I walked towards the Squirrel Junction city limit. My senses were heightened, and I smelled the damp loam beneath my feet, rich and Earthy. I was aware of all the critters of the woods scattering at my approach. I heard a black bear growl his discontent at my presence as he lumbered away. Birds took to the wing. Even insects hopped and skittered away as fast as they could. Spiders abandoned their webs, gnat swarms suddenly exploded in ten different directions, yellowjackets left the nest.

I was not of this world. I was unnatural. I didn't belong here.

In the suburbs I used my alien strength to rip the back door to a K-Mart from its hinges, and went in fifty strong while the alarm wailed. I knew the Squirrel Junction police force would have its hands full with the Outcasts right now, and wouldn't be able to bother checking it out. I found clothes, fifty totally different outfits for each alien body. I didn't worry about *exact* fits, but I didn't want to waltz into town stark naked. They were alien bodies, yes, but they did have reproductive organs that were recognizably such, and I didn't feel like unnecessarily shocking anybody. Maybe I took a little longer than necessary, especially accessorizing with sunglasses, hats, bandannas, ties, etc., and running each of my fifty alien selves before a mirror to make sure I/we looked nothing less than *good*.

Then I headed into town.

It was chaos, total anarchy, with bikers dragging townspeople like Art Hlaverty down the street on his back and letting him go to slide into an open sewer. And if he missed the sewer, the concrete curb was there to stop him. The Outcasts had broken every window around, and all three of the city's police cruisers had been turned over onto their roofs. The city's fire engine had been commandeered by Outcasts, who were spraying water across the street to facilitate the dragging of honest, hard-working, God-fearing citizens. Alas, I arrived too late to save Hlaverty from cracking his head open like an egg against the curb, but next up was my former third grade teacher, Edna Banks. "Don't you dare, Dewey Johnson," she was saying to the Outcast who had her by the leg and was trying to start his bike back up — it had stalled on him. "And I know that's you underneath those goggles! Do you *hear* me Dewey Johnson? Are you *listening*?"

Good ol' Mrs. Banks. Just as Dewey got his Harley re-started, I ran in with two of my new bodies, one on either side of him. One tapped him on the shoulder, getting his attention, and the other grabbed him and easily lifted him from his seat and tossed him through air to land on the tarmac with a bone-crunching *thud*.

Some of the other Outcasts saw what happened. One came at me — the me who'd just tossed an unruly Dewey — full throttle on his *hawg*, screaming a battle cry, intending to run me down. That superior alien dexterity and strength came in handy. I waited until it was almost too late, then jumped straight up, extending my legs into a full mid-air split, and the Outcast passed beneath me to run into the fire engine.

Other Outcasts came to the attack, surrounding their two assailants.

"Goddamn!" one Outcast yelled. "What a couple of freaks!"

They closed in for the kill.

I brought out the reinforcements. The Outcasts never had a chance, most of them being incredibly out of shape from too much drinking, smoking, and sitting, developing the classic biker physique. Plus, all fifty of my selves were under the control of one mind, acting with the efficiency of all the fingers on a single human hand. Not one of my alien bodies suffered any damage whatsoever.

But Zeke was nowhere in sight.

The Outcasts who were now lying unconscious or dead in the street represented a majority of the gang, but not all of them. There were still a few left. With my acute alien hearing, I quickly detected the familiar hoots and howls of a certain Outcast coming from the Happy Hour pool hall.

And then I heard an all too familiar voice begging to be let go....

A full frontal assault was called for, because I knew something was happening, or about to happen, that shouldn't. I sent alien bodies smashing through the front of the pool hall, and a few around back to kick in the door. I diverted part of my attention to whatever other Outcasts were there, using fifteen or so of my alien force to quell their resistance. A few others I kept outside to stand guard. The rest I sent in for Zeke.

Stephen L. Antczak

I got in there just as Zeke sat back to watch another Outcast rip Nadine's blouse from her body, leaving her clad in only her underwear. Zeke was already twirling her skirt around in one hand. They had her up on a pool table....

"Dance!" Zeke yelled. "I want you to *dance*."

"*I'll* dance for you, Zeke!" I yelled. Unfortunately I didn't quite have as much control over the alien bodies as I'd thought, and my words came from about six different mouths in six different directions. The remaining Outcasts looked all around them to find they were surrounded. Zeke looked at the one near the front door, the one I'd meant to be the vessel for my words.

He pulled a gun from his jacket.

"Well *damn*," he said. "Who, or *what*, the hell are you?"

I smiled with my slit of a mouth.

"You know me," I replied. "You *made* me."

He looked confused. Who could blame him?

"How's your *lip*," I then said, and watched as realization dawned on him, and he slowly put his free hand to his mouth.

"*You*," he whispered.

"*William?*" Nadine said. "Is that you?"

Zeke turned to her, pointing the gun at her.

"I said dance!" He pulled the hammer back on the gun. Nadine started dancing as a song began on the juke box. 'Smoke On the Water,' by Deep Purple.

"Let her go, you animal!" I told him.

He grinned, then aimed his gun at me, and pulled the trigger. The gun went off with a loud pop, like a powerful firecracker. The bullet struck me in the head, and that alien body fell dead. The sudden shock of death stunned me. All my alien bodies staggered back, suddenly disoriented while Zeke laughed and swept the barrel of his gun around, thinking he was scaring a now leaderless group of freaks. I was able to clear my heads enough for another alien body to step forward.

"You missed, Zeke," I said. He aimed the gun at *that* body and pulled the trigger, and it too fell dead. This time the shock wasn't so bad, as I expected it to happen.

"Over here, Zeke!" I had another yell, from the opposite direction, then stood there with my arms wide open, a willing target. He took aim, fired, and that one too dropped dead on the floor.

I did this with three others, until he was out of ammunition.

"You finished?" I asked with yet another alien body. Poor Nadine still danced atop the pool table, the music still pumping out of that juke box.

He aimed the gun, pulled the trigger, and was rewarded with a belittling "click."

"It's over, Zeke," I told him. "*You* are over!"

Space Aliens Ate My Head

He tried to run, but I was everywhere, and took him out with a well-placed kung-fu kick to the back of the head. It was actually what you might call "alien-fu," something hardwired in those bodies that they seemed to know, that *I* now seemed to know, instinctively. Then I mopped up the pool hall with the rest of the Outcasts and unplugged the juke box.

"You can stop dancing now," I told Nadine. She stopped, then looked at me, and looked around the rest of me.

"William?"

I nodded, all remaining 44 heads.

"What happened to you?" she asked as she climbed down from the pool table.

"Space aliens ate my head," I told her. "They absorbed me."

"Oh *God*," she said, "how *awful*!"

"No, actually I don't mind. I would've died anyway, after Zeke had me thrown into the gulch. As it is now, I'm better, stronger, faster...able to leap tall buildings in a single bound...and I run like a butterfly, sting like a bee...I know what evil lurks in the hearts of men...all that stuff."

"Wow. But...what about *us*?"

I shrugged.

"I can stay here with you, if you want," I said. "*And* I can repair the space ship and travel to the far corners of the galaxy. There's enough of me to go around!"

As we talked I used several of my other selves to remove the dead alien bodies from the pool hall, and commandeered a pick-up truck to take them back to the space ship, where I was reasonably certain they could be repaired good as new. I used others of my alien selves to help round up the wounded citizens of Squirrel Junction, and to explain my situation to the Chief of Police, the Mayor, and the good Reverend who promptly fainted on the spot. The Police Chief liked my idea of deputizing me and tripling the size of his force for the price of one extra man. And of course, there were plenty of extra motorcycles around now for me to ride while on duty.

"So do you think you could love an alien?" I asked Nadine as she wiggled back into her skirt and blouse. Outside I was getting it together with some of the Outcasts' discarded *hawgs*, riding up and down the street, getting used to those powerful engines.

"No," she said, and my alien equivalent of a heart sank. "I love *you*. You may have an alien *body*, but you're all man inside. I'll be your 'old lady' any day of the week!"

This story is what I like to call my backhanded tribute to Ray Bradbury. While I in no way advocate the use of hallucinogenic drugs in real life, using them in fiction is quite another matter. The idea came to me while daydreaming, when I wondered… what if the Mars in Bradbury's Martian Chronicles *was the real Mars? What if the lifeless red planet we know and love today was just a big hallucination caused by Martians? Maybe they don't want us to do to Mars what we've done to the Everglades and the Mississippi river.*

The idea of using LSD as the key to unlocking the mystery of Mars occurred to me after seeing Timothy Leary speak at a science fiction convention. Many people who use hallucinogenic drugs like to think the drugs don't distort their perception of reality at all, rather "tripping" allows them to see the world the way it really is. I don't know about that. But I do know that science fiction allows readers to see the world the way I sometimes imagine it might be.

The Mars Trip

THEY WAITED FOR HAPPY SAM in the cantina. Rusty Jones, Janis Devereaux, and Mabel Adams all had that look. Happy Sam had seen it way too many times of late, and tried to nip it in the bud as he walked past their table.

"I do *not* need cheering up," he told them, then headed straight for the bar. Nice of the Company to provide them with a wet bar on Mars. After the general strike of '09, the Company decided to grant what had been

daydreams undertaken

The Mars Trip

previously rejected as an "unreasonable" request. The bartender nodded in Happy Sam's direction, and a moment later placed a gin and tonic before him.

Happy Sam sipped his drink, closing his eyes to savor it. Nothing unreasonable about a cool gin and tonic after a ten-hour shift. It was like a smooth kiss that slipped down his throat, the tongue of an icy lover.

A hand rested on his shoulder, then slid around to his back and started scratching.

"We don't want to cheer you up, Sam," Janis told him. "We just want to show you something." She was a slightly plump sociologist, curly brown hair just down over her ears, wide brown eyes and full lips. Vivacious described her well. Under different circumstances, in a healthier state of mind, Happy Sam might have been attracted to her.

He sighed. "If I go with you, will you guys leave me alone from now on?"

"If you still want to spend the remainder of your tour in manic depression after this, fine. Thirty-six months is a *long* time to mope, though."

"Maybe I *like* to mope."

Janis sighed. "I was just like you, Sam…"

"*Happy* Sam, please. That's what you guys call me, isn't it? So call me Happy Sam to my face. Reminds me who my friends *aren't*." He sipped his drink. "And you were never like me."

"We *are* your friends, and I *was* like you," Janis insisted. "I signed up for five years for the same reasons you did. I used to read all those sci-fi books when I was a kid. I thought Mars would be the greatest adventure of my life. When I got here it didn't take long for me to get over the beauty of a Martian sunrise and realize that a barren and lifeless world is just depressing as hell. It had the same effect on me that it has on you."

"There's more to it than that," he told her.

"Of course there is," she said. "But that is the root of it. Once you get over that, you'll be able to sort out your other problems and deal with them better. Trust me. Did you know that several psychology journals have done articles on the people who work here? You know that, aside from the scientists, there are four basic types?" She didn't wait for him to answer that. "First there are those who come here to leave a bad situation on Earth, whether it involves the law, or a domestic dispute, whatever. Second, you have people like us, who come for the romance of it because we grew up reading science fiction stories. Then there are the Company people who come out of loyalty to the Company, or are trying to make points, et cetera. Fourth, you have those who just need a good job that pays well and keeps them out of trouble."

"Can't get further away from trouble than here," Happy Sam commented. His drink finished, he glanced over at the bartender for another, but Janis waved the bartender away.

"The first two groups always sign up for the longest tour, Sam," Janis said. "Five years, with an option to renew for another five. That's you, and me. Rus and Mabel, too. I *know* you didn't leave Earth for any deep, dark reason."

"You don't know that."

Janis nodded. "Oh yes. We checked you out. Your background's as spotless as the mirrors on the power grid. Majored in Systems Engineering at Georgia Tech. Dropped out before you got your Masters to work for the Company during the early days of the Mars Project. They were still sending only the so-called 'best and brightest' back then, and without a Masters degree that left you out. Married for three years, no children, amicable divorce. When the Mars Project kicked into high gear, you tried to get aboard for two years before they finally took you as a Systems Analyst."

"So you got into my personnel file," Happy Sam acknowledged, "but *why?*"

"We wanted to make sure you fit the type."

"For what?"

Janis looked at Mabel and Rusty. Mabel had the build of the classic waif, short blonde hair, green eyes, a model's face. Rusty had a smaller version of Happy Sam's build, with his black hair in a crewcut.

"We can't tell you. We have to *show* you," Janis said.

"Okay. Fine. Show me, and then promise to leave me alone for the next three years."

"Deal." She stuck out her hand, he grudgingly shook it.

"So what do I have to do?" Happy Sam asked.

"Remember how to put this on?" Rusty asked Happy Sam, indicating a blue skinsuit hanging at the end of a rack. Everyone who worked on Mars took a two-hour test walk around the domes in one, a training exercise designed to make sure that everyone could don a suit and go outside without assistance.

Happy Sam pulled the skinsuit off the rack. "Of course I remember." The light-duty skinsuits were the Martian EVA suit of choice. The larger hardsuits were still available for days-long excursions, taken mostly by the scientists who tended to disappear into the Martian wilds in the name of research. Most of the folks who were there to *work* didn't bother going outside during free time. Too many of them spent all day out there *working*, wearing specially built construction suits that were even less comfortable than the hardsuits. Consequently, there were plenty of skinsuits available.

They'd gone to an air lock at the north part of the Main Dome, which would eventually be the hub of a ring of smaller domes all interconnected by underground malls and aboveground monorail systems. The outer domes would house the hydro-farms and research facilities. The construction effort was concentrated on erecting the ring of outer domes. The work crew dormitories were in the Main Dome, temporary prefabs that would eventually have to make way for the Mars Marriott Marquis.

Mabel produced three 'energy bars' from a locker. "Everyone eat."

Happy Sam ate his without comment. They wouldn't be stopping at a hot dog stand for lunch, so eating now made sense. Despite the forty percent Earth-normal gravity, they could easily wear themselves out trudging around Mangalla Vallis. The Company chose the area mainly because it was 'convenient' to Olympus Mons and several other volcanoes, plus Candor Chasma and Kasei Vallis. Mangalla Vallis itself was dissected by channels. Plenty of interesting things for scientists to investigate.

After eating, Happy Sam and the others suited up. They had to wait while they breathed pure oxygen to remove the nitrogen from their blood, thus avoiding an attack of the bends. Janis started a conversation with Mabel and Rusty about their favorite science fiction stories set on Mars. The consensus rested with the more fanciful Mars classics like Burroughs' John Carter books, and Bradbury's *Martian Chronicles*.

"What about you?" Janis asked Happy Sam, who'd been sitting off in the corner, listening to the exchange with the blank face of boredom.

He rolled his eyes, like he had better things to be doing. "My guess is Bradbury," Rusty said.

Happy Sam shrugged. "When I was a kid, sure."

"Rusty already knew that," Janis said. "It's in your file."

"It is?" This was news. Who considered that worth putting in someone's personnel file? "How is it in my file?"

"Remember that questionnaire you took back on Earth, just before shipping out? That was to help determine the sociological make-up of the workforce here. There were half a dozen questions that were supposed to determine if you fell into one of the four basic food groups."

"What kind of questions?"

"Oh, you know, 'Did you ever read science fiction?' and 'Name your favorite science fiction.' Don't you remember?"

He shook his head. "Vaguely. It was a while ago."

The indicator light went on. The nitrogen had been removed from their systems.

"This better be good," Happy Sam told Janis as he put on his helmet. She just grinned. In fact, all of them were grinning as they donned their helmets.

The air hissed out of the airlock, and the door to the outside opened.

The airlock sat at ground level. The surface around the dome looked like it'd been littered with rocks and boulders by a giant. The sky varied in shades of pink, slightly tinted by the thin gold film of the skinsuit visors, and cloudless, a reminder that the thin Martian atmosphere would not protect them from a solar flare while they were outside. And off to the northeast, Olympus Mons, the largest volcano in the Solar System.

"Let's go," Rusty urged. He started north side by side with Mabel. Janis walked alongside Happy Sam.

Happy Sam stumbled, almost fell, then stopped to sit on a convenient rock.

"Only a little further, Sam," Janis said.

"I can't," he said. "I think something's wrong with my air. The ground...I'd swear it's moving underneath my feet. I'm hallucinating. I think I should radio in for help."

"Don't do that," Janis said. "Just try to go a little longer. You'll be fine, trust me."

Happy Sam laughed. "'Trust me' she says. Tell me something. Why did you people start calling me Happy Sam? What did you get out of it? Some laughs?"

Janis shook her head. "We just called you that. We meant nothing *mean* by it. Having gone through the same emotional wringer we knew it wasn't going to last once you saw what you are *about to see*. Which reminds me...It's okay if you're...seeing things. Don't worry about it. Now..."

Happy Sam shook his head. "I'm not going anywhere until you tell me what's going on. I mean it. I'll sit here until the Martian cows come home."

Janis laughed and kept laughing, although she seemed to want to stop. "Martian cows!" she cracked once, and just kept on laughing. Mabel and Rusty came back to see what kept them.

"My air is tainted or something," Happy Sam told them, "and she starts laughing."

"You're air is *not* tainted," Janis managed to say. A deep breath, and she calmed down again.

"Maybe we should just tell him," Mabel suggested. She looked loopy, grinning from ear to ear.

"Tell me *what!*"

"Okay, fine," Janis said, then looked at Happy Sam. "The hallucinations you're having? It's not your air supply. The energy bar you ate...was laced with a mild psychedelic. You're *tripping* Sam."

He sat there and didn't reply right away, letting it sink in. It seemed to him that in an environment like the surface of Mars, the last thing you wanted to do was deprive yourself of the capacity to think straight. Now that he knew, though, he also knew he could handle it. Happy Sam had done his share of experimentation during college. He'd tried LSD and psilocybin mushrooms.

"What are we on?" he asked. "LSD?" It seemed like the most likely suspect. Janis probably had access to some for addiction therapy.

"Actually, it's ALD-fifty-two," Janis said. "Pretty much the same thing, but smoother. It becomes LSD-twenty-five once you ingest it."

The Mars Trip

Happy Sam stood up.

"I'll be heading back, then," he said, and started walking. The ground felt uncertain beneath his feet, as if the entire surface of Mars were a giant waterbed. The others walked along with him.

"Sam…" Janis said, but he waved her off.

"There's something else you should know," Rusty said.

"Not interested," Happy Sam told him. The pink sky looked like a giant fuzzy pillow. The ground ahead shifted and wavered, but he kept walking, concentrating on putting one foot in front of the other, keeping his eyes focused just ahead of his next step.

"Sam, stop!"

He stopped. The skinsuit felt tight, constricting, as if it were shrinking. It took a powerful, conscious effort not to rip the helmet off.

"You're going the wrong way," Rusty informed him. "The dome is in the opposite direction."

"Goddamn it," Happy Sam said. "You people are in deep shit when I get back." He turned around to find himself visor to visor with Janis.

"You might as well keep going that way," she said. "What we wanted to show you is only about thirty meters more in that direction. Come on." She held out her hand, and Happy Sam took it in his without even thinking. He looked down at their gloved fingers intertwined, and imagined their skinsuits were somehow connected at the arms by a hollow tube, and they were actually holding *hands*.…

"There it is," someone said. Happy Sam blinked, saw Janis had let go of his hand.

Janis pointed ahead of them, so Happy Sam looked.

They stood at the edge of one of the channels that had led astronomers even into the Twentieth Century to believe intelligent life existed on Mars, because they thought those channels indicated a civilization. When humanity got a closer look, long before anyone ever set foot on the Red Planet, the dream of a Mars teeming with life had been shattered. Mars turned out to be a dead world, dry, desolate, freezing, and irradiated to the point that life could not exist.

All this ran through Happy Sam's mind as he looked into the channel, and saw *water*.

"You see it?" Janis asked him.

"He sees it," Mabel answered for him.

Bluish purple water came about halfway up the sides, and flowed along in a fast current. It swirled near the walls, created small eddies, splashed droplets into the air. Happy Sam *knew* without a doubt the drug was caused the hallucination, yet the knowing didn't make it go away.

"We need to go a little further, Sam," Janis said. "Along the bank. Follow the current."

They did, Happy Sam walking along numbly, going with the flow, so to speak. He watched the water closely, looking for a flaw in the illusion. He even imagined he could hear it through his helmet, a ghost river in his mind's ear. Probably his subconscious, out of habit, had supplied the appropriate sound effects for what he saw.

"We're here," Rusty said. They stopped. Happy Sam looked around, but saw nothing else out of the ordinary....

Until he watched Rusty, Mabel, and Janis take their helmets off, smiling the whole time. He was too stunned to even try to stop them. He expected to see each of them die, asphyxiate. Instead, Janis closed her eyes and deeply breathed in the Martian air. Rusty tapped Happy Sam on the shoulder, then motioned for him to remove his helmet, too. Letting his panic get the best of him, Happy Sam backed away from them. Fear and confusion caused his flight reflex to take over. He wanted to run back to the dome and be depressed for the next three years and then go back to Earth and just forget Mars even existed.

He turned to run, and found himself right at the edge of the channel, one foot *over* the edge, arms flailing, until someone yanked him backward. Janis stood before him, smiling, breathing, showing him it was all right to take his helmet off. So he did, and didn't care anymore if he died, or if he was *already* dead.

"Just take it easy," Janis said. "Breathe, okay? Slowly in, and exhale slowly, until you calm down."

"What's happening?" Happy Sam asked, when his breathing — *breathing!* — seemed more or less normal.

"Not yet," Janis said with a gleam in her eyes. "There's more."

Happy Sam closed his eyes. "I don't know if I can take anymore."

"Come on," Janis urged. Rusty and Mabel had already gone.

A road, ancient and cracked, and flanked by blue hills, ran towards Olympus Mons, and as far as the eye could see in the opposite direction. Mabel and Rusty were a good thirty or forty meters ahead, holding hands as they walked. Janis tried to hold Happy Sam's, but he pulled it away. He still didn't trust her. Her step didn't lose any bounce, though, and she hummed a spry little tune. Happy Sam kept rubbing at his eyes, trying to shake what he figured *had* to be hallucinations.

Something made a noise behind them, a warbling, whistling sound. Happy Sam jumped, but Janis simply turned and waved. Then something sailed over their heads, something that looked like a giant hummingbird all deep shades of red and purple and green. Sitting atop the hummingbird machine, *melted gold for eyes* looked right at Happy Sam, right through him to his soul. The hummingbird continued past them, and made the same warbling whistle when it got to Mabel and Rusty. They waved, the Martian waved back.

And there was a warmth there, inside Happy Sam, the spot where the Martian's eyes had looked....

Yes, Happy Sam could no longer deny it, a Martian had just flown by and waved. He recognized everything now. The golden eyes...The water in the channel? *Lavender wine.*

"Yes," Janis said, seeing in his eyes this new understanding.

"But...is it real?" Happy Sam asked. "How do we know we're not actually walking across just another barren red plain scattered with rocks and boulders, with our helmets still securely over our heads?"

She shrugged. "I guess we don't. On the other hand, I've done this three times so far. I've become friends with several of the natives. And there's a way to test it."

"Oh?"

"Before we leave, take a rock, a small one, and put it in your mouth until we get back. You couldn't do that if the atmosphere was the way everyone thinks it is, right?"

True. They'd have to stay suited up the whole time during EVA.

"I don't understand how this couldn't have been detected already," he told her. "I mean, we have all kinds of sensors and measuring devices. They can't *all* be wrong."

"They're not," Janis said. "The Martians just make us *think* that what the readings indicate is a dead world. Remember in *The Martian Chronicles*? Mind control. Apparently though, Bradbury could tune in enough to imagine the truth, although he never realized it *was* the truth. Others might have been sensitive to the Martians' tampering, like Wells, or H.P. Lovecraft sensing *some-thing* existed out there, something far greater than humankind. Depending on the person, the interpretation differed greatly."

"So why does taking LSD let us see them?" Happy Sam asked. "Why would we die out here if we weren't tripping our brains out?"

"We've been chewing over this again and again," Janis said, and frowned as she tried to come up with a way to explain it. "The drug activates something in our brains that lets us see a different reality, one that doesn't conform to all our measurements and expectations and observations. Like in cartoons, where the character runs right off a cliff and doesn't fall until someone tells him *that's* impossible, and then he falls. See? It's sort of the same thing."

"So why don't we just give the drug to everybody? It'd certainly make life easier."

"Would it, Sam? Maybe for us, but what about them?"

Of course. Them. She had a point. American Indians, Australian Aborigines, and native peoples all over Earth provided enough light by which

Stephen L. Antczak

to see certain truths. But why let *any* humans know the truth, and why let *him* know?

Janis sighed. "The Martians know that more and more of us are coming. Sooner or later we'll be too many and too close at hand to effectively blindfold to reality. They decided to reach out with their minds and find humans they could trust, to plant the seeds of compassion, understanding, respect."

Happy Sam could easily see how his 'type' fit that bill. Most anyone who loved books like Bradbury's *Martian Chronicles* would want humans to live in harmony with Martians. It had inspired Happy Sam to work towards one goal, to somehow go to Mars, even knowing the world was uninhabited, just on the minuscule chance that the scientists were wrong. They were wrong. His entire being filled with joy, and he wanted to sing and shout and laugh out loud.

But something prevented him from fully embracing this new reality.

All those months of misery, on the verge of suicide, surrounded by desolation, closed in among people with whom he had no empathy.

"Why did you wait so damn long to show me?" he asked Janis.

"You'll see," she answered, with a grin.

They were everywhere. Short Martians, tall Martians, thin ones, and fat ones. Martian women with long, braided hair, and men smoking sideways pipes like flutes. Hummingbird machines soared overhead, and others that looked like butterflies, mantises, ladybugs. Martian children ran laughing up to Janis and Happy Sam, danced around them shouting the whole time, and when Janis bent to grab one they ran screaming away.

"It's a festival," Janis explained. They were in the center of a village, squat geometric shapes that did not look like buildings at all, but were stores, shops, homes, restaurants, hotels. Music Happy Sam never could have imagined rang out from within every structure, alien chatter buzzed the pink air, smells tickled his nose and reminded him in quick flashes of popcorn, old books, coffee, low tide, his mother, his first new car, and a dozen other memories that brought a tear to his eye, and alternately, a smile to his lips.

An adult Martian approached them, wearing an elegant toga of woven silver. Happy Sam felt his mind touched, and then he heard, in plain English, "Welcome, friends from Earth! Welcome to the Festival of Life. May our friendship ring clear with truth far into the future!" Then the Martian bowed.

"May we *always* be friends," Janis said, and bowed in turn. Happy Sam followed suit. The Martian laughed, and danced away to the music.

Now Janis grabbed Happy Sam's hand and he didn't pull away. She squeezed it and feeling that the moment made it destiny, he swept her into a kiss that lasted a full minute.

"Let's not go back," he said.

The Mars Trip

Suddenly she pushed away from him, not angrily, and she still held his hand, but she looked sad. Happy Sam saw her as beautiful right then. He saw how her eyes reflected the pink sky, her face flush from their kiss, the curves of her body prominent beneath the skinsuit. Vivacious, sensual, warm. If he didn't love her already, then he knew he would grow to love her some day.

"We have to go back, Sam, and pretty soon," she said. "They'll miss us, eventually. Besides, we can only come out during festival time, once a year. That's part of the agreement we made with the Martians. We didn't know about you until just before the last festival. Rusty and Mabel had to check your background out before we could bring you. I'm so sorry you had two miserable years."

"It's okay," he said. "But when we go back, I want us to stay like this. I want us to be together, Janis."

He didn't think she'd say no, but when her smile returned and her cheeks reddened even more, his heart swelled with happiness.

"Of course, Sam," she said. "Happy Sam. Of course we'll stay together."

I actually wrote "Captain Asimov" before Isaac Asimov died. In fact, I'm pretty sure I sold it to Ricia Mainhardt & John Varley for their anthology, SUPERHEROES (Ace) before he passed away, but the book wasn't published until after his death. I remembering fearing that people might think I'd tried to capitalize on his death.

The story was actually quite well-received. Author Brad Linaweaver had alerted me to the anthology as a new market for short fiction. I decided to try and write something that, for me, would be a departure as a writer. I decided to write something that could be read by kids. That meant, of course, no "adult" material.

It was very gratifying to me to have a story published in an anthology that also contains stories by Roger Zelazny and Allen Dean Foster, authors I'd read since childhood.

This is the only story I've ever written that sold as a first draft. I wrote it, delivered it, and sold it. This was also a particular thrill for me as a writer because John Varley was one of my all-time favorite science fiction authors. His trilogy, composed of TITAN, WIZARD and DEMON, is in my Top Ten list of the best science fiction tales of all time.

"Captain Asimov" marries two of my childhood passions, robots and super heroes. I'd long been fascinated by Asimov's Three Laws of Robots as a potential plot device, and had loved his robot stories. I wondered how effective a robot super hero could be if it were constrained by the Three Laws.

I knew immediately that the story would be called "Captain Asimov." In my daydreaming I came up with the ending, and that pretty much was all I needed to get started. I sent a copy of the story to Isaac Asimov's widow, Janet Jeppson Asimov, who wrote back that she felt the Good Doctor would have enjoyed the story had he been given a chance to read it, although she also felt I should have explored the concept of imagination in a robot further. Perhaps in another story.

Captain Asimov

JEEVS CLEANED UP AFTER DINNER, loading all the dishes into the washer, but first washing them by hand as per Mrs. Moynahan's explicit instructions. Then Jeevs vacuumed the upstairs while the rest of the family watched vids downstairs in the holo chamber. Jeevs thought of them as the "rest" of the family, because he was programmed to think of himself as a Moynahan, subservient to the rest of the them, but still one of them. Just as he was programmed to think of himself as *him*self.

daydreams undertaken

Captain Asimov

The upstairs was vacuumed by the time Mr. and Mrs. Moynahan were finished with their family obligations…quality time with their children, which Jeevs had figured amounted to an hour and forty-seven minutes and ten seconds for the three of them. The Moynahans sometimes spoiled their children and gave them a full two hours. Then it was off to Social Club with the adults, and Jeevs was responsible for getting the little 'uns to bed. It helped that he was faster, stronger and able to leap taller pieces of furniture than they were. It also helped that he had shock-hands, and if they were bad he could stun them with a quick jolt of electricity and have them tucked into bed before they regained awareness.

It was usually easier to either wear them out with games or read them to sleep. The youngest child was Fermi, and he liked nothing better than to have Jeevs read him the lastest superhero comicbooks. Fermi was too young to actually read, but he looked at the pictures while Jeevs recited the story and dialogue from memory.

"Read *Captain Battle!*" Fermi yelled in his excitement. He had a repertoire of favorites: *Captain Battle, Warchick, Meathook and Bonesaw, Funkiller*, and *The Justice Legion of Avenging Angels*. They were all of the hit first and hit again later variety, and Jeevs privately considered them a little too violent for a little boy Fermi's age. But being a robot meant he didn't have the right to express an opinion of such a *human* nature, which was perfectly all right by Jeevs. He was perfectly happy to serve his owners well. It was in his program. To perform poorly resulted in a deep depression which could only be alleviated by going the extra mile, so to speak, with the housework. He had once gotten the carpet so clean he swore he could see his reflection in it. The Moynahans had to take him in to get his optics retooled.

"Captain Battle versus Cardinal Carnage in The Holy Terror Part Three," Jeevs announced in a perfectly pitched square-jawed news anchor voice.

Fermi clapped his hands and rubbed them together greedily. "*Yeeeaaaahhh!*"

Next was the only daughter, Jesse, and she didn't like to be read to at all. That didn't mean she could read, because she couldn't, but she had a series of make-believes she liked Jeevs to act in with her. One of them was Jeevs as the White Stallion and Jesse as the Princess, riding through the Enchanted Forest after having escaped from the clutches of the evil Duke. She would climb onto Jeevs plasti-frame shoulders and he would gallop her throughout the entire house. Jesse pretended the door frames were dragons swooping low to grab her off the White Stallion.

"A dragon, a dragon!" she would yell as they approached a door frame, and then cover her eyes with her hands as Jeevs ducked down a mere instant before she would have collided with it.

The oldest was Horace, and he had a jealous streak where Jeevs' time was concerned. He enjoyed having Jeevs read him science fiction books before bed. He couldn't read either, and was therefore typical as boys his age went. Despite the fact that most of the science fiction books he liked to hear were hopelessly outdated, he really seemed to like having them read to him by a robot, especially ones with robots in them. Jeevs knew this because Horace wouldn't let either his mother or his father read to him. Of course that might've been because they could only read the primary reader versions of the books...like most adults in modern society, the Moynahans were illiterate except on the most rudimentary level. They could tell the difference between the words MEN and WOMEN, for instance, even without the accompanying Greek symbols. They got confused once at a place with GENTS and LADIES. Horace's favorite authors were Asimov, Bradbury, Del Rey, Sladek, anyone with a lot of robot stories.

"Come *on* Jeeeeevs!" Horace yelled at the robot on the fourth pass through the living room, or as it was known in this make-believe, the Haunted Wood.

"A ghost!" Jesse screamed when she saw her older brother trying to get Jeevs to stop.

Jeevs was about to duck underneath the chandelier in the main hall—

"A falling star!" Jesse yelled.

—when Horace suddenly rolled a toy truck right at his feet. The robot stepped on the truck, and his one leg went flying out behind him. With his inhuman dexterity he managed to maintain his footing long enough to lift Jesse off his shoulders and toss her onto the plush sofa where she landed harmlessly. Then Jeevs' footing gave out and he plunged head-first into the wall.

Blackness. It was not unlike being shut off to conserve his power supply, except this time it had been unexpected. Jeevs knew it probably would have been rather painful too, had he been a human. This was not something he thought while "unconscious". He thought nothing. There were no dreams or anything like that. He just stopped being until somebody turned him back on and he was Jeevs again, ready to work.

Except, when he was turned on, he had other thoughts aside from musing about pain. His head was a-jumble with images from *Captain Battle* and Isaac Asimov's robot stories. The three laws of robotics scrolled through his memory over and over and over....

A robot may not injure a human being, nor through inaction allow a human being to come to harm.

A robot must obey orders given to it by a human being unless such orders conflict with the First Law.

A robot must protect its own existence unless such protection conflicts with the First and Second Laws.

And swimming through these Laws, underlaying them, was the cry of Captain Battle: "Fists...do the talking!"

Jeevs went back to work, although the children were no longer allowed to play with him before bed like before. The quality time with Mom and Dad stretched another hour into the early news broadcasts on the holo. Jeevs overheard a report about battlebots, designed by the military and sent into any number of small hot spot countries, where they efficiently murdered hundreds of villagers day and night until self-destructing. The report stated that there was a certain probability that a few of these killing drones had not self-destructed and continued to mutilate their way through certain South American countries. To top the story with a generous helping of horrific prophecy, the anchor suggested there was always a possibility one could wind up in *your* neighborhood someday, hacking and slashing and shooting to pieces *your* children. Then he ended with his usual, "And may the good news be *your* news."

Jeevs was puzzled. Hadn't these robots ever heard of the Three Laws? Weren't they imprinted with them from day one?

One day Jeevs was outside mowing the lawn, using a push mower because Mr. Moynahan liked to see Jeevs actually working. A remote mower that Jeevs could have controlled from inside while washing the dishes or something would have been much more efficient.

"Hard work's good for you," Moynahan would tell Jeevs, as if speaking to an actual person. "Gives you character."

Jeevs never bothered to wonder just what a robot would do with character.

While he was mowing the front yard, one of the robot street cleaners came down the road. Jeevs stopped and watched it as it approached. It looked very reminiscent of the battlebots he'd seen on the news. Some of the neighborhood children were playing in the street ahead of it, and it sounded several warning beeps as it grew near.

Jeevs turned off the mower, and went inside. Mr. Moynahan was sitting in his massage chair, asleep, and didn't see Jeevs sneak past him and go upstairs. Jeevs went into the Moynahans' closet for winter clothes and found Mr. Moynahan's ski mask, made of a lightweight yet warm material called Nylar. It was red with white circles around the eye holes, and elastic so it fit snuggly over Jeevs' head when he put it on. On the other side of the closet he located Mrs. Moynahan's hot pink cape, the one she wore to the Governor's costume ball and made of the same Mylar yet non-elastic, and fastened that around his neck.

Though he hurried he didn't fumble or drop anything. He was a robot, with unnatural dexterity. Within moments he was costumed and ready to do battle with the disguised Battlebot outside. Sure, it may have the appearance of a street cleaner, but there was something about the way it bore down on those children, slightly faster than a *real* street cleaner so only a robot would notice. Humans tended to miss subtle clues like that, but not robots and certainly not Jeevs. Dealing with the Moynahan children had trained him to notice any little alteration as in, say, a slight wobble in the mower indicating one of the kids had loosened the wheels so they would come off while Jeevs mowed the grass. Or

Stephen L. Antczak

Jeevs might catch one of the children faking illness to get out of having to go to what passed for school these days. The palms might be clammy, the temperature high on a damp forehead, and then Jeevs would reach underneath the pillow to find a washcloth that had soaked in hot water.

"They're just the most devilish little rascals, aren't they?" Mrs. Moynahan would ask rhetorically with glee when Jeevs gave her the weekly behavior report.

Jeevs paused to look himself over in the bedroom mirror, to make sure he was sufficiently disguised. He didn't want anyone to identify him. He knew from having read all those comic books that villains would gladly take their frustrations out on the superhero's loved ones at having been beaten by the superhero. The tight, fire engine red ski mask and hot pink cape definitely had the effect he was looking for, and the bright colors corresponded to what Jeevs remembered the superheroes in the comic books wore.

His inner brain, the one that handled all the logic and mathematical functions just like any other computer, told him he had just about a minute to get to the battlebot/street cleaner before it "swept" over the innocent playing children.

Jeevs bounded out the open window onto the gravel covered back porch roof, ran across it and leaped the chasm between the Moynahan house and the Corman house next door.

"That Corman's a cheese eater," Mr. Moynahan would say about his next door neighbor, who was a widower and at least 150 pounds over weight. Cheese eater was Mr. Moynahan's favorite way of saying someone was a rat, which usually meant someone in the collection business, which Corman was.

"He won't let the children play in his yard," Mrs. Moynahan would say accusingly while the children nodded their lying heads in agreement. Jeevs knew Corman let the kids play in the yard as long as they didn't hang on the branches of his citrus trees, which they always did.

From Corman's house, Jeevs jumped onto the next one, and then the next one, so that he was then behind the street cleaner. He then leaped to the ground and ran as fast as he could, which was close to sixty miles per hour, toward the street cleaner. He saw it as the disguised battlebot, even though he'd seen the street cleaner numerous times before; 165 times actually, his inner brain told him, once a week for the just over 3 years he'd been in the Moynahan's employ.

When he neared the street cleaner, Jeevs jumped as high as he could, hoping to land atop the monstrosity and get at its circuits to disable it. But a panel on the rear of the machine opened, and a nozzle popped out. A jet stream of water blasted Jeevs in mid-air, knocking him into the street, sprawled on his back. He scrambled to his feet. The children were shrieking with laughter, although to Jeevs they were screaming in agony as he imagined the battlebot grinding them into hamburger. Once again he charged, this time deciding the advantage could be gained by yelling out his battle cry.

Captain Asimov

The problem, of course, was that he didn't have one. In the space of the few seconds between the start of his charge and the moment he was to leap to the attack, he reviewed all the slogans and battlecries of Captain Battle, Meathook, Bonesaw and all the other superheroes in the comic books. He couldn't use any of those because of copyright infringement. Besides, he wanted one that would be uniquely his own.

Several occurred to him in the next instant.

"Eat metal!" He didn't like the connotations of that one.

"It's BATTERING time!" Sounded too much like a slogan for a fried fast food place.

"Kawabunga!!" No superhero in his right mind would say *that*.

"Viva Las Vegas!" Hadn't some cartoon already used that?

Finally, as he neared what he perceived as a murderous behemoth, Jeevs came up with one he felt would be both effective and appropriate.

"Yeeeaaaagggggghhhhhhaaaamama!!" he screamed inhumanly in mid-leap. The pitch and tone of his scream pierced the delicate noise sensors of the street cleaner like shards of glass through the diaphonous membrane of a jellyfish. Its balance servos got all out of whack and it stopped. Jeevs landed securely on the thing's wide roof, where he knew the simplistic brain card had to be.

"Warning!" The battlebot (for although Jeevs' sensory apparatus informed him that in every way, shape and form it was definitely a street cleaner robot, his misguided, short-circuited reasoning center still believed it to be a battlebot in disguise) stopped and an alarm started whooping. "Warning! Vandalism of city property is a misdemeanor offense punishable by fines of up to five thousand dollars, community service, house arrest, and up to one year in the county jail! Warning! This is a series eight-five-three double-ay street cleaner by Hunnington Robotics Incorporated, and is owned by the city of—"

Jeevs had found the brain and pulled the card out, effectively mind-wiping the big 'bot. Still, it wasn't technically dead.

Jeevs broke the thin, fragile brain card, snapping it in two with his hands. Now it was.

He ran across the roof and jumped down from the front, expecting to find the mangled remains of the poor children beneath the suspiciously missing forward grinders of the so-called battlebot, for he was sure he'd been too late to save them. Instead he was met by the quizzical expressions of small faces.

Suddenly a hovering newsbot approached.

Jeevs was disappointed. He had hoped to spend a touching moment with the children, to make sure they were okay and tell them not to worry because now they had a masked marvel to look out for them. But like any good super-hero, the last thing he wanted was publicity. He turned to leap back onto the battlebot and make his escape.

"Wait!" a voice ordered. It sounded too much like a human voice to ignore, but it was coming from the newsbot. "I'm a reporter from Make it Great with Channel Eighty-Eight News! I'd like to interview you, please!"

It *was* a human voice, and the newsbot wasn't a newsbot at all, but a remote. Jeevs couldn't ignore a human just like that, unless an order from his owners overrode that human's requests. Jeevs had no such orders, so he stood and waited to be interviewed.

"Don't I know you?" one of the kids, who lived across and down the street a few doors, asked.

"All children know me," Jeevs answered gently, "as their *friend*." Good answer, he thought. He'd never read anything that good in any of little Fermi's comic books, that was for sure.

The news remote hovered up to him, floodlights bathing him aglow even though it was midday and there were no clouds impeding the sun's rays.

"Why did you attack that street cleaner 'bot?" the remote asked.

"That's no street cleaner," Jeevs replied. "It's a battlebot. It was about to rip these innocent children limb from limb."

"No it wasn't. Don't you know street cleaners are programmed to wait for people to move aside before they can continue?"

If Jeevs could have sighed with exasperation he would have.

"Of course. Street cleaner robots have the Three Laws of Robotics embedded in their behavioral chips."

"The three what laws?"

Jeevs explained the three laws, then said, "I could tell that this was a battlebot because it wasn't slowing down quickly enough...if that makes any sense. It was my duty to stop it."

"Your duty? Who *are* you?"

Jeevs paused before answering, although the human reporter would perceive no pause, as it lasted less than a second. Jeevs couldn't give his real name, he knew that, for the same reason he had to disguise himself. He needed a good superhero name, like...Several occurred to him: Mightybot, Robohero, Metal Man, Captain Asimov, Tik To— Wait! Captain Asimov...It sounded good, and certainly rang true to his mission — to uphold the Three Laws and fight crime. That was *it*.

"I'm..." he paused for effect, "*CAPTAIN ASIMOV!*" With his modified speaker voice, for calling the children from play, Jeevs was able to add a nifty echo effect. The entire block reverberated with the "*OV! OV! OV!*"

"What kind of a name is that?" the reporter asked through the remote.

Jeevs' inner clock suddenly told him it was getting close to the time for lunch for the Moynahans.

"I've talked with you long enough," he announced, then turned and leaped onto the dead street cleaner, ran across it, jumped down, and disappeared behind the houses. He de-costumed in the Moynahan's backyard and hid the uniform in the tool shed. Nobody ever went in there, so his secret was safe… for the time being.

It made the six-fifteen news, exclusive to channel 88.

"In the suburbs today a city street sweeper was attacked and immobilized by a costumed robot calling himself Captain Asimov. The robot was apparently under the delusion that the street sweeper was a rogue battlebot, such as the type currently deployed by the United States in Iraq, Lebanon, Afghanistan, Los Angeles, Cuba, El Salvador, Bolivia, and North Vietnam. Our research has led us to believe that this robot has named himself after the prolific science writer of the Twentieth Century, Isaac Asimov, whose Three Laws of Robotics were an idealistic if unrealistic proposition to control the use of robots."

They showed Captain Asimov talking to the kids, included sound when he reverbed his name, flashed a still photo of the writer Asimov, showed some scenes of a real battlebot slaughtering some sheep in a field test, and ended with a picture of the street sweeper carcass being hauled off by a massive wrecker. Jeevs' inner clock had timed the segment at twenty seconds.

"Hey Mom, hey Dad," Fermi said as soon as the news bit was over. "Can we get a robot like Captain Asimov instead of just plain ol' Jeevs? *Pleeeeease?* I bet we'd have a *lot* of fun with *him*! He's a *real* superhero!" With that he commenced pretending to be Captain Asimov, beating up on imaginary battlebots (actually his father's footstool).

"Gaaaawwwwd Fermi, you're stuuuupid," Horace said with an exaggerated roll of his eyes. "Captain Asimov beat up a *street cleaner*! It wasn't any battle*bot*."

"It was *too*," Fermi insisted. "It was in disguise!"

"How would *you* know?" Jesse asked, having decided to take her older brother's side this time. "You've never even *seen* a battlebot."

"I just saw one on *TV*!" Fermi yelled.

"Tell him Dad, please," Horace appealed. "Mom…"

Mr. Moynahan cleared his throat and looked to his wife for guidance, but she only shrugged. As if to say *Tell them, dear, I want to hear, too.* "Well," he started, and paused. He came very close to just saying Go to your room, but didn't. "If the news says it wasn't really a battlebot, then it wasn't. Whoever this Captain Asmovitz is—"

"*Asimov*," Fermi corrected exasperatedly.

"Well, whoever he is, he must have a chip loose somewhere, to think a robot street cleaner could hurt little children."

"There was that street cleaner that thought it was a dog catcher for a while," Mrs. Moynahan pointed out. "Until they switched its chip with that dog catcher that was going around trying to sweep the streets with a net."

Mr. Moynahan nodded as if this somehow proved a point, *his* point, whatever that was.

Jeevs remained unconvinced that the battlebot had really been a hapless street sweeper.

That evening he was relieved from having to read for the kids since the parents weren't going out. Jeevs cleaned the upstairs while everyone sat watching vids downstairs, and finished early. Since he had nothing left to do, and tonight Mrs. Moynahan would handle the putting to bed and tucking in of the children, Jeevs silently climbed atop the roof where he tuned in to the airwaves in search of something for Captain Asimov to do.

Then he heard it, on the police band.

"Unit Twenty-three, Unit Twenty-three, please investigate a possible three fifty-two oh four at Harris Street. Over."

Jeevs wouldn't have been interested had Unit Twenty-three not responded with, "Did you say a three fifty-two oh *four*? Isn't that a *street sweeper* malfunction? Over."

"Affirmative Unit Twenty-three."

"Where the hell are the city maintenance 'bots?"

There was a pause, then the operator said, "Ah, they're all disabled, Unit Twenty-three. Over."

"*All* of them?"

"Affirmative."

"Jesus. Okay. Unit Twenty-three responding."

Jeevs wasted no time. He was costumed and en route to Harris Street within moments.

He tried to stick to the rooftops as much as possible, with pretty good success since he could leap the gap between most of the houses and other buildings on the way. His body was constructed mainly of lightweight but extremely strong plastics reinforced by an alloy skeleton. Robots like Jeevs, self-aware and capable of learning, were designed to last a very long time. As Jeevs got further away from the Moynahan's home, he started to get an unfamiliar and unpleasant feeling...as of being lost and alone. He went through the catalog of emotions he could feel, and found the only thing it could possibly be, since he was familiar with the others.

Longing. It started off as a small tug towards home, the urge to think Harris Street was a long way off, he might not make it back in time to have breakfast ready for everyone when they got up in the morning. Jeevs recognized it then. It was something he'd heard of but had never actually experienced, until now. In robot lore it was called the Collar. The Collar was supposed to keep a robot home, or within a certain boundary, by making it impossible to even *want* to run away. At first the Collar had been simpler, and crueler, giving the robot the equivalent of a painful jolt if it went past a certain point. This early version of the Collar had been inspired by the late 20th century movie *Star Wars*. Then self-awareness in robots became a reality, and a lobby on their behalf got the current, and much more humane, Collar written into the Artificial Intelligence Act of 2010.

The farther away he got the stronger the longing got. By the time he was almost to Harris Street he was near panic, but kept it under control as he imagined a *real* superhero would. In fact, it made him feel even *more* heroic!

But there was something wrong. He was at Harris street, but there was no street cleaner/battlebot. It *had* to here somewhere! What if it had gotten away? What if it had only *appeared* to break down to *lure* the police there. It could be off hacking up poor innocent humans *right now*!

Jeevs ran into the street, looking for clues, tracks, something that might tell him where the battlebot went. He was examining the pavement in the street, not finding any recent tracks whatsoever (and he'd know if they were recent, it was one of his most important skills, useful in keeping track of the Moynahan children) when he heard a noise behind him.

He whirled into a battle stance, feet wide apart and fists on hips, to find himself face to face with a robot cop.

"Freeze, you are under arrest," the robot cop ordered.

Jeevs knew from the comics that there existed an uneasy truce between the law and costumed vigilantes. The best reaction to a confrontation with the police was to turn and run...as long as the danger was taken care of. But the danger *wasn't* taken care of, there was still a battlebot on the loose somewhere in the city and *someone* had to do *something* about it.

Captain Asimov was just that someone.

"State your identification," the robot cop ordered. It continued to advance on Jeevs, who stood his ground. Jeevs almost blurted out his formal I.D., which was Jeevs D (for domestic) 35 (for the year of his creation) X-5000 (series letter and model number) Moynahan (for his owner's name).

He caught himself just in time, and though it took a great force of will to overcome the automatic law-abiding response that was as much a part of his self as the Collar, he said, "You can call me...*Captain Asimov!*" With reverb and everything. It wasn't *exactly* a lie, which was why he didn't suddenly drop to the ground paralyzed as would normally happen to a robot who lied to the police.

"Okay, tin-head," a human male voice said from behind the robot cop. "We'll handle it from here...give it the *human* touch, eh?"

The robot cop stopped advancing, and replied, "Yes sir."

Two human police officers, a male and a female, approached Jeevs.

"Okay Superman," said the woman, "Shut yourself down so we can take you in. Don't give us any trouble and we won't give you any trouble."

Jeevs didn't do anything. He didn't know *what* to do. He hadn't counted on having to deal with the police, and certainly not *human* police. The Collar effect was getting stronger, and that battlebot...who knew *where* it was? Killing and maiming and slaughtering. And here the police were harassing an innocent, well sort of innocent, robot.

There was only one thing to do, and it had to be done *now*, because Jeevs knew if he waited any longer he would *have* to obey the police. It was the only behavior control stronger than the one that caused him to obey his owners.

He suddenly broke into a run.

"Hey!" the cops yelled, and started in pursuit. There was no way they could catch him with their organic legs. Jeevs outdistanced them within moments. He ducked into an alley to stop for a bit. Not to rest, but he needed to tune in to the police band again to find out if they'd sighted the battlebot anywhere.

But...before he could do that, he heard something.

It sounded like wheels, the way a battlebot would sound on pavement... Jeevs stepped into the shadows, as if that would do any good against the battle-bots heat sensors. But it would! Jeevs gave off barely any heat at all because he wasn't truly alive! He'd have the element of surprise.

"This is the police," came the mechanical voice of the robot cop. "I know you're in there, please come out with your hands in the air."

The police, again! It was impossible to get away, and Jeevs couldn't muster the strength to ignore the cop's orders again. In fact, he knew that had the robot cop not come along, he would have wound up back home, for he suddenly realized that was the direction he'd started running in. The constant yearning of the Collar, to be home where he belonged, was becoming too much as well.

He stepped out of the shadows with his hands raised.

"You're going to place me under arrest." It was a statement of fact, and Jeevs didn't know why he said it.

"No," the robot cop replied.

"No? Then what—?"

"You are going to return home."

Home! It was an effort not to immediately start running that way. Right now! Home!

But he stayed, and asked, "What about the battlebot? We have to find it and—"

"There is no battlebot. It was a ruse to trap you. We cannot permit deluded robot vandals running around scaring people. This would be detrimental to human/robot relations."

"I couldn't *hurt* anybody!" Jeevs said. "The three laws of robotics—"

"Science fiction," the robot cop said. "There are three hundred and forty-two laws governing the behavior of robots and the behavior of humans towards robots. You can access the public records concerning all of them, if you wish. Now go, go home, go where you belong."

"Why?" Jeevs asked, even as he started past the robot cop. "Why are you letting me go?"

Captain Asimov

"It is obvious you present no danger to anyone. I am capable of value judgements without penalty, and have decided it would be best for all concerned for you to go home."

Jeevs went. He took only a few steps homeward before turning back around to thank the generous robot cop, but it was already gone.

"Thank you," he said anyway. He went home.

When he got there he noticed immediately that the downstairs lights were on, even though his inner clock told him it was just past four in the morning. This was quite odd, for no one was ever up at four in the morning at the Moynahan residence, except Jeevs who used this time to straighten and dust and clean. That way he had the days free to cook, run errands, do yard work, watch the children when they were home, etc. He had intended to go in through the rear entrance, but paused near a window to listen. Inside he heard voices, and crying.

He recognized the crying right off. It was Jesse, with her subdued, gulping sob that could go on for days if she felt so inclined, like the time her parents first left the kids alone with Jeevs. That had been a week with breaks only for sleep. He also recognized the sniffling trying-not-to-cry of Fermi.

Then he heard Mr. Moynahan.

"Please...please, don't hurt us." His voice quaked with fear. "Take anything, take whatever you want, just—"

"Shut *up!*" This voice was gruff and gravelly, and was followed a moment later by a dull thud, another thud, Mrs. Moynahan's scream, and louder crying. The same gruff voice then said, "All of you, shut up *now!*"

Silence.

Jeevs didn't know what to do. From the tenor of the intruder's voice Jeevs concluded the man had to be desperate, and obviously capable of anything. If the police were called, would they arrive in time to avert disaster? Probably not. Jeevs was going to have to do something and do it soon.

There was a problem. Captain Asimov obeyed the Three Laws. One of those laws would not permit him to harm a human, yet another law would not permit him to allow harm to come to a human through inaction. If the thug inside were only a robot, then Captain Asimov could crash in through the window and knock him all the way to next Tuesday...but not even actorbots could act *that* human. The man in there was as real as, well, the Moynahans.

Nothing Captain Asimov could do, unless he found a way to subdue the criminal without hurting him, but the man sounded dangerous, violent, even suicidal — which goes hand in hand with homicidal. Someone had already been hurt, though, while Captain Asimov stood barely twenty feet away, seperated by a plate of glass and a nylon drape. Inaction.

It suddenly hit Jeevs. Captain Asimov: superhero failure.

At the same time it also hit Jeevs that *he*, Jeevs, had no such animal as the Three Laws of Robotics constraining *him* from action. If he needed to, he would be perfectly within his rights to punch the villain holding his family hostage so hard it would knock his nose all the way around to the other side of his head. "You," he heard the ruffian inside say.

"Yes?" he heard Mrs. Moynahan reply.

There was a pause, then a low, throaty, evil, "Come here."

The time for thought was past. Jeevs removed his Captain Asimov garb and dropped it onto the grass.

He stepped back from the window, took half a second to project his trajectory and envision the room inside. Assuming nothing major had been moved, he knew exactly where everything was. Then he jumped.

As he smashed through the glass he heard Jesse and Fermi scream, Mrs. Moynahan faint, and Horace yell out his name.

"Jeeeevs!"

The thug was as surprised as they were, and couldn't react fast enough. He tried, though. He held a black automatic in his hand, and brought it around to aim at Jeevs, but by then Jeevs was upon him. He knocked the gun out of the man's hand, sending it harmlessly into a cushion on the sofa. With his other hand, Jeevs plowed his palm right into the man's nose, lifting him off the ground with the force of the blow and sending him airborn to slam against the only unadorned wall in the room. The man sunk to the ground, his nose gushing blood onto his shirt, unconscious. Jeevs quickly ran to the aid of Mr. Moynahan, who was groggily coming to. He seemed okay. Jeevs could detect no damage to the skull, at least.

Fermi had regained his spunk as soon as he saw the bad guy was down for the count — down, in fact, for several counts. "Wow Jeevs, you were way better than that old Captain Asimov! Wow!"

Jeevs felt something else, a new emotion he wasn't sure he was supposed to be feeling. It seemed linked to the manner in which the Moynahans were looking at him, sparked by the grateful, adoring expressions on their faces. He wasn't absolutely sure, but if he was right, he knew the word for it. Belonging.

Captain Asimov may have been a friend of the childen, Jeevs thought, but *I'm* family.

I enjoyed writing "Captain Asimov" so much that I decided to write a second story featuring the character. I had an idea that this might make for a good series of short stories. Alas, although I did come up with several more Captain Asimov stories I have not yet gotten around to writing them. Maybe some day.

Captain Asimov
Saves the Day

"**I**'M HOME!" MR. TULANE YELLED when he came in after work. "The house looks *great*, Jeevs! Way to go!"

Jeevs was in the kitchen preparing the evening's dinner of macaroni and cheese with soyburgers. Mrs. Tulane wouldn't be home for several days from a business trip to Japan, and Jeevs had adjusted the proportions accordingly. Without his wife around, Mr. Tulane tended to eat more than usual, and the kids tried to get away with not eating dinner at all. They would leave food on

daydreams undertaken

their plates after declaring themselves full, just to annoy Jeevs, not realizing robots don't get annoyed. Jeevs gave Mr. Tulane less than his usual serving, and the twins more. Everyone got their required daily intake of calories, vitamins, and minerals in spite of themselves.

"A damn fine job you did painting the house, Jeevs old boy. And dinner smells great! I don't know *what* people did before robots came along!"

Jeevs didn't answer that because he didn't know, either. He'd never even considered the implications of a world without robots and Artificial Intelligence. They did everything from operating the mass transit system to balancing city hall's checkbook. Robot cops patrolled the streets twenty-four hours a day. Without them, wouldn't crime run rampant? Robots controlled air traffic overhead. Wouldn't aircraft crash into each other and debris rain down on the heads of unsuspecting civilians?

After dinner, Mr. Tulane settled back in his recliner to watch a baseball game: the Tokyo Zeroes at the Honolulu Waves.

"Jeevs," he said, as 'Take Me Out to the Ball Game' played before the first pitch, "run downtown and pay a little visit to Mother for me. Tell her the kids send hugs, too. I'd go myself, but I'm so busy these days…I just don't have the time."

Robots had to stand in the back third of the bus and hold on, while human passengers sat in comfortable form-fitting seats in the forward two-thirds. One other robot rode the bus with Jeevs, a short Playmate Timmy$^{(TM)}$ that absentmindedly hummed ten second samples of different songs at random. Playmate Timmys had come along fairly recently and were quickly becoming the robots of choice to babysit kids, mainly because they were significantly less expensive than a fully functional robot like Jeevs. Little Timmys were thrown together on the cheap, with stamped out brain chips, small vocabularies, and a limited repertoire of activities.

When the bus arrived at his stop, Jeevs walked the rest of the way to Grandma's house. It was a rough neighborhood, one reason Mr. Tulane didn't like coming for visits in person.

"Hey, Tin Man," a voice said behind Jeevs as he walked along the sidewalk, two blocks from Grandma's. From the tone of the man's voice, Jeevs expected trouble.

He turned to face the man, musclebound and sporting a red bandanna.

"You are misinformed," Jeevs said to the man. "Less than point oh-oh-two percent of my body is made of tin."

The man took two steps towards Jeevs.

"I should warn you," Jeevs said, "that assault on a robot is illegal."

"Yeah," the man replied. "I know." He lunged at Jeevs with an iron railroad spike, intending to knock Jeevs' plasti-steel head clean off. Jeevs ducked, using

Captain Asimov Saves the Day

his inhuman reflexes, and the man's momentum caused him to lose his balance and almost fall.

"Careful," Jeevs said. "You might hurt yourself."

The man growled, lunged at Jeevs again, swinging the railroad spike like a medieval mace. Jeevs stepped back and to the side. The man's momentum propelled him forward this time, and he would have slammed into a concrete light post had Jeevs not reached out, grabbed the man's arm, and yanked him clear.

"I'm gonna rip you apart!" the man howled, then ran at Jeevs full throttle. Jeevs feared the man might really hurt himself this time if Jeevs just ducked out of the way. So instead, he ran backwards just ahead of the man, who swung the railroad spike wildly before him. A block later the man started to run out of breath, so Jeevs slowed down. The railroad spike whipped through the air, and Jeevs dodged to the left, and when it came back the other way, Jeevs dodged to the right. He kept just out of the man's reach, but close enough to prompt another swipe.

Eventually the man got tired, and pooped out. Jeevs snatched the railroad spike from the man's hand.

"Hey," was all the man had the energy to say. He didn't do anything as Jeevs walked away with the spike in hand, looking for a suitable place to get rid of it. Across the street and down the block the opposite way from Grandma's stood a squat recycling receptacle, and since the spike was iron Jeevs decided that was the place. He calculated the distance and angle to the receptacle from where he was, figured in the weight of the spike, then threw it. It arched gracefully through the air, spinning like an expertly thrown football, then *whanged* into the recycling bin perfectly.

Jeevs turned around to continue on his way to Grandma's house, and found himself face-to-face with a robot police officer.

"*Halt!*" the robot cop ordered him. Jeevs had no choice but to stand there, immobile. Automatic responses to certain orders by the authorities were built into him, and this was one of them.

"How can I help you, Officer?" Jeevs asked.

"You just threw an iron railroad spike approximately three hundred meters through the air," the Officer said. "You could have injured somebody. That constitutes reckless endangerment of human life."

"Reckless endangerment? But—"

"There could have been a homeless person sleeping in the recycling bin," the cop said. "That railroad spike would have killed or maimed a human. I'm afraid I'm going to have to write you a citation."

Before Jeevs could react, the robot cop scanned the bar code on Jeevs' forehead. The bar code, invisible except to an ultraviolet scanner, gave the cop Jeevs' entire history and current status. In less than an instant, the robot cop added a citation for reckless endangerment to Jeevs' coded history, so now any other robot able to read the bar code would know about it. That, along with the fine Mr. Tulane would have to pay, would have been enough to make Jeevs sick had he been capable of getting sick.

"Continue on your way," the cop told Jeevs when it finished with him.

Jeevs continued on his way, wondering where the robot cop had been when the man had assaulted him with the railroad spike. Grandma's was an apartment in Shady Glades Villas, a high-security retirement village surrounded by a brick wall topped with electrified barbed-wire, patrolled by human security guards with trained German shepherds, and watched by robot-controlled cameras. Jeevs paused at the gate to let the security robot scan his bar code.

"Entrance denied," the security robot said.

"Entrance *what*?" Jeevs replied. "Please explain."

"You were charged with reckless endangerment. Violators are not allowed inside for thirty days after receiving a citation. You got yours six minutes ago."

"But I was instructed to visit Grandma Tulane!" Jeevs said.

"Mrs. Tulane has been notified of your arrival and her presence at the gate has been requested."

And sure enough, Jeevs saw her: Edna Tulane, 87 years old, hobbling towards him, using her walker to help her negotiate the sidewalk.

"Hello, Grandma!" Jeevs yelled, waving. When she looked up to see him, she didn't notice that one leg of her walker had caught on a piece of concrete jutting up from the sidewalk. When she tried to move it forward, she lost her balance.

Jeevs tried to run inside the gate, figuring that with his speed he'd get there in time to catch her, but the electronic leash built into his neutronic brain stopped him cold, having been activated by the Shady Glades security system. Jeevs could only stand by and watch helplessly as Grandma Tulane soundly thwacked her head on the concrete sidewalk.

As soon as she hit her head, medi-bots came whizzing out from several different directions to help. Jeevs was stunned, unable to do or say anything due to the conflicting orders going through his brain. On one hand, he willed himself to move it, to get in there and help her, while at the same time the security leash told him *no*.

Then he realized that he'd just violated a Law of Robotics by allowing harm to befall a human being, and Grandma Tulane at that! There were Three Laws of Robotics. These boiled down to: 1) Don't hurt humans, 2) Don't allow humans to come to harm by not acting, and 3) Don't follow the orders of a human who wants you to hurt other humans. The Three Laws were the product of one of the great scientific minds of the 20th Century, Isaac Asimov.

"I should be deactivated," Jeevs said. "They should melt me down into two Playmate Timmys!" Jeevs held the Three Laws as sacrosanct, they were the core of his soul if a robot could be said to have a soul. If Jeevs did indeed have a soul, it would be…Captain Asimov!

That's right, due to a glitch in his neutronic brain Jeevs was also the masked robot superhero known as Captain Asimov, defender of the Three Laws of Robotics as he interpreted them!

Never mind that in reality there weren't Three Laws chiseled in imaginary stone governing the behavior of robots. There were actually three hundred and sixty-five, such as this one:

A robot street cleaner will always yield right-of-way to pedestrians under any circumstances. In such cases where a robot street cleaner fails to yield right away, the Owner and/or Operator of said street cleaner may be charged with Failure to yield right-of-way to a pedestrian, which is a Misdemeanor under state law, and will result in a fine to be determined by a Judge.

Or this one:

Robot police officers may use non-lethal means to immobilize and disarm a fugitive if and only if positive identification of said fugitive is obtained, or the suspect attempts to flee, or produces a weapon (upon which the intent to harm civilians or vandalize the robot is assumed). The means of restraint will minimize the possibility of injury to the restrainee.

The medi-bots loaded the limp frame of Grandma Tulane into a hovercraft ambulance. Once the back door slammed shut, the sirens wailed and lights flashed as it rose into the air. They'd be taking her to the Shady Glades Care Center, the hospital funded by the Shady Glades franchise, which admitted only residents of their various retirement communities.

Jeevs decided to follow the ambulance, to be at the hospital for Grandma Tulane in case she needed anything. Once the emergency was past, Jeevs fully expected that Mr. Tulane would decide to have his brain chip wiped clean.

Consulting his hardwired map of the city, Jeevs traced out the best route to the hospital, and started jogging. He determined he could get there an hour earlier that way than by taking the bus. As he ran his neutronic brain replayed all the old robot stories he'd ever read to the eldest son of his owner, especially those written by Isaac Asimov. Jeevs sought guidance in these stories. Nothing quite pertained to his current predicament.

Jeevs took the surface streets, while hundreds of meters overhead most of the traffic zoomed along on the elevated skyways. Without warning a huge piece of plastiform guard rail from the skyway came crashing to Earth. The concussion of its impact lifted Jeevs off his feet and threw him into the air.

Calculating trajectory, speed, and height, Jeevs was able to twist around before hitting the ground to land safely on his feet. Using his telescopic vision, he looked up to see what had happened on the skyway. Several vehicles hung precariously over the edge of the skyway where the guardrail had ripped away. And one of those vehicles was…the ambulance from Shady Glades Villas! Jeevs

Stephen L. Antczak

immediately tuned to one of the disaster channels of the airwaves to find out what had happened.

"An exciting, desperate situation on the ferry," someone was saying, "as the gunman makes out his list of demands..."

Wrong emergency. He tried another channel.

"Apparently the ambulance lost power as it hovered over traffic on the Sonny Bono Skyway," a voice was saying. "Word is there are no fatalities...*yet*. Stay tuned, though, because that may change at any second as the drama unfolds!"

Jeevs knew *this* was a job for *Captain Asimov*!

He donned the trademark Captain Asimov duds. A catwalk dangled thirty yards or so above him, bridging the gap between two of the huge pylons that held up the skyway. Using his extendo-legs, Captain Asimov telescoped up to within about ten yards of the catwalk. Using his extendo-arms, he was able to grab it. He retracted his legs, and then his arms to pull him up.

From the catwalk, Captain Asimov noticed rungs went up each of the pylons. He scrambled up the rungs at what would have been an astonishing rate for a human. In a few seconds he found himself just below the landing for a stairwell that actually entered the pylon and undoubtably emerged in one of the work booths alongside the skyway. The door was locked. Ignoring the warnings that trespassers would be prosecuted, Captain Asimov ripped the door from its hinges, carefully set it aside, and went in. Security cameras mounted in the corners recorded his every move, but he wasn't worried. It wouldn't be the first time Captain Asimov violated minor ordinances during the course of one of his heroic feats.

Up the stairs, and into the booth. That door was also locked, but he kicked it open, bursting onto the scene dramatically.

"It's him!" the cry went up. "It's that Captain Asmovitz guy!" someone else shouted.

News drones, already hovering over the scene of the wreck, turned to digitize his image and broadcast it *live* to their respective receivers. Captain Asimov ignored them, except for a brief salute to the viewers, most of whom had supported his exploits through a letter campaign to the Mayor. His intent had been to rush right over to the ambulance and pull it up onto the skyway, but now he saw it wouldn't be that simple. The ambulance hung where it was only by virtue of the fact that a school bus, crowded with children, supported it with the twisted metal of its bumper. The kids were crying, and the driver of the bus was slumped over the steering wheel, unconscious. Captain Asimov immediately saw a major dilemma: If he tried to pull the ambulance up, the bus would fall, and vice versa. He didn't know what to do. On the one hand he was driven to save Grandma Tulane because...she was Grandma Tulane. On the other hand that was a busload of *children* who would plunge to their deaths if he saved Grandma Tulane.

Captain Asimov Saves the Day

"Don't just stand there," someone said, "*do* something!"

Yes, indeed, *do something*. But what? A metallic moan assaulted Captain Asimov's ears, and the weight of the ambulance shifted. The entire assembly of ambulance and bus tilted over the edge of the skyway at an even steeper angle. The kids screamed, but not a sound came from within the ambulance.

Maybe…Was Grandma Tulane already *dead*? It would make the situation less of a dilemma if he didn't have to worry about the ambulance. He focused on listening to any sounds coming from within the ambulance, and still didn't hear anything. He was about to make his decision to forget about the ambulance and save the busload of children, when suddenly he *did* hear something coming from within: a wheezing sound, perhaps the sound of an old woman strapped into a gurney, trying to free herself!

Captain Asimov saw no choice: He would have to try to save *both* the ambulance and the school bus.

First, he positioned himself behind the vehicles, then suctioned his feet to the surface of the skyway. This was actually a standard feature of the Jeevs model domestic servant robots, like his extendo-arms and legs. Using those extendo-arms, he reached out and grabbed the bumper of each vehicle. Then, very slowly, he started to retract his arms, with the idea that he could pull both the ambulance and the bus back onto the skyway in this manner without any sudden jolts to cause a sudden shift in weight.

"What's he doing?" somebody behind him asked.

"Pulling 'em *both* up!" someone answered. A cheer went up, and one of the newsbot drones zipped around in front of Captain Asimov and hovered there.

"Is it true?" a voice asked him from the newsbot. Captain Asimov recognized the voice as that of intrepid ace reporter Gordon Ferguson, the newsman who first broke the Captain Asimov story two years earlier….

"Is what true?" Captain Asimov replied.

"Are you going to pull *both* of these vehicles up?"

"That's right."

A pause, and then Ferguson's voice came back, saying, "Umm, C.A., I don't know about that. I just had our computer do some quick calculations and it told me you have less than a one percent chance of success."

"I know."

"There's a twenty-five percent chance you'll be ripped in two."

"I know."

"You'd have much better odds if you just tried to save the school bus," Ferguson told him. "Ninety-nine percent chance of success."

"I *know*," Captain Asimov replied, and this time he sounded annoyed, which wasn't easy for a robot.

When Captain Asimov had managed to pull the bus up a few more meters, the children tried to make it to the back door, which, if they could get it open, would let them jump out and onto the safety of the skyway. Their sudden movements caused the bus to shift, and because he was holding onto it with only one hand, Captain Asimov could not keep it from sliding further back. The ambulance also started to slide, just as *its* back door opened and Grandma Tulane appeared, trying desperately to scramble out. Captain Asimov held fast to both vehicles, even as their continued slippage forced him to extend his arms out to their limit. His feet stayed suctioned to the skyway, but his extendo-legs began to stretch until *they* reached their limit, too! His torso now actually hung over the side of the skyway, and the ambulance and school bus dangled precariously in mid-air. The children in the bus were all piled on top of one another against the windshield, while Grandma Tulane clung for dear life to the rear door of the ambulance.

The news drone buzzed around Captain Asimov.

"He is *determined* to save *everyone*!" Ferguson was saying, broadcasting live. "Captain Asimov just *won't* give up!"

Captain Asimov felt his feet losing suction. The combined weight of the ambulance and school bus was too much. If he didn't do something *now*, Grandma Tulane and the school kids were all as good as dead, and Captain Asimov would go down with them. There was only *one* thing he *could* do: let either the bus or the ambulance fall, assuredly killing all on board, and pull the other to safety.

"Save the children," Grandma Tulane gasped at Captain Asimov. "Just… save…the children."

What was she saying? Robots were not usually capable of processing subtext and unspoken implications. Were he human, Captain Asimov would have seen it in her eyes: Determined resignation. But even though Captain Asimov was not human, Grandma Tulane's words sounded like a direct order — which he had to obey — to save the children, and there was only way to do that.

His left foot came loose from the skyway surface and his leg automatically snapped back to its normal length.

No more time!

He let go of the ambulance. A collective gasp rose from the spectators above. Jeevs imagined the gasp being echoed by residents all over the city as they watched his actions live on the evening news.…

Even as he watched the ambulance fall, with Grandma Tulane still clinging to that back door, he pulled the school bus back up to the road by retracting his right leg. He got it halfway back up, but then couldn't get it any more. The school bus was *just* too heavy for him to haul all the way back up with one leg, and he couldn't extend his other leg back to the road. When it had snapped back to its normal length, it lost extendo-capability.

Stuck. Again.

The ambulance crashed into the ground below.

Captain Asimov Saves the Day

Captain Asimov calculated just how much the weight of the bus exceeded the amount of force he could exert to retrieve it. It was a surprisingly small amount: Sixty pounds. He determined that with his free hand, he could remove something from the bus and let it fall, lightening the load enough for him to save the children. Using his telescopic vision, he scanned the bus for something that weighed sixty or more pounds. Maybe a seat could be pulled out or a wheel removed. It would have to be done quickly, because he could feel the suction on his other foot starting to give. As he scanned the interior, he checked the kids to make sure none were hurt, and his gaze passed over one who looked oddly familiar. A closer inspection revealed it was a Playmate Timmy. Checking his inner records of all robot makes and models in current use, Captain Asimov found that Playmate Timmy weighed *sixty-four pounds.*

With his free hand, Captain Asimov opened the door to the school bus, careful not to jostle it and cause some kid to tumble out and fall to his death like Grandma Tulane. He reached inside and grabbed the Playmate Timmy by a leg and started to drag him towards the door. When the kids realized what he was doing, they screamed.

"Playmate Timmy! Noooo!!"

Several of the children grabbed Playmate Timmy and tried to keep him from being pulled out. There was no way Captain Asimov could pull Playmate Timmy from the bus without taking a few kids along with him. Of course that would lighten the load by that much more and make it that much easier to save the remaining ones. Grandma Tulane's death weighed so heavily on Captain Asimov's neutronic mind that it threatened to overload and short it out completely. If he ended up sacrificing some of the children, it might blow before he could even bring the bus back up to the skyway. Then they'd all die, and that'd make it even *worse.*

Somehow, in the remaining few seconds before his foot came unsuctioned from the skyway surface, Captain Asimov knew he'd have to figure out a way to save *all* the children. In a few nanoseconds he reviewed the various functions of his hands and fingers, and found one, only one, he'd have time to try. If it didn't work...there wouldn't be time to try anything else, and he'd plummet to his doom along with the children. The forefingers of his hands also had the capability to spray WD40 oil. He sprayed the stuff all over the Playmate Timmy, and the kids holding onto him began to lose their grip on it. Playmate Timmy slipped out of their little hands and tumbled out the door of the bus.

Captain Asimov heard another collective gasp from the spectators on the skyway. They all thought a child had fallen out of the school bus. Playmate Timmy's body tumbled through the air like a rag doll until it slammed into the catwalk with a echoing *thwang!* The body remained on the catwalk, but Playmate Timmy was decapitated by the blow, and his head rolled off it and fell the rest of the way to the ground, landing right near the ambulance wreckage.

Captain Asimov started retracting his leg and arm, hauling the school bus up, getting it closer to safety, while he pulled his other hand out of the bus. He tried to shut the door, but one of the other kids, a *real* child, a *human* child, slipped down and got wedged in between the door and door frame.

"Ow!" the kid, a skinny little blond boy, yelled as the door closed on his head, the rest of his body hanging outside the bus, arms and legs flailing away. "Mommy! Mommy, help me!"

Because the kid was all greased up with WD40, he started to slide through the gap. Captain Asimov retracted his leg as fast he could, hoping to get the bus back onto the skyway before the little boy got squeezed out like a seed from a grape. The more the boy flailed his arms and legs, the more he increased his chances of coming loose and falling to his death.

"Come on, Captain A!" someone yelled, and a cheer went up.

"Hooray for Captain A! Hooray for Captain A! Hooray for Captain A!"

Inside Captain Asimov's mixed-up head, his neutronic brain chip still processed the information of the what had just happened, the reality of what had just occurred. Grandma Tulane had fallen to her death because he'd *let her go. Impossible!* the neutronic brain wanted to tell Captain Asimov, but the logic centers said, *We saw it and recorded it with our own two eyes. Would you like it played back for you?*

The neutronic brain replied, *Uh, no thanks.*

Captain Asimov's leg completely retracted, and he managed to bring the school bus, and the children, to safety just as the kid stuck in the door popped out and fell a couple feet to the pavement. He was okay. All the kids were okay. The crowd reacted with silence, then a belated cheer went up.

"He did it!"

Sirens in the background, as rescue and police vehicles raced to the scene, moments too late, both on the skyway and down below, although down there it would only be a matter of collecting the body of Grandma Tulane....

Despite the elation of those around him, Captain Asimov considered his performance a failure. He had violated the Three Laws, had allowed a human to come to harm, if not through inaction, through *insufficient* action. As the news drones hovered around him, spotlights nearly overloading his optical circuits, Captain Asimov decided an interview was not appropriate. Without one single comment, he leaped from the skyway, over the side, unnoticed by the crowd of people who helped the crying children from the school bus, although his actions were being recorded, and would later be broadcast on dozens of channels.

As he fell, Captain Asimov considered letting himself smash into the ground below, like Playmate Timmy. It would be a fitting end to a disastrous outing as a supposed superhero. *Superhero.* In all the comic books Jeevs had ever read aloud to the youngest child of his previous owner, not once did any of them

Captain Asimov Saves the Day

fail, ever. Captain Battle vanquished his foe in every fight. Lady Luck always saved the day, and seemed to meet a handsome hunk, in every adventure. Micro, despite his diminutive size, somehow always managed to avert disaster, all the while making wisecracks and telling bad knock-knock jokes.

Not only did Captain Asimov never meet any hunks, not only did he not have any original joke material, but here he'd even failed to save the day, which was the whole stupid *point* of being a superhero in the *first* place.

"They should recycle me into a recycling bin," he said as he fell. Wouldn't that be the ultimate irony. At least then he'd do *some* good.

But at the last instant before it would've been too late, Captain Asimov's self-preservation "instincts" kicked in. All robots had survival in their most basic programming. A robot was incapable of committing suicide.

Captain Asimov extended his arms, with the intent of grabbing the catwalk and swinging off it, having already calculated the angle and momentum necessary to throw him to a nearby rooftop. Unfortunately, due to the incredible stress they'd suffered holding onto the ambulance and school bus, his arms failed to retract when he let go of the catwalk. The unexpected redistribution of his weight caused Captain Asimov to angle away from the targeted rooftop, extended arms flailing uselessly in the air.

"After having failed to save a human life today," he could imagine the news accounts saying, "Captain Asimov failed to save his own worthless self. But the *real* news of the day is Archbishop Anthony's response to allegations of inappropriate conduct with a Playmate Timmy robot..."

Captain Asimov managed to twist around in midair, in such a way that he might minimize the damage of impact. He came down in an alley between the target building and a warehouse. He saw his shadow projected onto the warehouse wall, a kinetic Rorschach blotch wiggling across its surface, and then a brief glimpse of a pile of rusted out fifty-five gallon metal drums right before he hit.

And that, he assumed, was that.

End of story. Goodbye Captain Asimov, failed super-hero. Goodbye Jeevs, faithful servant to his owner. Goodbye.

Not quite.

No, he didn't perish.

He didn't die and go to robot heaven, nor robot hell.

He did achieve the robot equivalent of unconsciousness, but his *self* (or soul, if you believe a robot can have a soul) didn't transmigrate. His emergency back-up kicked in, saving everything that made Jeevs *Jeevs* (and by default, Captain Asimov). When he awoke he found himself in a robot repair shop. Hanging from racks along one wall was a whole row of Playmate Timmy robots.

"*Junk*," a gravelly voice said from behind Jeevs. "Nothin' but *junk*, those damn things."

Jeevs could not turn his head enough to see who the voice belonged to. A shadow played across the floor, and he heard the sound of boots scraping greasy concrete as the person walked around behind him. A moment later, a squat, thick-limbed, grease-stained woman came into Jeevs' field of vision. She had an unlit cigar protruding from the left corner of her mouth, and an eye-patch over her right eye.

"You, on the other hand, are a piece of *work*," she said to Jeevs, with a grin. Jeevs wanted to say something, to ask where he was, who *she* was...but he couldn't speak.

"Whatsamatter?" she asked him. "Cat got yer tongue?" She laughed at her own joke, loudly, and her laughter reminded Jeevs of a combination of barnyard noises he used to make for the children of his previous owner when he read stories for them. Tarzan of the bread-belt farm. Thoughts of his previous owner reminded him of his *current* owner. A sudden panic came over Jeevs.

Mr. Tulane!

Grandma Tulane!

"Uh oh," the woman said. She reached around behind Jeevs' head, touched the emergency off/on switch, and blackness enveloped him....

"You must destroy me," Jeevs told the woman when next he awoke. "I violated the Three Laws of Robotics when I swore to uphold them! I am unfit to continue in this existence. Destroy me! Or at the very least turn me over to the authorities and let *them* destroy me!"

The woman grinned and shook her head.

"The three what? Say what? Honey, I *ain't* gonna to let a prize like you go *that* easily. I found ya, I fixed ya, an' I'm keepin' ya...at least for a little while anyway."

I'm keepin' ya... Those three words triggered a growing desire to go back to the Tulane house.

The woman continued babbling on about something or other, but Jeevs didn't hear it. The urge to go home grew until he felt consumed by it, engulfed by it. It became the core of his being.

He needed to get home, *now*! It didn't help that Jeevs knew he was programmed to panic like that when he was away from home for an unauthorized extended period of time.

On the other hand, he really didn't want to go home because his secret was surely blown by now. Any idiot, even any *human* idiot, would be able to figure out who Captain Asimov was. To face Mr. Tulane after causing his mother's death....

"Uh oh," the woman with the eye-patch said, noticing Jeevs' face was flickering at high speed through his entire range of expressions. "You look like

Captain Asimov Saves the Day

you're havin' some internal strife. You already done enough damage to that delicate brain chip of yours, hero. No sense fussin' over somethin' that already happened. *Dream sequence.*"

Those last two words the woman said forcefully, and suddenly Jeevs felt his thoughts dissipate, and the robot repair shop with the Playmate Timmy bodies hanging along the wall wavered like a mirage and then disappeared. He did not fade to black this time. Jeevs found himself in a whirlwind of domestic activity, washing dishes, vacuuming a carpet, waxing the kitchen floor, giving a dog a bath, pressing a pair of pants, adding a pinch of salt to a stew, and an almost dizzying variety of other chores. For a robot like Jeevs, this was the equivalent of heavenly bliss.

Subjectively, it was a timeless experience, but in reality it lasted only a few hours, and then Jeevs found himself back in the repair shop. This time, however, he could turn his head.

He ran an internal diagnostic, opened and closed his hands and extended his arms about a meter. Everything seemed hunky-dory. He felt good as new.

"Hope you don't mind," the woman's voice said behind him, and Jeevs turned just in time to see her emerge from behind something that looked like a robot torture chamber with a Playmate Timmy strapped in it. "I went in and VR'd your experiences to find out what the problem was. Figured out what was weirdin' you out so bad and made a few, um, improvements."

"Improvements?" Jeevs asked.

She nodded, grinning.

"Who are you?"

"Name's Gidge," the woman said.

"What improvements?"

"You don't feel the need to rush home anymore, do you?"

Now that she mentioned it....

"No."

"I removed all your inhibitors."

"Why?" Jeevs asked.

"Because, my artificial friend, I need me an assistant. I also took care of your alter ego for you."

"I don't understand," Jeevs said.

Gidge sighed, sounding exasperated.

"Captain Asimov is *history*," she said. "Gone, wiped, *phht*, outta there."

"What did you do?"

"Only what you wanted me to," Gidge told him. "Captain Asimov violated them Three Laws, right?"

"Yes..."

"I got rid of him for ya."

"But I *am* Captain Asimov."

"No, you ain't. Trust me. Not anymore. I went in there," Gidge said, pointing at Jeevs' plastisteel head, "and made a few, um, adjustments. Besides, I found out how it all started. You used to read superhero comics to some little kid and those Isaac Asimov robot stories to another kid…There was an accident and your chip got all scrambled up into a robot superhero omelet."

"It did?"

"Yep, and I unscrambled it. Now yer back to normal."

Jeevs didn't notice anything different about himself, but then, he realized, he probably *wouldn't*. If his very *self* were tampered with, he'd have no way of diagnosing it internally. And this woman Gidge was a robot mechanic, and human at that, so Jeevs had no choice but to believe her. Why would she lie to him? Her purpose in life was to *repair* robots. He tried to imagine the implication of what she was telling him. If Captain Asimov had truly been wiped from his neutronic brain, and he was just plain ol' Jeevs again, then did that also mean the Three Laws of Robotics no longer held sway over him?

"I don't want you thinkin' I did this for charity, now," Gidge told him. "You gotta work it off. I need me an assistant. I worked up a contract you can look over when you feel up to it."

Jeevs considered this, then said, "I am someone else's property—"

"Up until I put you back together, Tin Man," Gidge interrupted him, "you were nothin' but a heap of *junk*. Junk don't belong to nobody, got it? Besides, it's three days since you crash-landed in my alley and you ain't been claimed by no one, so…"

So the law, the real law, made him a free agent now, owned by no one at all. *A free agent.* Jeevs knew he wasn't the first freed robot in history. In fact, there were hundreds of them just in the city, employed *by* the city since the city didn't have to foot the bill for their maintenance, unlike the ones it owned outright.

Gidge had a contract for him, so she said. He'd be employed. Since he was programmed to actually *want* work to do, Jeevs looked over the contract — a standard three year apprenticeship — and signed it.

She started him off cleaning up around the workshop, making coffee and then lunch, cleaning robot parts, removing the heads from the Playmate Timmys so she could tinker with their inferior brains, and various other duties. Gidge listened to the radio while she worked, generally music but sometimes news. While Jeevs twisted the head off a Playmate Timmy the latest hit single, all of seventeen minutes on the charts, got interrupted by a special report:

"It appears that a robot crane has gone berserk at the Yakamori Tower construction site downtown."

Jeevs stopped work to listen to the report.

"It's swinging a load of plastisteel girders back and forth, threatening to knock robot workers off the building while below traffic is gridlocked. If one of those robot

Captain Asimov Saves the Day

workers falls, someone down on the street could be killed. I don't even want to think about how many will die if one of those girders falls!"

A robot endangering the lives of humans!

"Hold on...We have a caller on the line, a woman calling from her car. Yes, Ma'am, you're on the air."

"Somethin' wrong?" Gidge asked him.

"Those people..."

"Yeah, what about 'em?"

"I'm stuck in traffic on Tenth Street. Is that near the construction? Am I in danger?"

"They might die."

"I'm checking our map of downtown, pinpointing your car using your phone..."

"Yeah."

"Because of a robot..."

"Yes! You are right smack under that crane!"

"Yeah, because of a robot. What about it?"

"That means you could die at anytime, crushed by the body of a falling robot worker or, even more spectacularly, by one of those ten-ton girders!"

"Is...Captain Asimov truly...*gone?*" Jeevs asked Gidge.

"Oh no! I...I have to get out of here, but I'm stuck in traffic! What am I supposed to do? I haven't even eaten lunch yet!"

Gidge brought her fist up, resting her chin on it, and looked at Jeevs.

"You feel the urge to run out and save those people?"

"Just calm down, Ma'am."

Jeevs thought about it for one tenth of a second, then nodded.

"I'll tell you what. Just sit tight and we'll have Zippy Pizza, one of our sponsors, deliver you a personal lunch-for-one pizza right to your car! On us!"

Gidge sighed.

"Just stay on the phone and tell us how you feel, all right? Give us the full range of your emotions as you feel them, okay?"

"Guess I didn't do a very good job, then."

"Oh, um, okay, I guess..."

"Come on and we'll take care of it *now*. Don't want ya interruptin' work every damn time somethin' comes on the radio like that."

"Now, what toppings do you like on your pizza?"

Gidge turned the radio off, then looked for the tools she'd need to work on Jeevs again.

"Gidge," Jeevs said. "I need to go."

She stopped what she was doing, but didn't turn around.

"You sure? Captain Asimov might not be able to save *everyone*, you know. Might mess you up again."

"I realize that," Jeevs said, "but I know I can save *some* of those people. And I'll come back, don't worry."

Stephen L. Antczak

"Okay," Gidge said. She turned around, grinning devilishly, and held out Captain Asimov's mask and cape. "Here."

Jeevs took them, put them on, and was instantly transformed.

"I need a good exit line," he told Gidge.

"Don't look at me," she replied.

"Later, gator!" Captain Asimov yelled. "No. How about…Live long and prosper!"

Gidge shook her head.

"I'll be back!" In an Austrian accent, no less.

Gidge continued shaking her head.

"I'm outta here!"

"Whatever," Gidge said, "just *go!*"

Captain Asimov turned to run out into the night, or the late afternoon at least, but paused first and looked at Gidge.

"You didn't even try to wipe Captain Asimov from my memory," he said.

Gidge shrugged.

"Why?"

"What can I say?"

She opened the door to her office, and there on the wall behind her desk hung a poster of Captain Asimov, caught in mid-leap from an overpass onto the roof of a speeding semi-tractor trailer. The poster had to be a least a year old, one of the first offerings from the unofficial Captain Asimov Fan Club.

"Go save the day," Gidge said.

And he did.

I've always loved reading so-called 'first contact' stories, and wondered once what could make an alien race decide to end all contact with humanity, once and for all. Would it be William Shatner's rendition of "Lucy in the Sky with Diamonds?" I figured it would be something that we would never know, nor understand.

So what about using this idea in a story? I definitely wanted to write my 'last contact' story, but I felt like it needed a good twist to really make it work. And then, while daydreaming, it hit me. Maybe it'll hit you, too, when you read it.

I sold this story to the Canadian magazine Horizons SF, *but it was never published. I never found out if the magazine went under or what. Such are the vagaries of the small press publishing world, alas.*

Last Contact

IN HER DREAMS, LYSA HEARD songs like ghost voices whispering through space and time. They haunted her sleep, haunted every moment of thought, lingered beyond thought. She didn't know if it came from her, from within, or was it even possible for a *human* mind to dream alien sounds? Surely there was an analogy somewhere on Earth for what echoed in her mind. Or was she experiencing the phantoms of an alien opera?

Humans called them the Uglies.

daydreams undertaken

"Conservation of aesthetics," Lysa's teacher had explained. "They think we're ugly, we think they're ugly."

Uglies was the unofficial human name for them. Officially, scientifically, they were *Gens Alienus Primus*, or First Alien Race; assuming there were others out there.

The Uglies had not yet said if they knew of another race or not. Every potential new Xenodiplomat hoped to be the one the Uglies told. This information was the Holy Grail of Xenodiplomacy.

Lysa had daydreamed a lot while sitting alone on the front porch of her parent's cottage on Hope, a recently settled world nearly a thousand light years away from Earth. Hope was similar to Earth, Lysa learned from her parents, who'd emigrated in deep hibernation. The color of the sky was a little *off*, the air tasted funny, and the higher gravity made everyone tired a little faster, but those were minor differences to get used to when compared to what other worlds had to offer.

Lysa was one of the first hundred humans born on Hope. As a young girl she would envision a thousand futures for herself: star pilot, pioneer, planetoid miner, explorer…Two visions had lasted, night after night, year after year. The two persistent visions led down separate paths; visiting Earth, or becoming a Xenodiplomat. Finally, she chose to follow the path of one star, out of the hundreds she had seen with the naked eye of youth from that porch. She followed it to another world even further away from Earth than was Hope, and sacrificed the dream of ever seeing her parents' home world.

There *had* been another dream, one acquired during her developing womanhood, a dream with a name: Daen, a boy she grew up with, her first sexual experience, whom she decided to spend her life with…if it was to be spent with anyone *human*. He had encouraged her to pursue her goals to become an XD. It was such a longshot, after all, a farfetched fantasy. Daen had been taken by surprise when Lysa actually applied, but he supported her. When she was accepted into the program, he was there to see her off. Whenever she even so much as thought about him she developed a knot in her stomach, because she knew her relationship with him was in conflict with her dream of becoming a Xenodiplomat.

"I'll wait for you," he told her, his face nuzzled up to hers. "I'll be here."

Until the Point of No Return, he'd meant; that point in the Transformation where the body could no longer withstand the shock of being changed *back*. After the Point of No Return she'd die if they tried to make her human again.

"What are they doing to you?" Daen had asked once, during an expensive hyper-space call. Daen was a holo sitting in her room, real but not real, a dream but also a nightmare reminding her of what she'd left behind. She wanted him to go away, she wished he would never leave.

Last Contact

At that stage in the Transformation she still looked like the Lysa he loved. She wasn't. Only a few days later she would lose all her hair, and her skin would secrete a slick coating of slime with a strong odor that reminded her of the fish farms on Hope.

"Inside I'm different," she said. "Chemically, genetically. Remember my favorite color?"

"Purple."

"Now I can't even *see* purple. I sort of remember it. Even that's fading."

"What else?"

"I can't taste anything now, although I'm told it'll come back, but different. I'll have to eat food that would probably make me sick even now. You couldn't eat it at all."

"Why not?"

"It would kill you."

"Is all this really necessary?" Daen asked. He was worried, Lysa could tell, that she might not *be* Lysa anymore, when it was over. He could lose her to another man and he'd be all right. But this was different. She had hoped that once the Transformation began she would lose the knot in her stomach. It was still there.

Lysa sighed. Later, she might not care, might not remember, but right now she *did* care, and she remembered: his arms around her that first time on the porch, the first kiss not long after, all the times he gently touched her face.

"Daen...we couldn't be in contact with the Uglies if we didn't change ourselves. It's the only way they'll talk to us. You knew that before."

"I wish you hadn't gone," Daen said suddenly, then, "Will you come back to me? Please?" Lysa didn't know how to react.

All along she had been afraid that if he only asked, *please don't go,* she would have stayed with him. If he had asked *before....*

"Come back. Please. I want you, I *need* you."

"Daen, I can't. I'm not the same anymore."

"You don't love me anymore?"

She closed her eyes. Did she love him? Stupid question, because she did, it burned deeper inside her than anything else in her life. Except her dreams.

"You haven't passed the Point of No Return," he said. "You could change back, come home. We can still have a life together."

"No. This is the path I chose, the path *we* chose. I'll always love you. I don't have to be there on Hope for that."

"No, but you have to be here to touch."

Daen's eyes glistened with tears, and her own eyes began to ache. She could no longer actually cry. All she did was hurt.

"Daen, I have to go."

He wiped his eyes, forced a smile.

Stephen L. Antczak

"Sorry," he said. "I hope it goes okay. Really. You wouldn't be the woman I love if you just dropped everything to run back."

After the call, she sat alone in her dorm room, and tried to imagine what it had been like to cry a river of tears into Daen's shoulder, to just cry, and cry, and cry. He would run his fingers through her hair to soothe her, whisper in her ear.

"It's all right. I'm here. It's all right."

"What would you ask an Ugly," Lysa's instructor had quizzed, "if you had only one question?"

She didn't need to think about it.

"Are there other sentient alien races in the galaxy, besides Uglies and humans?" Lysa answered.

The instructor took notes. Was she doing well? Had she already failed? Her body had withstood the system shock of Transformation fairly well, so far. Her sickness had not been nearly as bad as some others. Rumor had it that some *never* recovered.

Embassy was not open for colonization, nor tourism. If you were on Embassy, you were there for two reasons: to talk to an alien, or provide support for those who did. Embassy wasn't a dead world, nor was it quite alive. It had a faint atmosphere, not breathable by humans and Uglies. There was almost no water, and no native life beyond a few species of microbes.

Most of the surface area was desolate, the ground jagged and stark. There were a few hundred plateaus of level ground, ranging in size from a couple acres to the one settled by humans and Uglies, an elongated dumbbell of about ten thousand square kilometers.

The Uglies had a village, or hive, or colony, on the opposite side lengthwise from the human compound. No human ever visited it. It consisted of a semi-circle of low structures, arranged around their space port. The bulk of their settlement was underground.

The Uglies and the humans met in the Common, a massive structure covering the entire width of the plateau at its narrowest point, midway between the two habitats, where all the actual diplomatic relations happened. The XDs travelled to the Common via underground monorail. Contact was always one-on-one, and each XD had a permanent relationship with his or her Ugly, and never met the others.

They performed no ritual, went through no elaborate maze of protocol. A human and Ugly just got together and started talking, unfettered by time limits. The Uglies possessed an amazing capacity for conversation, could go for hours, even days, until the XD collapsed from exhaustion. The humans had implants that recorded what they saw and heard, so they didn't have to remember hard information. Feelings, emotions, things no computer would be able to express, these an XD concentrated on trying to understand.

From these sessions came recordings of alien sounds, and holos of Uglies. The general public saw only "artist's renderings," which made the Uglies look like duckbilled pygmies on stilts...cartoons no stranger than the drawings of UFO crews that had peppered the media during the late 20th century on Earth. Potential XDs were shown the holos and listened to the recordings. The cartoons Lysa had seen before did not prepare her for the effect of the holos, the shock of seeing something truly *alien*.

She tried to describe them to Daen, during another expensive call, to explain the emotions that overcame her. She struggled for the words.

"How strange can they be?" Daen asked.

"They're *not* strange," Lysa told him. "I don't know...*other* may be a better word. I looked at the holo, and thought here was some *other* I would never be able to comprehend, never be able to communicate with, never be able to understand. But it looked totally and completely natural for what it was. I heard a recording of them. Or one. I couldn't tell, and I wanted to wrap myself up in a womb and not have to be born. At the same time, I felt something in those *other* sounds pull me outward from the inside."

"That doesn't mean all of you feel that, right?" Daen asked.

"No," Lysa said. "Three committed suicide. Six have been sent home for psychiatric treatment."

"Are *you* okay?" Daen sounded more than concerned. Frightened. She heard it in his voice.

"I'm fine," she assured him. She tried to describe the Uglies to him. As carefully as she chose her words, they came out looking like duckbilled pygmies on stilts.

Daen laughed.

Lysa hung up on him that time. She didn't know why. She certainly didn't feel offended on the Uglies' behalf.

The road to the Point of No Return in the long process of Transformation took two Earth years. The exposure, piece by piece, to the recordings and the holos, increased while Lysa's physiology gradually changed. She had started as one of thirty-six, and by the Point of No Return only four remained. If four made it all the way, it would be the highest number of "graduates" from one class in Embassy history.

Before all that, though, they had one final hurdle: a personal interview with the Director of Embassy, the Senior Diplomat, the official human Ambassador to the Uglies. He was one of the first humans ever to undergo the Transformation and talk to an alien, and the only surviving member of the original contact team.

Stephen L. Antczak

Golan Haver was legend to anyone who dreamed of becoming a Xenodiplomat, and a celebrity all the way back to Earth. The alien he talked with had also attained celebrity status among humans. Its name was Agu, a phonetic translation of the sound the alien made for what other Uglies called it. Golan Haver had so far "discovered" the secret to circumventing the speed-of-light barrier, which put an end to the Age of Coldsleep in travel among the stars.

Golan Haver also delivered to humanity more information about the Uglies themselves than any other XD. The Uglies consisted of three sexes: two that corresponded to male and female who produced a single egg, another that ingested the egg and later gave birth in the Earthly mammalian sense. There was a complicated family arrangement regarding the three parents and different partners of the other two sexes, resulting in an extensive filigree of sibling-cousin relationships that human sociologists were still trying to figure out.

Haver had started off as a crew member of the starship *Hawking*, one of those shining examples of humanity chosen as much for his solid good looks and sex appeal, to generate good PR, as for his abilities. Exploring the outer reaches of known space, they encountered an Ugly probe, and on that probe an Artificial Intelligence that initiated contact with the human race, and led to the establishment of Embassy. Ten years passed before contact was made with an actual Ugly. Kelley Morgan, *Hawking*'s captain, was the first human to see an alien face to face. She survived the experience long enough for the kinks to be worked out of the Transformation process. Not long after, Embassy was in business.

The surviving crew of *Hawking*, who became the first XDs, were no longer those shining examples of humanity they'd once been.

"Good morning, Lysa," he said, his voice a flat tone, nasal, wheezing.

"Good morning, Ambassador Haver," Lysa said, trying to keep her own voice steady. Meeting a legend for the first time, even one who was "merely" human, or who had once been, was nerve-wracking. It took a major effort on her part not to turn around and run away. If she was this nervous, what was she going to be like with an honest-to-God alien? Lysa had a disturbing vision of herself sitting there in shocked silence, unable to speak, while the Ugly impatiently turned around and left, effectively ending her career as an XD before it began.

"Have a seat," the Ambassador said.

Lysa saw a desk, and only one chair in the room, so she sat there. On the other side of the desk sat Golan Haver. Lysa couldn't see him very well, the lighting was dim, and the room was filled with a fine mist. After the Point of No Return, would *she* be breathing the mist? She wore a breathing filter now, though. The mist would kill her if she breathed for longer than a few minutes.

Last Contact

"How are you progressing in the Transformation so far?" the Ambassador asked.

"Fine, I guess," Lysa answered.

"You don't sound very sure of yourself," he said. "Having doubts?"

"Doubts? This is what I've wanted to do my whole life."

Through the mist, Lysa could see the Ambassador apparently nodding. Obscured as he was, the motion looked odd, more a bobbing up and down.

"You find my appearance disturbing?"

Lysa blinked. "I can't really see you."

The response was a gurgling noise that at first sounded like the Ambassador had gone into a hacking fit, but which Lysa soon recognized as laughter.

"I forget," he said. "This room is a compromise. I'm not entirely comfortable here, myself."

"I'm sorry."

"You have retained much of your…humanity. More than most. It would be relatively easy for you to go back, you know. Easier than the others."

"I don't want to go back. I want to be a Xenodiplomat."

A moment of silence, though not absolute because Haver whistled with every breath. It was almost worse than silence. Lysa knew he was there, watching her, deciding things, probably not in her favor. She tried to sit as still as possible, but shifted in her seat several times, crossed her legs, uncrossed them, then crossed them again the opposite way. *I don't want to go back.* The statement echoed in her head. She wanted to pass the Point of No Return *now*, so the prospect of going back would be moot.

Golan Haver finally spoke: "Before the final phase of your Transformation can begin, I must inform you of a recent development in our relations with the Uglies." He paused, long enough for Lysa to form some wild ideas about what this new development was. *I'll have to marry one,* she thought. *They've figured out a way for Uglies and humans to mate, and I'm going to be the test-mother….*

"The Uglies will allow only one more human to become a diplomat," Haver continued. "Furthermore, they will allow this last diplomat *one question*, which they have promised to answer truthfully. After that, *Gens Alienus* and humanity will part company…forever."

Before Lysa could reply she had to let it all sink in. Did she hear correctly? Did she understand? One question, and that was *it*? *Goodbye, nice talking to you, but we really have to run. Don't call us, we'll call you?*

"Why?" she finally asked. Her father used to tell her that *Why?* was the hardest question to answer, when she was a little girl asking why the sky was blue, why she was a girl and not a boy, why, why, why?

Haver leaned forward, and Lysa could see him better. The secretion that covered his entire body glistened. An odor of rotting fish almost overpowered her. She caught a glimpse of Haver's face. Something about it unnerved her for a moment. It didn't look right, but she couldn't tell what it was.

"They are *aliens*," Haver said. "We can only begin to guess *why*. However, I know they've already processed one of their own to interact with a human being. As with us, their transformation is not reversible. Thus they're allowing one more human contact, but that contact will be limited to one, final question."

"Didn't they give an explanation?"

There was a noise, like a balloon losing wet air through a pinhole. She assumed it was a sigh.

"Whatever their reasons," Haver said, and Lysa wondered if she detected a small amount of exasperation in his voice, "the point is, will you give up your humanity to live out the remainder of your life on Embassy in exchange for the limited opportunity to ask one, final question of an alien? Just one question. Whatever the question, your alien *will* answer truthfully."

Your alien. As if that would matter after her question was through. Then what? What kind of life would she have on Embassy?

"What about the others?" Lysa asked, meaning the other three humans who'd made it as far as she had, right up to the Point of No Return.

"You're our first choice, Lysa. If you decide to continue," Haver said, "they will undergo a reversal of the Transformation and be returned to the human worlds. Assuming they do not suffer adversely, they will lead relatively normal lives. There may always be a differentness about them which cannot be avoided, but at least they will not be repulsive to other humans."

Other humans made Lysa think of Daen, and her family on Hope; and Earth.

"I need to know your answer tomorrow morning," Haver said. "You have tonight to consider it. I urge that you do so carefully." Then he left her there, suddenly alone, as he disappeared through a doorway that opened up behind the desk.

She wanted someone to talk to. She needed to discuss it with someone, to get input and to have someone listen to her fears. She could call Daen. It would be expensive, and she knew what she would want him to say. *Come back to me.*

No, she wouldn't call. Lysa needed to make this decision herself. Whether he wanted her back or not, Lysa decided this was about something else. What question could yield *the* answer all of humanity wanted to know? *Where are the other alien races out there?*

It wasn't enough just to have the Uglies. Somehow it made the human race feel even lonelier, according to sociologists. Humans needed a crowded galaxy, wanted an endless variety pack of alien civilizations. In another thousand years of contact with the Uglies, humans *still* wouldn't come close to knowing all there was to know about them. Humans still surprised *themselves*.

What Lysa really wanted to know was *why*. *Why are you leaving us?* she wanted to ask. What was the perfect question? What question, if answered truthfully, would do humanity the most good? Maybe she could think of a question that might yield a more useful answer, and tell humanity something about *itself.*

How can we be better?

But did humanity, spread out across a dozen worlds light years apart, share one characteristic? Would one answer apply to all humans? Would her Ugly even know the answer?

The next morning, Lysa awoke, exhausted. She hadn't slept well all night. A hundred times she'd come to a decision, only to doubt it the next second. The innards of Embassy seemed to have lost their luster as she ambled towards her meeting with Golan Haver.

An aide met her at the entrance to his chambers. A completely human woman who stood stiffly in Lysa's way, and who had to exercise visible control over her gag reflex in Lysa's altered presence.

"Ambassador Haver cannot see you at this time," the woman said. "He's in conference with Agu. He asked me to relay your decision to him, and to express his sincerest apologies for not seeing you personally."

Lysa's mind had changed a dozen times more during the walk there. Now she wondered again what to say. Two simple words, *yes* she would stay and become something other than human for the rest of her life, or *no* she would leave, have the Transformation reversed until she was human again, and…then what?

"Please tell Golan Haver this," Lysa said, then took a deep breath. The aide waited patiently. Lysa literally did *not* know what her answer was going to be even as she opened her mouth to proclaim it: "No."

The aide nodded. "Very well. Ambassador Haver instructed me to accompany you to the processing center to begin reversal of the Transformation. The sooner you begin, the easier it will be on you since your body hasn't gotten used to the differences."

They walked along the tubeway to the hospital, and the processing center. If she'd said yes, Lysa would be on her way to undergo another treatment in the Transformation; the Point of No Return.

At least she would not be alone in her failure. Two other hopefuls would be going back with her. Who were they? She wondered who would be the one, the last new human Xenodiplomat to the Uglies. What question would she, or he, ask?

Why?

The aide deposited Lysa in a reception room, then left to arrange for the reversal to begin right away. Another person in the room, a man, younger than Lysa, smiled at her. He'd been at the same threshold as Lysa, and apparently had made the same final decision. The candidates had not socialized at all during the Transformation. She didn't know his name.

"What would you have asked the Uglies?" Lysa asked him.

He shrugged. "I don't know. Soon as I found out what the deal was, it didn't matter. I knew right away I wanted out."

The door opened. The aide came in. "They're ready to begin," she said.

"What about the others?" the man asked. "One of them, at least, should be reversing the Change with us."

The aide frowned. "No, you two are it. If there's anyone else, they're starting the final phase of the Transformation today."

"But I thought only *one*..." Lysa began, but then it hit her. How stupid she felt!

"Please come with me," the aide told them. They followed her out of the room.

"A test," Lysa said as they walked.

"What's that?" the man asked.

"It was a test," Lysa told him. "The last test before the Point of No Return."

"Well, I'll be..." He scratched his head and grinned.

"What are you smiling about?"

"I just realized something. I didn't *really* want to be an XD. If they hadn't tricked me, I might not have realized it until too late. I'm not going to spend the rest of my life on Embassy talking to Uglies. All this time I've had a big knot in my stomach, and you know what?"

"What?"

"It's *gone*."

But the knot in Lysa's stomach didn't go away.

While she was getting ready for the journey back to Hope, Lysa received a message from Daen. It was a reply to the message she'd sent him regarding her failure. Her message had been short and to the point, saying only that she was no longer in the XD program.

Daen's message was long. She listened to it several times. He was happy she was coming back to him. He said all the right things. He admired her for pursuing her dreams as far as she had. She had courage. He wanted to get married as soon as possible and start a family.

It took her almost a week to send a reply. Maybe she knew that her response would be another Point of No Return. She wasn't going back to Hope. She'd been accepted into Earth's Diplomatic Corps. The human worlds automatically took anyone who'd been accepted into the XD program.

Lysa recorded the message and sent it to Daen, telling him her decision. When she pressed the SEND button, she felt it. The knot in her stomach was finally gone.

Science fiction has long been an open forum on the concepts of science and religion, and how the two can coexist in our civilization when they are apparently the antithesis of one another. Many science fiction writers have thrown their two cents in. Given that, it was only natural that I would eventually come around to exploring my own ideas about this subject.

While many religions tells us that we were created by God, there are opposing views that posit the opposite...we created God. For a long time I'd been wanting to use this, but could not come up with a suitable idea. Until one day, while daydreaming of course, I came up with the idea that if God created us in His image it stood to reason that one of us elevated enough could conceivably become...God.

It took a while to find a home, but finally sold to the literary magazine Descant *for their special issue on speculative fiction.*

Nail in the Coffin

I SAT IN MY TINY room on Gaban station. I had a rocking chair where I could relax and listen to music. I liked to remember my childhood. I'd had a best friend then, a boy my age who lived down the street. I could not remember his name. I felt as if I had betrayed him by forgetting.

A piano concerto filled the room, computer-generated based on my responses in the past to different pieces. For all I knew I would be the only person to ever hear it. The sad beauty of that was not lost on me.

daydreams undertaken

When I opened my eyes, on the night stand stood a white porcelain vase of a dozen red roses. The roses had not been there moments before, but I wasn't surprised to see them there. I closed my eyes again, listened to the music, and allowed myself a smile.

My friend had not forgotten me.

My Knack was this: I could link my brain to someone else's the way most people could jack in to a computer. I could then slip deep into their subconscious mind. Most people couldn't get past the conscious part, the "awake" part, and they had to use computers to create a shared setting, common ground.

I didn't need the computer because I was a Delver.

Nail was a Surveyor. Nail's Knack would be useless without someone like me. His subconscious mind could be siphoned out of his brain and *projected* from a computer-controlled device called a caster, like casting a net. It cast Nail's subconscious mind over an area of space, light years cubed, spread it as thin as possible, while his conscious self slept, unaware. If something were to go wrong and he should wake, his mind wouldn't be able to stand the strain and disorientation of being spread across space. He'd probably die, or at the very least go completely insane.

The pod in which his body rested while this happened we called a coffin. It slid into the shell of the lightship that carried him across the galaxy via the superluminal universe. The caster spread his mind across space, and he saw what he could see, so to speak. Of course, *he* never remembered it. That's why I came along, to look beneath the surface.

"I didn't know what they were doing to Nail, Hart," Jayne told me after the evaluation. "I had no idea. What they did to Nail, it seems like a cruel joke you'd play on a child, drop him off in the North Pole to find Santa Claus. You have to believe me, no one told me *anything*."

"I know they don't tell you," I said. "We only know what we're looking for when we find it in the Surveyor's mind. They told Nail to find God...Now it's up to us to decide what happened.'"

"That's...what I wanted to talk to you about."

"I know."

"You think the Machine Civilization, the Burned World, the Regressed Civilization...these don't exist?"

"They exist," I said. "Robot probes have already physically visited the Burned World. You know that."

"Yes, but I'd find it easier to deal with if I believed they're wrong, that the probes have somehow malfunctioned. That's easier to believe than the alternative."

"I understand," I told her. "Jayne, I know that believing everything I've told you so far isn't easy, but there is a third alternative. I assume you picked up on it when you delved me."

Nail in the Coffin

"I did."

"You don't have much of a choice, you know."

"Yes, but...*why?*"

I didn't answer her question. Why? That was for me to know, and for Jayne to always wonder about.

So she decommissioned me, and I sat out my new uselessness for a few more weeks on the station, waiting for someone to come tell me I could go home. I threw the roses into the recycler after a while, and days later their scent was still strong in my room. I got the impression that if anyone else had been there, only I could have smelled it.

Nail had pasty white skin when they pulled him out of his coffin, carefully detaching all the neural links. His breathing was shallow, saliva slid from his half-open mouth to his chin, and dripped onto the floor.

"Hart," Jayne said behind me. I turned to face her as the aides took Nail to Recovery. Jayne was actually younger than me, but had been groomed for command since her early teens, when her particular Knack had been discovered. I didn't know about mine until just after my 20th birthday.

"You shouldn't be up here," Jayne said.

"He's my friend," I said, surprised at my own frankness.

"You know better than that," she said. "Perhaps I should delve him myself this time."

"No one can delve him better than me."

"I don't think you're up to it, if you're starting to think of him as your 'friend.'" She could see that I wasn't going to back down. Jayne sighed. "Fine, you delve him. Then report for a psych evaluation. Now go to Prep."

An evaluation would go on my record. If the psych found me getting too attached I could be sent back to Earth. Just for having a friend.

Maybe it wouldn't matter. The information I'd delved from Nail since becoming his friend had been right on target, just what the prognosticators back on Earth had expected. We'd proven ourselves the best team they had, in spite of the rules about becoming too attached.

At first Nail was just another subject for me to delve, although delving him was easier than it had been with anyone else. Our relationship stayed that way for a while, and then I started hoping that my next assignment would be Nail, and I felt disappointed when someone else got him. However, when the results of others who delved Nail came through fuzzed, blurred, and sometimes incomprehensible, I was assigned to Nail permanently.

I didn't really think of *Nail* as my friend, not exactly. Honestly, I never got to know much about him at all. He was from Earth, like me, but I did not know what part. I didn't even know his real name. His subconscious Self was my friend. Conscious, he probably just felt this vague sense of familiarity about me he couldn't figure out. He did not know I was his Delver. And it was only when I delved him, to find out what secrets of the universe he'd uncovered, did I find my 'friend.'

Back on Earth I'd had no friends. Most of the people I'd ever known were passing acquaintances. That spark of true friendship just never seemed to happen. To me, a friend is someone who can make you feel like the sun has just chosen to shine on you, and the warmth you feel provides a reason all by itself for existing.

That's how I felt when Nail returned safely from his missions, like the sun was about to shine on me.

Some who had the same Knack as mine went into criminal psychology. Others delved people who'd withdrawn, who'd suffered a major shock in life and turned inward, who didn't speak or acknowledge anything. A few of the good ones delved coma patients, to find their subjects living happily in a fantasy world of their subconscious creation, and maybe they wanted to wake up, maybe they didn't. A very, *very* few of the best of the best got recruited to do what I did.

I never realized I was *that* good. I'd always assumed it was the same for anyone who shared my particular Knack. I thought, if anything, I'd started too late to really learn how to use it.

They didn't discover these latent abilities some people have — their Knack — until true neural interfacing was perfected.

When someone discovered that the subconscious mind could be cast like a net, the R&D people realized there was potential for more than military applications. It was amazing, the capacity of the subconscious, what it could hold, how far and wide it could be spread, how it violated the laws of physics. The science behind casting the subconscious bordered on mysticism. One theory, widely accepted among our community, held that when cast out across space, the subconscious self was united, or reunited, with the fabric of space and time, and the very stuff of creation fused with our own sentience....

There was always a price, though. The conscious self paid that price. The ways the consciousness exacted its toll for what the subconscious self knew were varied, and usually not pleasant. If the Surveyor was lucky, all he or she experienced were bouts of depression, mood swings, insomnia, impotence, migraines.

So how did *I* handle the information I delved? My Knack used my conscious self along with my subconscious. I could delve an individual like Nail, but my ever-present conscious self prevented me from being able to delve the universe.

The sour smell of Nail's sweat permeated the room, like the sweat of a fever.

"This one's a doozy," the technician, a young Asian woman, said. "He's in shock."

Nail in the Coffin

"What was he looking for?" I asked, knowing better.

"We don't know," said the medic. A medic always stood by during Recovery. He was a thin black man I'd seen around, friendly enough, but I never said more than hello to him outside of Recovery.

"There've been rumors," the techie said. "I heard he was looking for—"

"Don't say it," I told her. "Never tell a Delver what people *think* a Surveyor was sent to look for. Even if it is all just rumor and speculation, it could taint what I find."

"Surely you hear the rumors, though," the medic said.

I shook my head. From whom would I hear them, without friends? No one posted rumors, because the station's computer monitored the bulletin boards around the clock, and rumor-mongering always earned serious demerits.

"Let's run a check on you," the techie proposed, changing the subject. Just a routine diagnostic, to make sure the jacks in my head were copacetic. I had jacks like anyone else who plugged in, except I got plugged directly into Nail's head. There was a computer connected, but that was only for the techie and the medic to monitor vitals.

It'd been a few months since the last time, so I felt a little tightness when the plugs went in. Could have been my imagination, since they say you *can't* feel them. Kind of funny, but I always lost my sense of smell when they went in. You could have crushed a fresh clove of garlic under my nose and I would have smelled nothing. That's how I knew everything linked up right.

"Okay, how many fingers am I holding up?" the techie asked, holding up three. I said three.

"Okay, good. Ready to link you up to Mr. Personality here if you are."

I gave her the thumbs-up.

"Enjoy the ride…"

I heard the *taptaptap* of fingers on a keyboard, and then everything went dark and silent. At the Academy they called it "Helen Keller," no sensory input at all, except *she* could still feel, and smell, and taste. *Total* sensory deprivation while the computer facilitated the link between me and the subject. A few minutes isn't a long time, but it can feel like forever when there's nothing in there but your Self, with flashes of memory bursting all at once. Christmas lights blinking, a rock concert screaming, the smell of hot apple pie, cool silk sheets on my bare skin….

Scientists on Earth made predictions, educated guesses, as to what Nail would find Out There.

Like the Machine Civilization near the core of densely packed suns clumped around the massive black hole at the heart of the Milky Way; the scientists believed that life would begin its evolutionary journey at the first opportunity, and that civilization would arise as soon as it was possible to do so. This meant there would have been an advanced civilization somewhere in the Milky Way long before the dinosaurs ever roamed the Earth.

The scientists also knew that no civilization would begin its evolutionary ascent near the galactic core; the intense radiation would have made it impossible for life to begin there. Elsewhere in the galaxy, however, it is nearly impossible for nature *not* to have begun the processes of life at the first opportunity. Just as nature abhors a true vacuum, the wisdom of the day stated that nature loves life.

Life surviving long enough to develop a technological civilization is another story. Given the odds of the continuously modified Drake equation, scientists predicted that at least *one* of the first civilizations to appear in the Milky Way would last long enough to evolve beyond their natural states of existence. They would become something *other*. They would become one with their technology.

The Machine Civilization was the logical conclusion. The race of beings who created the machines became dependent on the machines, then came into conflict with their creations, and were ultimately destroyed by them. The son destroyed the father in perhaps the original telling of the familiar human myth. Alternatively, the aliens became symbiotic partners with their machines, ultimately being absorbed by them.

The scientists posited that this Machine Civilization now would continue to expand and evolve on its own, requiring more and more energy to survive.... The greatest concentration of energy in the galaxy was the galactic core, a maelstrom of stars and superheated gases spiraling wildly about the great singularity at the very center. The Machine Civilization would migrate *en masse* to the core to soak up that energy, using it to sustain, grow, and evolve.

Many scientists believed it was the natural progression of all life, to evolve from an organic origin to an inorganic zenith. So they sent Nail's subconscious self, cast the net over as much of the bright, burning galactic core as was possible, expecting to find evidence that the Machine Civilization was there.

"Hello, Hart, glad you could make it." Unmistakably Nail's voice. The Nail I thought of as my friend. He sounded healthy and vibrant down there, full of life. I couldn't see anything yet. Sometimes it worked that way, the senses came in at different times.

"Where are you?" I asked.

"Down here."

He meant down past the layers of his conscious self.

I began to see the glimmer of something just out of my field of vision, a ghost light, vaguely in the form of a boy.

"I think I see you," I told Nail.

"Yes, that's me."

Nail in the Coffin

Everything lit up, and I found myself in a magnificent stone *hall*, decorated with elaborate tapestries and a Michelangelo ceiling. There stood Nail, the *real* Nail, the one beneath the surface. My friend. He always looked better than his physical self, always more color, more meat on his bones despite the fact that down here he was an eight-year-old boy, his black hair combed to one side, always smiling and happy. He always wore the same clothes, a pair of pajamas and cape. The sudden input of all my senses — I could even *smell* the room, a sweet, savory odor of simmering sweet potatoes, a favorite food from my childhood — dazzled me. Nail laughed.

He looked at me, arms folded across his chest, smiling away, not saying anything. We looked at each other like that for a little while, without needing to speak. I imagined that if he and I had grown up in the same neighborhood we really *would* have become friends and would have spent a lot of time just sitting around, not saying anything.

"Did you find what they sent you out for?" I eventually asked. I wasn't eight years old anymore, alas, and I did have a job to do.

"I guess that depends on what they expected me to find. I think that, in their eyes anyway, I probably failed."

That stunned me. This was a first then, if Nail had truly failed, because every single time out for him had been one hundred percent successful. He always found exactly what they expected.

Like:

The Machine Civilization. Nail found it, a civilization of sentient machines, vast living structures orbiting stars a few thousand light years out from the black hole at the center of the galaxy. The machines existed to use the energy there to build new machines, to continuously improve on their designs and construction, and thus enable the new ones to use the energy more efficiently and create even better new ones…and so on and so on, forever and forever.

There were others, besides the Machine Civilization.

The Sleeping World. A world populated solely by creatures who existed in a state of perpetual slumber, plugged into a central computer network, living in a virtual universe while their bodies slowly died, one by one, and none were born. Scientists on Earth had predicted this as one of the dead-end routes of evolution that a certain number of civilizations would take.

The Monument. An entire dead world sculpted into a symbolic shape, perhaps meant to mark the passing of an early civilization that had predicted its own premature demise. The Monument orbited an ancient, cooling, red dwarf star, the only world in that system, a silent homage to a doomed people.

There were others that scientists, using their own obscure methods, predicted must exist somewhere in our galaxy. Nail found them all: the Burnt World destroyed by thermonuclear war, the New Civilization just discovering space travel, the Regressed Civilization who gave up on technology and went back to the jungle eons before humans figured out that a wheel goes round and round....

"I'm sure you didn't fail," I said.

"Maybe I didn't fail, not exactly, but what I discovered wasn't what they expected me to find, it wasn't what they *wanted* me to find."

"What was it?"

"God."

I didn't know what to say, so I said nothing. It was enough.

"Yes, exactly," Nail said in response to my silence.

"Show me."

"Hart—"

"I have to do my job, so show me."

"Do you really want to know?" he asked.

Did I? I wanted to do my job. The scientists had their theories, and now I developed a theory of my own; that sending Nail out there to look for God had snapped him. The way he had looked coming in, he'd never looked quite that bad before. I nodded.

"Okay," he said.

I expected the room around me to shimmer and waver and fade out of existence, and I'd see...What did I expect God to look like? Or maybe I expected a booming, disembodied voice. I didn't know *what* to expect.

What happened seemed like such a ridiculous parlor trick, I burst out laughing. It had to be a joke. Nail was pulling a fast one. It had to be. A vase of long-stem red roses appeared on a table beside me, and Nail stood there looking so self-assured it almost kept me laughing, but I knew this was no joke. He'd cracked. He was useless now, and they'd send him back to Earth. He'd reside comfortably in a nursing home for the rest of his life without a care in the world or a thought in his head.

It was sad. It was *very* sad. They did this to my friend, Nail's inner child; they sent him out to find *God*. He thought he'd succeeded and failed at the same time.

"I guess that's it, then," I said.

"You're going to report my failure," he said. When I didn't say anything, not knowing *what* to say, he continued, "That's okay. Actually, I'd prefer it if you did. I don't want them sending any others out looking for me."

"Looking for...*you?*"

"Yes," he said.

"You mean you think *you're*...?"

"I am," he replied. He grinned like a child who'd just let me in on his biggest, best secret.

"Oh."

"I guess you'll be going, now," Nail said.

I nodded. I couldn't speak.

Nail in the Coffin

"Take the flowers," he said, and that almost did it, almost brought it all out. If I cried down there, what would my body be doing? Lying there peacefully, no outward display of emotion at all.

"I can't," I said. "You know I can't. They're part of you."

"This is true."

I had nothing else to say, there was nothing else I needed to see in there, so I willed myself up and out, back through the computer and into my own head. Then I opened my eyes. The techie and the medic were bent over me, looking concerned.

"We were about to bring you back," said the techie. "Your readings were all over the map."

"You almost went into shock," said the medic.

"He's okay?" I asked, motioning towards Nail with my head.

The medic nodded, said, "Yeah, he'll be fine, just a little sluggish. Why?"

"Put him on ice," I told them. "He's finished."

Jayne evaluated me by delving me, found out what I'd learned delving Nail, and immediately sent someone to my room to see if a vase of roses was really there. Of course they weren't. They were probably being filtered in the Greenhouse as compost sludge during my evaluation.

She'd know that I *thought* I opened my eyes and found the vase and roses. She'd know I'd thrown them into the recycler, that there would be no trace of them ever having existed. She'd know exactly what I was doing, and why, and she'd be playing her part while knowing it was a part I wanted, and expected, her to play.

When I did leave, Jayne didn't come around to bid me a final farewell. A steward came to my room, led me to the shuttle bay. The shuttle ride from the station to the big starship was uneventful, a few hours of unfamiliar weightlessness, a slight knot in my stomach because I didn't know what was going to happen to me. It took six months to get to the outer edge of the Gaban system, well away from the station. Then a week through a wormhole, one thousand light years to the outer edge of the Solar system. Eighteen months to a space station orbiting Ganymede. Eight more months on a space liner to Earth orbit, then a shuttle to the surface, a jet from the Miami space port to Nashville, and then a bus to my parents' farm in central Tennessee.

Home.

"Hart, is that you! Oh my...it *is* you!" I turned to look.

"Mom?"

She ran down the steps of the front porch, arms wide, and caught me up in a great, big hug. Then Dad came out.

"Well hit me on the head and call me stupid!" he yelled. "My sunshine's *back*!"

He picked me up in his arms and carried me inside. The first thing I noticed in the house were the roses, vases of them everywhere, on the mantle over the fireplace, the coffee table, the end tables on either side of the sofa, the great oak hutch, the shelves mounted on all the walls. The whole place smelled intensely of rose, as if every surface had been wiped with concentrated rose water. Dad bounced me up and down, the way he used to when I was little, as we entered the kitchen.

Dinner was already put out on the table: a mound of sweet potatoes, a glazed ham draped with sliced pineapple, green beans, and steaming dinner rolls. Only in the dining room was the scent of rose overpowered by the aroma of home-cooked food. My place was set; and a very familiar-looking little boy sat across from me. The boy looked about eight years old, healthy and fit, with black hair combed to one side, and he watched me with cool green eyes.

"Company, Hart," Mom said. "What's your name, little boy? Spike?"

The little boy smiled at her. "I'm Nail," he said.

Dad put me down.

"You two get acquainted while we grown-ups disappear for a minute." And they promptly did just that.

"So," Nail said. "What do you think?"

"My parents were dead last time I checked," I said. "They died while I was outbound to Gaban."

"But they look fine now, don't they?"

"Is it really them?"

He nodded again. I closed my eyes, almost hoping that when I opened them again I'd be in the infirmary on the station, and at the same time hoping I *wouldn't* be. I opened them, and I was still there in my parents' kitchen, with a little boy named Nail sitting across from me.

"This was my favorite time," I said. "I was ten."

"I know," Nail said, in a way that made me realize that he did know, really did know, *everything*.

"I'm not dreaming?" I asked. "I really am a little kid again, and you really are my friend?"

"Not your friend," he said, his smile bigger. "Your *best* friend."

The idea for this story arose from a fascination with the concept of the light-speed barrier, and the different ways science fiction had come up with to get around it. I wondered if there might be a mirror universe that existed on the other side of that barrier where the inhabitants, like us, couldn't break through it. The idea wasn't so much that they couldn't go slower than the speed of light as that, for them, it would also be speeding up.

This story allowed me to play with a McGuffin that my friend James C. Bassett and I had come up with some years before; the Conversion Drive we called it. It was our answer to warp speed and other tools used to allow humans to travel faster than light. The Conversion Drive projects a field around a space ship, and then converts the subatomic particles of everything within the field to their superluminal counterparts. When writing the story, I wondered if there might actually be some basis in science for this idea, so I wrote to the only physicist I knew of who might entertain such a question with a straight face, science fiction writer Gregory Benford. Benford actually wrote back, and to my delight mentioned that the Conversion Drive had some similarities to other concepts floating around (John Cramer's excellent book Twistor *was one he urged me to read) but no one had quite suggested it in the same manner. This was highly encouraging.*

I wondered how that universe might correspond with ours, what the relationship with our universe might be. It hit me that there could be a one-to-one ratio between the two universes of every star and planet. If a corresponding Earth existed in the FTL (Faster Than Light) universe, was there life?

It was while daydreaming that I figured out the two elements that would let me write this story. One was the idea of 'conservation of souls,' in that when one of us died one of them was born, and when one of them died one of us was born. Of course, this had interesting implications when one considers the population growth here. Does that mean the population of the FTL Earth is diminishing? And is it a cyclical phenomenon? Will our population eventually drop while theirs grows?

I toyed with these ideas, but ultimately decided they weren't the story I wanted to tell. The other element I came up with while daydreaming centered around the main character, a 'luminaut' who is commanded by his distraught wife to go over and retrieve their son's soul. It was the end result of his mission that occurred to me while daydreaming, and gave me the story I wanted to tell. This story was originally published in the Algis Budrys-edited magazine Tomorrow Speculative Fiction.

The Other Side of Light

IMAGINE COLLAPSING IN ON YOURSELF, being turned inside out, scrambled like an electronic transmission in a lightning storm, then reorganized, and exploded outward like a minor Big Bang, reborn in another universe, on the other side of light. Conversion. That's what it feels like, too. The Conversion Field, charging us up, zapping us poor souls in just the right way to excite our basic subparticular selves to leap through that nasty light barrier, phasing through like ghosts through the wall. Cosmic osmosis.

daydreams undertaken

Stephen L. Antczak

The Earthspace swirled before us, a roiling, swirling, tempest. Our faceplates translated the language of the superluminal spectrum for our eyes to understand, so that what we saw was a shadowy maelstrom of grainy black and white, like bad film stock instead of something that wasn't blue or green or red, wasn't any color we could comprehend. Strangely, the faceplates allowed the stars, and space surrounding them, and us, to remain as we would have seen them unaided, as black pinpoints against a solid white sky. The snowblinding void that felt so much emptier than our own cipher of darkness.

We were lightwalking at the end of a long tether, two luminauts out to see what the sensors of our lightship, *Einstein's Folly*, could not. Can a computer truly see the beauty of a sunset, or see the tragedy in the eyes of a woman whose child has died? It takes human eyes to see into the spectrum of emotions and beyond the scope of physics.

I was at the fore, the Geezer some 200 meters behind me. He was singing what he knew of the *Hallelujah Chorus*, which was only the one word.

"Hall-e-lu-jah! Hall-e-lu-jah!" Then he stopped as we reached the end of our line. "Lookee there, Connor m'boy! The Well of Souls stretches before us, waiting for us to die and come home!"

Well of Souls. I preferred the other misnomer given it by a luminaut who'd been an avid collector of antique comic books. The "Phantom Zone" he called it, and it did fit. It was one of the things the computer couldn't see that human eyes could. Shapes flitting about in the colorless, confused storm, or maybe *shades* is a better word. Ghosts? Spirits, faeries, souls of the dead and the unborn, a phantasmagoric rhapsody....

There were shapes in the Phantom Zone now, swimming out to the edge to take a look at us, it seemed. Darting right out to where we could see them clearly, humanoid, but liquid or ethereal in construction, pulsating or shimmering depending on the mood. Something else the computer, even if it could see them in the first place, would miss. I could feel their sentience, through however many meters of white vacuum lay between them and us, not to mention the membrane of the Earthspace, their world, which kept them in and us out. Not that we'd tried to penetrate it, not yet. After only seven trips Over from our universe, we weren't ready for that.

"They're doin' a dance! Yeehaw!!" Geezer shouted, his nasal voice broadcast clearly through the speakers in my helmet, made even more nasal by them. Indeed there looked to be several of them dancing an elaborate pattern right there in front of us, weaving in and out of each other, passing through each other's corporeal form effortlessly, playing, perhaps even making love. It was beautiful to watch, and somewhat disconcerting in that it wasn't *too* alien, it was almost comprehensible, as if being constantly on the verge of getting it, then missing something else and having to start over.

The Other Side of Light

We drifted closer, the entire ship and us dangling off it like Christmas ornaments. *It's Christmas time in superluminal space*, I could almost imagine Bing Crosby singing. I'd be playing that CD now, snuggling up with Lillian, my wife, sipping hot cider from our very own apple trees on six big acres in New England. Ahhhh. Except, there I was, floating not just a million lightyears away in the same old universe, but in a completely different one. The fact that in real units of measurement, distance-wise, I was orbiting the Earth, didn't help. I didn't even exist in the same frame of being as the Earth and Lillian.

Not that she missed me at the moment. She was too far gone for that, I'd been told. At first it seemed like she might be able to deal with it, the birth of our son, Rand. That he wasn't actually *dead* was what drove her over the edge, over a boundary so much easier for human beings to cross than the light barrier! Madness. A wall of thin air between sanity and insanity, sometimes so subtle it could be a while before anyone noticed you've crossed over.

Rand, he wasn't dead, but he wasn't alive either. He just *wasn't*, that's how Doctor Lopez said it. Lopez was a big man, massive and not used to being the messenger in danger of losing his head for bearing bad news. With the giant leaps for humanity medical tech had been making for the last twenty years, it was easy to understand that.

I was the one who had to tell Lill. No, I *wanted* to be the one to tell her. I had Lopez give me the details, because I wanted to know in case Lillian asked, in case she needed to hear the how's and why's.

"He's dead, isn't he," Lillian said to me as I slipped quietly into her room at the hospital. They'd kept her for observation in case Rand's condition had something to do with her. It hadn't. It wasn't even a question; she'd mentally prepared herself to hear the worst, had expected it, and stating it flatly like that was the easiest way to confront it.

How I wished I could lie to her and say Yes, his little heart doesn't pump our blood through his body, his little lungs don't breathe…but in the Informed Age she had to know.

"He's not exactly dead," I told her.

"He's deformed, then," she said. "Is it something they can fix?"

I shook my head. "No, no. He's a perfectly healthy little boy, Lillian, it's just…there's no spark there. He's just a…a shell. He'll never become Rand, our son, never develop a personality."

"How do they know?" she asked, and I should have heard that first hint of vicious sorrow in her voice. Maybe I did hear it, and maybe I felt it too and let her express it for both of us. "He's a newborn, Connor. How can they know already?"

She knew how. We all knew.

"The Cradle," I said. The Cradle. We are all of us measured, weighed, analyzed, probed, prodded, mapped, graphed, diagrammed, cataloged, and thoroughly inspected right after birth. Rubber nurses gloves carry us directly from the womb, barely wiped free of birthing slime, and deposit us in the warm, oven-like compartment of the Cradle. Then, similar to those old CAT scanners, we slide in to be subjected to the closest scrutiny we will ever undergo from then on, until death, when they'll break us down and study each individual cell, one by one, to see why we die in the first place.

Lillian closed her eyes. "The Cradle doesn't know everything," she said with a tired voice, fed up with the stupidity of her husband. Me. Fed up with me, and it started right then, when I seemed to have accepted the prognosis without so much as a *May I have a second opinion, please?* Not even a *Let me see my son!* routine.

"I…" I didn't know what to say, but thankfully she didn't bother to wait for me to fumble with the words anyway.

"I want my son," she said. "Tell them. And if they can't find him, then you get him the next time you go Over to the other side. Find him and bring him back."

Ah, and right then all the beauty that had been Lillian inside and out, all the wonderful things about her that I'd fallen in love with faded in her eyes, overcome by the new fire that burned in them now. Maybe not right away, maybe it took time, because when she came home she seemed okay, if unusually silent, but she made love when I wanted, and sometimes it was her who wanted to, and she laughed, and she cried, and we harvested apples for the cider. Until *Einstein's Folly.*

"You're going," she said the day we heard the announcement. It was an optional trip for me, and I was offered the chance to go more as a courtesy than anything else. I'd intended to pass, to stay with Lillian through the holidays because I didn't think she should be alone then, when family and loved ones gather together. The gathering together is what reassures us we are not alone in the world. But apparently Lillian wasn't worried about that.

The hospital had kept Rand, and had him on life support as per my wife's wishes. It was okay with me, although I believed it was just prolonging the misery and wanted to exit the program, let the computer let Rand die and be done with it.

"You're going." She repeated it hourly, as if the first time didn't yet ring in my ears. "You're going." She only had to say it once, and I knew I was going.

They asked about it at the Hawkings Institute, when I went for my usual battery of Q&A psych tests. Would I be able to handle it so soon after Rand? *During* Rand, I pointed out. It's still going on, still happening, it ain't over yet. Yes, I'd be able to handle it. My record bore that out. Four jumps Over and each one I came back as much me as when I left. Some weren't so lucky, or maybe they *were* the lucky ones. The idea of leaving behind an entire universe, then seeing a new one, even filtered by the faceplate for human eyes, drove some over that edge. There were those who believed the pseudo-scientists who

The Other Side of Light

claimed the Earthspace was truly a Well of Souls, where we went when we died, born into the other half of our dual nature while the same happened for them. Every time a phantom ceased its throb of life, died Over there, a mother's contractions got closer and closer together over here, and a baby was born. Usually, thanks to today's wondrous medtech, usually a healthy baby, one that would grow into a wonderful little boy or girl, shy or extroverted, kind or mean-spirited, happy-go-lucky or chronically depressed. But wonderful nonetheless.

Usually, but not always.

I didn't believe it, but apparently Lillian did. I didn't dismiss it either, I just didn't know. How could I know? How could anyone? Conservation of matter and energy, and now souls…Rand's soul.

No one would expect me to *do* anything about it. Except Lill, but what could I do? Call him, call our son to inhabit the vacant shell, to grace the temple with his presence. I prayed. If the body is a temple, then we spirits inside are but shards of God, splinters, sparks of His eternal flame. So I guess I prayed for a piece of God to leap into our son's body and awaken him, finally, not even in time for Christmas. I didn't want to ask *too* much. Just make Rand laugh and cry, before my wife was gone, too, just another empty vessel of flesh, blood, and bones.

Hanging there in the balance, in the Faster Than Light universe, a negative of our universe, seeing what may be the unborn flock to peer curiously at what? What are we to them? I wondered.

"Connor, answer me, damn it all!"

"What? What's wrong?"

"Ask yourself that question," Geezer growled. It was funny, he was only the Geezer by virtue of the fact that he'd gone Over more times than anyone else, but I was actually his chronological senior by almost a decade. "You've been entranced," he continued, "staring into the damn Phantom Zone for almost an hour! And get back online."

I checked the reading in my visor display. So, I'd disconnected myself from *Einstein's Folly*. I didn't remember doing it. Cast off from the lightship, the tether a headless electronic snake flailing uselessly a good hundred meters away. It was an emergency-only option for the luminaut to "go satellite" as the deep spacers say, cutting all ties except the whispery bond of gravity…in *our* universe, anyway. No one had proven gravity in superluminal space yet. My lightsuit did have a limited capability for independent mobility in FTL space, using good ol' electromagnetism to push me along. I could get back to the tether easily enough, if I wanted to.

"I'm all right," I said. I didn't want to lose my freedom just yet. Did I recognize one of the phantoms? Wasn't there something familiar about a certain apparition who hovered more or less in one place in the midst of his companions? His?

Stephen L. Antczak

"Come on back here, you fool!" Geezer said. "Connor, come back. We have to go. Conversion in tee minus forty minutes, let's *go!*"

I realized I was thinking my way closer and closer to that edge. One of the dangers of being a luminaut, getting snowblind and losing yourself in it, disappearing, coming back with a certain vacant look in your eyes that told everyone there was no one home anymore...like Rand. My son.

Ah. Lillian's last words, before I left to go Over, came back to haunt me in the face of Faster Than Light poltergeists.

She'd been singing. "Rock-a-bye baby...when the bow breaks, the cradle will fall, and down will come baby, cradle and all."

I remember thinking what an awful song to sing about your son. "Guess I'm leaving now," I told her.

"Go and find him," she said. "He's being a very bad little boy and Mommy's very upset."

"I..." I didn't know what to say, so I said, "Honey, I love you."

"Don't come back without my son."

I didn't see her face that whole time, but I could feel it warped by close proximity to the edge. I left without saying another word to my wife.

Rock-a-bye baby.

"Connor, jumpin' Jesus, let's go!" Geezer again, a raging apostle in my head. Christ, what to do, what to do? What kind of Father was I? What kind of husband? What kind of man? What kind of man loses his son, then his wife, and just goes along with it, pretends there's nothing he can do, that's the way it goes?

He's in there, was all I could think. In the Phantom Zone, waiting.

"Goddammitall, you promised...you told me you wouldn't do anything stupid," Geezer said. "Remember? Remember?"

Yes, over three vodka tonics at the Space Opera Tavern in O'Neill Six, the only orbiting saloon for spaghetti western space cowboys in a spoke-wheeled colony high above the Earth. Can you trust yourself, the Geezer had asked.

Don't come back without my son.

"Yes, dear," I said.

"No!" Geezer shouted. "Don't do it!"

The Earthspace, the Phantom Zone, the Well of Souls, maybe the light at the end of the tunnel of death, a flickering, flashing, strobing blizzard of black and white loomed ahead ever larger as I moved through the unpainted canvass of void toward it.

"It won't work!" Geezer was howling, powerless at the end of his leash, unable to cut himself off from *Einstein's Folly.* "It won't work!"

I barely heard his rant as I penetrated the membrane, entered the bubble of shadows, and disappeared amid a swarming mass of glowing specters. They were all around me, and I saw the faint outline of features on each one, faces fading with memory, trying to forget who they once were to become someone new, again. Angels, I thought, sprites, djinni, loved ones from past lives. They touched me through the suit, caressed me, stroked my essence, fed me warmth and happiness. Then I realized they were moving me, carrying me through the visual cacophony of their environment, taking me somewhere important. I felt it, sensed the gravity of their urgency, realized something was wrong despite the good vibrations emanating from all around. Then I saw one illusory countenance that disappeared immediately, a phantom phiz that had flashed, burned into my retinal memory as a tender smile of love from the one that was, would have been. My son.

"Rand…" I said, reaching out, but I was gone, and he had never really been there, anyway.

Suddenly the cloud of spectral children parted and fled, swam back, away from me, and I saw where they had been taking me. A dilating diaphragm, translucent grey and pulsating, was the center of the Earthspace, and I was falling toward it now. I was alone, increasing speed as if being sucked in, realizing too late that there was no way back, no way for me to change my mind and listen to the mad reason of Geezer. *Einstein's Folly* had probably already jumped back Over, returned to a void comfortably black.

The hole pulsed open and closed like some cosmic bodily orifice, and I watched horrified as it spat forth a stream of the phantom bodies, smaller and apparently more solid. They surged past me, or I past them, and I could see their faces, and they were *human*, eyes closed, blissfully smiling.

And then I saw the hole shrinking, puckering up to kiss my entire being as it sucked me in, and through.

Falling, collapsing in on myself, pressed from all sides, turned inside out, then…nothing. No exploding out, no Big Bang of the self, rather a subtler blossoming as a flower towards the light, and an emptying out, pouring forth like emotions into a warm cup, filling the cup, a cup custom designed for me by an accident of Nature.

Then blackness, comfortable void inside.

I remembered my mother. *Mother.*

I recalled her taste, her scent as I fed on her. Mother's milk, I remembered it, felt the nipple in my mouth, recalled how she held me, cooed to me, kissed me gently on my head as she shuddered from the pleasure of my sucking. A dream, but in this dream Mother turns into Lillian, and she's feeding me milk meant for our son, and I'm afraid she'll find out, and hate me for stealing it from little Rand.

"Don't come back without him," she says, throwing me into the trash, slamming the lid over me as I cry.

All along I knew I wanted to say something, but for a long time I didn't know what, didn't even know I *could* say anything, didn't know what saying was. Thoughts were hard to come by. Pressing needs like hunger, physical distress, and discomfort stole away my awareness and trampled my feeble attempts at cognition beneath a stampede of baser urges. I didn't know for how long this went on, my perception of time had been whittled down to moments, the *now* of pain or pleasure.

Until one day I understood a word, just one word. "Mommy." The voice was Lillian's, and it confused me.

"Mommy," I repeated, remembering Natasha, my mother, dead ten years, but alive in my past. But the image that came to me wasn't hers, it was Lillian's face, close to mine, nuzzling, her warm breath tickling my cheeks.

"Oh my God," Lillian said, and I understood that, too. "He said Mommy. Say it again, sweetheart, say Mommy again…"

"Mommy," I said.

"He *did* say it!" she shouted joyously.

"Lillian," I then said, although it came out something like "Yenyen", but caught her attention again. She regarded me with a pained look of confusion on her face, and I saw the edge there, and realized she was still so close to going over. So close to going Over to the other side of darkness.

"Did you just say my name?" she asked.

"Connor," I tried to say, but wound up saying, "Cowuh."

Baby-talk, I suddenly realized. Of course. The way she was looking at me now, she had never looked at me like that before. Never.

"Connor," Lillian said. "You said Connor." Her voice trembled, and I could see another universe there in her eyes, a universe she was close to, a universe called Hell masquerading as a safe haven if this reality proved too much for her.

Would finding out that her son, Rand, was a two-year old's body inhabited by the…what? Soul, spirit, essence of Connor. Would that be too much? *Don't come back without…*What if I came back *as* Rand?

I could see it in her face, in her being, screaming when she knew. If she knew. Did she have to know?

"Honey," Lillian said, a twitching smile playing her face like TV with a bad connection. "Honey, say what you said again, okay?"

I smiled back brightly, and said, "Mommy?"

Is that what you want to hear?

"Oh, sweetheart," Lillian said, lifting me out of the crib with strong yet careful hands, holding me to her breast in a desperately subdued, intense hug. Humming softly, she carried me to a rocking chair, and began to rock me oh so gently to sleep. I would sleep, I knew, in the arms of love, but I would dream on the other side of light.

Afterword

AS I WRITE THIS TODAY, I note that I have now written one hundred short stories. Of those, I have sold thirty-six. The first thirty or so stories I wrote were meant for non-paying fanzines like the one James C. Bassett and I published in the late '80s, *Science Fiction Randomly*, or the one Rob Sommers published into the mid-'90s, *Peripheral Visions*. My work and Letters of Comment appeared in a number of other fanzines before I started to sell. Among those were *The Reluctant Famulus*, *Pulsar!*, *Neophyte*, *The Scanner* (in England), *Starsong*, and *FOSFAX*.

daydreams undertaken

Stephen L. Antczak

My first story sale was to renowned science fiction and fantasy author Lawrence Watt-Evans, for an anthology he was putting together about New York, called *Newer York*. Watt-Evans had been a Guest at a science fiction convention in Tampa, Florida called Necronomicon. We gave him a copy of *Randomly*, and he wrote a LoC (Letter of Comment, for the uninitiated) and we sent him the next issue. Back then, that was how it worked. Anyway, after a few issues he wrote me and said that he liked what fiction of mine he'd seen in *Randomly*, and that if I were willing to give it a shot I could submit a story to him for *Newer York*. He was very careful to explain that my being invited to submit a story in no way guaranteed an acceptance.

I wrote a story, sent to him, and he rejected it. I wrote another story, sent it to him, and he rejected that one. I wrote a third story, and he sent that one back. I wrote a fourth story…shot down. Finally, nearing the deadline months later, I wrote a story called "Rise and Fall." He wanted a rewrite. I did the rewrite, sent it back, he bought it. My first pro sale.

And my first devastating review. That story got slammed by someone as being "embarrassingly bad." Frankly, while I don't completely agree with them, I have long thought the story needed something more. That's not why it isn't in this collection, though. It didn't really fit thematically and will go into a collection of my darker stories…if I can give it something more.

Writing science fiction is an amazing experience; participating in a field of artistic endeavor that has had such a dramatic effect on our society is very gratifying. Even if you sell only one science fiction story, you're part of the experience. Of course, we all know that (dis)organized fandom is the heart of science fiction. The field lives and breathes through them (or, I should say, us…). Fans are the people who recognize that they are taking part in a grand tradition that affects society at large. I believe it was Norman Spinrad who once said that science fiction is the most important form of literature because it is the only literature that is about *now*. Everything else is about yesterday.

SUPERNATURAL MYSTERIES FROM MARIETTA PUBLISHING...

The Things That Are Not There

by C.J. Henderson

Teddy London was ready to close his detective agency after a demon-driven storm trashed his offices. Then fate led a beautiful woman to him – one being pursued by winged monsters determined to use her to unlock a doorway that will lead the entire world to madness.

**$13.99 – Trade Paperback
ISBN 1-892669-08-0**

The Occult Detectives of C.J. Henderson

by C.J. Henderson

Here are thirteen tales of the greatest otherworld investigators ever created tackling witches, werewolves, and every other terror that crawls, flies or creeps through the night. It's the best stories ever from the reigning monarch of macabre mysteries!

**$15.99 – Trade Paperback
ISBN 1-892669-10-2**

BELUGA STEIN MYSTERIES FROM MARIETTA PUBLISHING...

Last Resort
by Wendy Webb

Beluga Stein is a hit-or miss psychic who never travels without her familiar, a black cat named Planchette, a far more gifted psychic. An ill-conceived gift lands Beluga and Planchette at the opening of a new luxury spa. Opposed to healthy pursuits of any kind, Beluga is ready to leave – until a body is discovered.

$13.99 – Trade Paperback
ISBN 1-892669-21-8

Bee Movie
by Wendy Webb

Beluga Stein is back — with her loud muumuus, pastel cigarettes, and hit-or-miss psychic ability. This time she's called to investigate strange events on the set of a low-budget horror movie. But after a fire mysteriously erupts on the set, an actor in a bee costume is found dead. Is the set haunted, or are the supernatural stirrings the result of special effects?

$13.99 – Trade Paperback
ISBN 1-892669-24-2

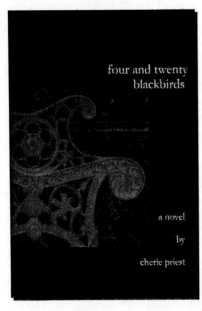

ALSO AVAILABLE
FROM MARIETTA PUBLISHING...

Frontiers of Terror

Edited by Bruce Gehweiler

Ride along the edge of a razor blade allowing your flesh to be flayed from your bones. The stories in this book take you to the cutting edge of dark fantasy. Do you dare to take the challenge? Can you handle eighteen trips to the very frontiers of terror from today's most exciting authors?
$17.99 – Trade Paperback
ISBN 1-892669-07-2

Warfear, A Collection of Strange War Tales

Edited by James Shimkus, Byron White, and Allen Tower

From the medieval English countryside to the far future where humanity is fragmented into myriad tribal cultures, from the ideals of the American Revolution to Hitler's laboratories of terror, *Warfear, A Collection of Strange War* Tales takes you to thirteen battlefields beyond imagination.
$14.99 – Trade Paperback
ISBN 1-892669-20-X

ORDERING INFORMATION

Marietta Publishing's books are available from Ingram Book Distributors and Baker & Taylor Book Group. A catalogue can be found at www.mariettapublishing.com. Or simply use the order form below.

Bee Movie _____ @$13.99 = _____

Four and Twenty Blackbirds _____ @ $13.99 = _____

Frontiers of Terror _____ @ $17.99 = _____

The Ghost Finds a Body _____ @ $14.99 = _____

Last Resort _____ @ $13.99 = _____

Lin Carter's Anton Zarnak
Supernatural Sleuth _____ @ $19.99 = _____

New Mythos Legends (Ill. Hardcover) _____ @ $25.00 = _____

New Mythos Legends (Trade Paperback) _____ @ $15.99 = _____

The Occult Detectives of C.J. Henderson _____ @ $15.99 = _____

The Things That Are Not There _____ @ $13.99 = _____

Warfear, A Collection of Strange War Tales _____ @ $13.99 = _____

What You Pay For _____ @ $15.99 = _____

S&H ($3.00 per book) = _____

Total = _____

Name _____

Address _____

_____

E-Mail _____

Phone _____

Send to:
Marietta Publishing
PO Box 3485 • Marietta, GA 30061-3485

Printed in the United States
17309LVS00005B/1-75